DRUMHELLER

THE PAINTER

A NOVEL

Susan Statham

BAYEUX

THE PAINTER'S CRAFT: A NOVEL
© Copyright 2011 Bayeux Arts, Inc. and Susan Statham

Published by
Bayeux Arts, Inc.
119 Stratton Crescent SW,
Calgary, Canada T3H 1T7

www.bayeux.com
First printing: November 2011

Cover and Book design: PreMediaGlobal

Library and Archives Canada Cataloguing in Publication

Statham, S. N. (Susan N.), 1951–
    The painter's craft / S.N. Statham.

Issued also in an electronic format.
ISBN 978-1-897411-31-5

    I. Title.

PS8637.T375P35 2011   C813'.6   C2011-905987-8

Library and Archives Canada Cataloguing in Publication

Statham, S. N. (Susan N.), 1951–
    The painter's craft [electronic resource] / S.N. Statham.

Type of computer file: Electronic monograph in EBOOK format.
Issued also in print format.
ISBN 978-1-897411-56-8

    I. Title.

PS8637.T375P35 2011a   C813'.6   C2011-905988-6

Printed in Canada

Books published by Bayeux Arts are available at special quantity discounts
to use in premiums and sales promotions, or for use in corporate training
programs. For more information, please write to Special Sales, Bayeux
Arts, Inc., 119 Stratton Crescent SW, Calgary, Canada T3H 1T7.

The ongoing publishing activities of Bayeux Arts, under its "Bayeux" and
"Gondolier" imprints, are supported by the Canada Council for the Arts,
the Government of Alberta, Alberta Multimedia Development Fund,
and the Government of Canada through the Book Publishing Industry
Development Program.

Canada Council   Conseil des Arts
for the Arts   du Canada

**Government
of Alberta** ■

LIVRES CANADA BOOKS

To Mark, Eric, and Chris.

Acknowledgement

I am grateful for the love and encouragement of my family and friends. I offer special thanks to Susan Weinstein, Finella Hughes, Lynn Hamilton, Dr. Muriel Henderson, Cst. Mike Vander Schaaf, Ashis Gupta, and the team at Bayeux Arts. To the legion of writers and artists, past and present, who have educated, entertained, and enlightened, thank you.

Chapter 1

"Art is long, life is short," Charles reminds me the last time I see him.

I agree, knowing my life will be too short if I can't eat and pay the rent. Though I promise to return to his studio when I've saved some money, he dismisses me with a flick of his wrist. Charles Philip Venable understood sacrifice for art; anything less was a waste of his time.

I cried both selfish and unselfish tears when I read of his death. At fifty-four, his life and work were unfinished. And as my instructor, his work with me was unfinished too. But I'm not thinking about Charles when I leave my second floor apartment and pad down the wooden steps to the foyer. He's not on my mind as I tighten the belt of my blue cotton housecoat and peer out the window at an overcast June morning. Only when I scoop up the mail by the front door and find the letter does he become my constant companion.

The envelope is so impressive I immediately check the return address—'Smith and Wilson, Attorneys at Law.' I read the contents twice before re-entering my apartment and though Charles was an important person in my life, I can't imagine why I'd be mentioned in his will. A bequest? I knew I had to wait three days to find out and patience has never been one of my virtues.

There's one person who might know the answer. Zarina Hughes was Charles's assistant—partner, she would have said, though behind her back we students referred to her as his dogsbody. An odd duck and possibly certifiable but after I left the art studio she was my only link to Charles.

At ten a.m. Zarina would normally be tending to Charles's many needs but as he now needed for nothing, she might be at home. She answers on the second ring.

"Hi Zarina, it's . . ."

"Ah Maudlin," she interrupts me.

"Maud," I tell her, as I always do, knowing she'll never say my name correctly.

"It's been months. You heard about the Maestro?"

"Yes, Zarina. I read the article in the paper. I also called Alissa to give her my sympathy, but two minutes into the conversation I wanted to ask for it back."

"*Entre nous*, Maudy, Charles had been spending more time on the cot in his studio than with his wedded bliss."

"I gather it was his heart, though Alissa did say something about his liver."

"Well," she drawls. "You know he cared more for his art than his temple and the wine was his undoing."

"I had no idea it was that bad. Zarina there's something else I'd like to talk to you about. Could we meet for lunch?"

"Umm . . ."

"My treat," I offer.

"Okay. Winston's, noon."

"Winston's?" She hangs up before I can suggest a cheaper venue.

Keeping to a strict budget, I put myself through my last year of university and three years of art school working for my Uncle Sid, a former police detective and present owner of a small P. I. firm. Although I expected to leave the clerical work when the world discovered my artistic genius, the world is turning a blind eye and I now work full time for the Gibbon's Investigative Services.

My job generally confines me to the office, but when I first started working for him, my uncle insisted I learn to use a gun and take a basic course in self-defence. Being young and naive, I thought he would involve me in some detective work. To date, the only case I've solved has been done on my own time. I found Charles Venable's father. There's one other call I need to make before leaving for the restaurant.

"Hi Uncle Sid."

"Maud, sweetie. Good thing you called." I hear the warm tone in his voice. "Can you get to the office now? Al needs his report typed and sent to General Contracting."

"Well, actually, I'm calling to ask if you could do without me until one-thirty. I have a lunch date with Zarina Hughes—did you ever meet her? No probably not. Anyway I knew her in art school and I've already promised to be there, so I'd rather not have to call her back and . . ."

"Maud. You're running off at the mouth." His tone is cool. There's an irritated pause before he says, "Okay, one-thirty."

I do a quick scan of my one-bedroom flat. I'm not innately tidy but I've been well trained by my often-annoying, yet ever-loveable cat, Kora. Anything that can be damaged or destroyed is carefully put away. Removing paw prints in oil paint is something I only want to try once.

There's little point in trying to match Zarina in attire. My wardrobe is limited to casual and tasteful. It's Winston's after all so tasteful seems the best choice and since summer is hiding beneath the long sleeves of spring, I will greet Zarina in a lovely periwinkle blouse and black dress pants and I will be on time.

Driving to the restaurant, I pass the studio where I first met Charles Venable. I'd been attending a distinguished college but was experiencing artistic frustration. It seemed to me that we were learning to pour our guts onto the canvas in a manner that looked like—well, guts. I wanted to learn to draw and I complained long and loud to my classmate and fellow sufferer, Jack. About three-quarters of the way through a year of trial and error, Jack arrived at class with great news. What he actually said was, "Maud, I have great news."

"You sold a painting!" I congratulated him because this is every art student's definition of great news.

The frown and shake of his head told me he hadn't sold a painting, but he tossed the emotion off like a wet towel and continued with enthusiasm. "I've found a private studio run by an instructor who studied in Italy with a master painter. His work is amazing, Maud. If you'd like to meet him I'll take you Saturday morning."

The offer was irresistible and Jack picked me up at ten. During the drive, he mumbled something about the art school being a little rundown but when I saw it I thought it looked run over. It was in an old section of Toronto where the buildings are only two storeys and like POWs made to stand too long in the prison yard, they seemed to remain upright only because each supported the other.

"Now, don't judge a book by its cover," Jack said, leading the way. He opened an old wooden door, much in need of a coat of paint, to reveal a staircase, its linoleum-covered steps listing slightly to the left. The pungent odour of varnish and turpentine grew stronger as we ascended. At the top of the stairs was another door. This opened to a small hall, which in turn lead to another doorway. I was beginning to feel like Alice in the rabbit hole when we paused in the archway of a large sun-filled room. An army of students stood before their easels—attention focused on a makeshift stage and a naked young man, his skin stretched taut over angular bones.

As we entered, a deep and melodic voice announced, "Let's take a fifteen minute break, shall we." Concentration broken, the students made their way to the small kitchen, while Jack and I pressed against the wall and waited. A man, taller than most, his white shirt and tie an anomaly in a studio of paint-splatter jeans, approached us with his hand outstretched. I automatically extended my own as he said, "Welcome, I'm Charles Venable."

Luminous cerulean eyes hid his inner darkness and my first impression was of a man with a major role on life's stage. Shaking his hand, I was reluctant to let go. I had to, of course, or look a fool. He exchanged one awkward moment for another when he turned to Jack and said, "So this is the dissatisfied art student you were telling me about." Cognisant of the startled look on my face he continued, his voice like a soothing touch. "Don't worry. Jack hasn't revealed too many secrets. Would you like to see my paintings before you decide if you want to join the studio?"

Though my eyes widened involuntarily I hid my surprise under a casual nod. In my experience, most art teachers judged a student's work prior to acceptance, but I was soon to discover, Charles Venable was not like most art teachers. Jack had said his work was amazing but that did not begin to describe the skill he displayed in still life, landscape and portrait. Not only did he excel as a draughtsman, his work radiated an inner glow I'd have walked through fire to achieve. After about three months at the studio, Charles learned of my job at the detective agency and hired me to find his father. It was through this investigation that I uncovered the details of a lost childhood.

Charles was the result of an ill-fated love affair between a flamboyant American pilot and a timid, lonely English girl. His father disappeared after hearing the word "pregnant," and in post-war England, his mother's embarrassing condition was dealt with by relocating her to an elder sister in Canada. Isolated and frightened, she allowed her personal tragedy to entangle her like a web and when it finally smothered her completely, Charles, at the age of nine, was left dependent on his maiden aunt. Aunt Theo seemed to lack any mothering instincts but she did provide her nephew with the tools for quiet amusement and in this way she played her role in his development as an artist. Also, if she had been a kinder, gentler woman, Charles may not have fled to Italy when he was eighteen.

He returned to Canada with his raison d'être but a life with purpose is not a life without problems and his first was financial. He could not avoid the artist's dilemma—to make money he needed to produce saleable work, but to create the work he needed the time, the space and the raw materials, which of course required money.

Charles turned to teaching but at the same time, nursed a fantasy in which his father played a starring role. If he could only find him, his fighter pilot Dad would be his patron. After years of failure, Charles hired me, but my success meant the end of his dream.

In time, a prestigious gallery in Yorkville accepted Charles's work and he began to receive some lucrative commissions. He gradually cut back on his teaching while keeping three 'fans' and former students close to hand—Alissa, whom he married; his most promising apprentice, Rupert Jaynes; and his assistant Zarina Hughes.

Punctuality is one of Zarina's cardinal virtues but at eleven-thirty, I'm on Dupont Avenue waiting for tow trucks to remove two cars crippled in accidental contact. I walk through the door of the restaurant at twelve-fifteen and feel Zarina's glare before I see her.

"You're late," she says, when I reach the table.

I know the futility of offering an excuse, so I simply agree with her. Battle-ready but finding herself without an enemy, her shoulders drop and a smile tickles her lips. In a final gesture I add a compliment. "Zarina, you look stunning." And indeed I am stunned to see the combination of a wide-brimmed purple hat and a ruffled blouse the colour of mandarin oranges. Sadly, the tablecloth hides the lower half of her outfit, but I anticipate another surprise when she stands up.

"Thank you, Maudy," she coos. "What do you want to talk to me about?"

I sit down and pick up the menu. Zarina uses one of her long, purple fingernails (they match her hat) to gently pull it from in front of my face. "Oh, Miss G., I've ordered us both the Lobster Thermidor. It's one of my favourites."

"Great," I say. I hate lobster.

"So?" Zarina rests her elbows on the table, her chin in her cupped hands and gazes at me through a forest of mascara.

"I received a letter this morning from Charles's solicitors. They're requesting that I attend the reading of his will. I didn't know they did that, you know, had a formal reading and all?" My attempt to be light and breezy fades under her intense stare.

Finally she says, "Ah yes, you two were once very close, were you not?"

"No! I mean well, yes, but not, not in the Biblical sense."

She winks at me. "Ah well, whatever. You did have a parting of the ways though, didn't you?"

"I left the studio for financial reasons. I intended to return once I paid off my student loan."

"But there was something else." She leans back in the chair and adjusts her hat. "Artists build fantasies, Maud. You should never have found his father."

"Zarina, Charles hired me to find his father and I can hardly be blamed for his condition."

"But you discovered more than that. I think Charles resented your prying into his past."

I want to smack that smug look off her face. "It was part of the job. I never disclosed any of it."

"Really, Maudy, there's no need to get testy."

I make a conscious effort to relax. "If Charles was upset with me then why would he leave me something in his will?"

"Perhaps it's a token of forgiveness."

"I didn't even know I needed to be forgiven but if that's true, what sort of token would he leave me?"

With the enigmatic smile of Mona Lisa, Zarina says. "I can't imagine."

The waiter arrives with our lunch and I watch my companion attack her lobster. Somehow I'd let Zarina lead me into the thorns of a conversational garden and before we reach a patch of barren ground I decide to be a little more personable. "I'm sorry Zarina. I know you were with Charles a long time and I haven't even asked how you are dealing with his death."

"Oh Matilda, it hasn't been easy. I miss him so much." She drops her fork and stares at the far wall as if willing Charles to appear. After a lengthy pause, she turns to me and continues. "He was more than just an employer, you know."

I assume she means he was also a friend—images of a romantic relationship between them are quickly cleansed from my mind. "Was it cirrhosis of the liver? Had he been suffering for a long time?"

"Many cases of cirrhosis go undetected for years and of course, Charles had a phobia of doctors. He began to complain of stomach pains during what was to be his final month." Her fingers idly press at the slight wrinkles of the linen tablecloth. "Perhaps complain is not the right word. You know, he never complained. But I knew. Oh yes, I knew something was wrong. Naturally, I begged him to seek medical advice but he put me off by saying it was just the flu and I shouldn't worry."

As she speaks, her eyes fill with tears. They spill out and flow down her over-blushed cheeks leaving a trail of diluted mascara. Reaching into my purse, I grab a tissue, but she shakes her head at me and produces a clean white hankie. Dabbing under her eyes, her voice quavers. "Then the week before he died, I wasn't there for him." She drops her face into her hankie and begins to weep.

I don't know if I should get up and hug her or sit and wait. I'm instantly aware of the silence and feel the glares of suspicion from my fellow diners. Two waiters rush to our table but Zarina waves her hand and shoos them away, which seems to vindicate me and people return, if somewhat warily, to their meals and their conversations. I wait, confused by her reaction. She'd always given the impression she was above the emotions of regular folk.

"Zarina, you don't have to talk about this."

She ignores me, and with great effort continues. "My father fell and broke his hip and I was called home to help my mother. I came back the day Charles was taken to the Toronto General. Of course, I immediately rushed to his side but when I got there, he was in a coma. He died without regaining consciousness." She takes a deep breath and tucks an errant strand of her crimson hair back under her hat. "Alissa, the dingbat, could tell me nothing. According to Rupert, Charles spent most of his final week at the studio." With the mention of Alissa and Rupert, Zarina seems to regain some of her composure.

"And how are Alissa and Rupert doing?"

"As I told you," she begins, the impatience in her voice making me feel like a bumbling student, "the marriage was nearing the end of its course. In any case, I think Alissa had found someone else's shoulder to cry on. Really, that woman isn't happy unless she's in the depths of despair.

"As for Rupert, he's got a part-time job, framing for the Tellman Gallery. He's also thrown himself into finishing Charles's last commissions—the mural for MetLife and the portrait of their CEO. But," Zarina sighs audibly, "I was feeling sorry for poor Rupert. I thought, when he didn't have Charles to orchestrate his every move, he would go completely catatonic. I must say, though, he is surprising me. In his effort to keep the studio going, he's taken over Charles's class and even added two more. Thankfully, he's asked me to stay on and help him. It's a real comfort knowing that what Charles started carries on. How about you Matty, are you still painting?"

"Not as much as I'd like."

"Well, why not come and join us for a class? They are filling very quickly, but at the moment you have your choice of Tuesday or Thursday evening," she concludes, the quintessential secretary.

"Perhaps I will."

Completely recovered, Zarina tugs at the shell of a large claw. "You know, the one who really seems broken up is Leona."

"Leona. Who's she?"

"Oh Matty, Matty," Zarina continues in that patronising way I especially hate in someone who is my contemporary. "She owns the Tellman Gallery, here in Yorkville. She and Charles spent an inordinate amount of time together." She winks at me. "Although things definitely had cooled off in the last couple of months. He was busy with one thing and another but he was avoiding her and let me tell you," Zarina leans toward me, "the ice queen wasn't taking it very well. Of course, if you knew her, you'd understand. She's a very demanding woman. Much like Charles's aunt Theo, but of course he failed to see the resemblance."

I consider defending the maiden aunt but decide to let it go.

Zarina scoops a forkful of rice, pausing only long enough to swallow it. "And then there's poor Teddy. You remember Teddy, Charles's agent. He and Charles had a 'battle royal' the day before Charles crossed over and he's been riddled with guilt ever since. And . . ."

"Wait a minute, what do you mean 'crossed over'?"

She moves her face closer to mine. "Died, Maudy, died. You really must try to keep up with the times." She looks at my plate. "And why aren't you eating your lunch? You are what you eat you know and this whole thinness craze just isn't healthy. I, for one, am glad to see there are a few Hollywood celebrities rebelling against the anorexic idol."

I voice my agreement and it launches her off on a dissertation about dieting. Well, at least it's a relatively safe topic. I pick away at my lobster, thankful for the large side order of rice, while my companion finishes her meal. My suggestion of dessert is met with a look of disgust and we finish lunch with herbal tea.

Although it means missing a view of the lower half of her outfit, I must get to work. To be honest, I'm looking forward to the routine of the office. "Zarina, you stay and finish your tea. My uncle's expecting me at one-thirty."

Without another word, she signals the waiter and while he scurries over, she gazes at me with anticipation. I know what she's up to and consider pretending otherwise, but since Zarina has no sense of humour, I pay the bill.

"Thank you, Maudlin," she drawls.

"Well, Zarina, I hope to see you again soon."

"Oh, you will Maudy, you will."

Chapter 2

My hopes for a great day are encouraged when my unruly curls dry without frizz, the spot on my tastefully sombre navy blue dress disappears with only minor scrubbing and I pull into the small parking lot outside the offices of Messrs. Smith and Wilson with fifteen minutes to spare. As I tug on the handle to check that I've locked the door, I notice that I've parked next to my most coveted automobile, a Mercedes Benz 500SL convertible. It's even in my colour of choice, champagne with black interior. The top's up and I'm peering through the tinted windows when a tap on my shoulder sends me bolting into an upright position so quickly I feel vertigo. Spinning round, I find myself face to face with Charles's apprentice. "Good God, Rupert!" I pause to catch my breath. "Sorry, is this your car?"

"No. It's Ted's."

"Ted?"

"You know, Ted Baer, Charles's agent." His voice is devoid of emotion.

"Oh, of course, Teddy."

"Stupid name."

I caress the roof of the car. "Well, it's a beauty."

"Yeah."

"So, Rupert, it's been a while. How are you?"

"Fine."

"I hear you're teaching now. How's that going?"

"Fine."

I give up trying to get a full sentence from him. "Shall we go in?" I ask.

"Sure."

Due to the nature of my job, I've had occasion to be in a few lawyers' offices and it's remarkable how much alike they tend to be. Perhaps there's a course in law school on how to decorate for success with specific instructions on the use of wood—pine for the new graduate, oak for the experienced and mahogany for the veteran. In which case, Smith and Wilson are definitely veterans—mahogany panelling, mahogany bookcases and a huge mahogany desk. My reverie on cabinetry is interrupted by the arrival of an ultra-prim middle-aged woman.

"We will be meeting in the conference room. Please follow me." She had the kind of tone that ensures you daren't do otherwise, so of course, Rupert and I trail after her. Perhaps I'd been making a stereotypical judgement in assuming I would be dealing with "Messrs." Smith and Wilson.

The conference room is in complete contrast to the office—floor to ceiling windows, soft pink walls, light floral prints—no heavy mahogany. Five people make a semicircle around a pale laminate table and as Rupert and I enter the room, four heads turn in our direction. First is Alissa, her bleached blonde hair flowing over black chiffon, tissues clutched in each fist. Then Teddy, his heavy salt and pepper beard obscuring a massive neck, completely fills the space next to her. To his left, the majestic-looking woman, with a precision cut to both her auburn hair and expensive suit jacket, could only be Leona Tellman and finally, Zarina, somewhat subdued in a deep green poncho, its hood shrouding her shocking red curls. The fifth individual, who is sifting through papers, looks up when Rupert and I walk toward the two vacant chairs and sit down.

"Good afternoon, and thank you all for coming. I'm Andrew Smith." Turning to the woman who had ushered us in he adds, "And this is my associate, Ms. Katherine Wilson." She nods to us as she takes her seat. "As everyone is here now," he continues, "we can begin. This meeting is at the expressed wishes of Mr. Charles Venable, as outlined in this letter to me dated May 2nd of this year, 2000. Although the bulk of his estate has been left to his widow, Mrs. Alissa Venable, he outlined separate bequests, which are to be recognised at this meeting. I will now read the following bequests in the order in which they were written:

To my wife, I leave my painting in oils, 'Hercules and Deianira.' To my faithful aide, Zarina Hughes, I leave my painting in oils, 'Guinevere and Sir Gawain.' To my most promising apprentice, Rupert Jaynes, I leave my painting in oils, 'Socrates and Meletus.' To my emperor of an agent, Evelyn (Teddy) Baer, I leave my painting in oils, 'Nero and Britannicus.' To the loyal Leona Tellman, I leave my painting in oils, 'Theseus and Medea.' To the ever-curious Maud Gibbons, I leave my painting in oils, 'Hamlet, Prince of Denmark.'

Mr. Smith tucks the letter back into its file while we each take surreptitious glances at one another.

"If you will follow me," Ms. Wilson interjects, "you can pick up your respective paintings. They have been packaged in brown craft paper and clearly labelled."

In a small lunchroom, we find them, just as described, laid out on two tables. The packages appear to be about the same size, approximately 16" × 20", easy enough to transport. As we walk around the tables, checking the labels, little is said, save such comments as "Here's yours, Teddy" and "Alissa, this one has your name on it." Although they are cordial with one another, I am ignored and begin to feel like the unjustly rewarded interloper. I decide to collect my painting, exchange polite good-byes and beat a hasty retreat. No one seems to mind.

Anxious to get home and unwrap this unexpected gift, I'm equally curious about the works bequeathed to my fellow heirs. I press the record button of the handy voice recorder I keep in the cup-holder between the car's seats. (I have a great short-term memory, it just loses something over time.) 'Okay, Charles's painting to Teddy was Nero and Britannicus. Nero was a Roman emperor, but I'm not sure about Britannicus. Maybe Teddy also had an interest in that period of history. Leona's was Theseus and Medusa, wait—she was the woman with snakes for hair, that can't be right, well it was Med-something. To Rupert he had given Socrates and Melita, who was probably a student—a nice way to commemorate their relationship. Zarina's was Arthurian, Guinevere and one of the knights, Sir Gawain, I think. Well, she did seem to live in a mythical world. And finally, Alissa—Hercules and something like Dejera.'

I turn off the recorder and as I navigate through the traffic, ponder past conversations with Charles, searching for clues that would explain his gift of 'Hamlet.' To my recollection we never talked about Shakespeare. Charles's focus was always on the great visual artists, seldom the literary ones. Perhaps the painting will explain itself.

My furry feline companion greets me at my front door and follows me into the living room, watching as I gently place my new treasure on the table before taking a minute to clear a spot on the fireplace mantel. My hands tremble as I struggle with the tape. At last, I have the wrapping pulled back and grasping the stretcher bars on either side of the canvas, I flip it over and place it carefully on the mantel.

Dark and brooding, it is wondrously painted. Here is Shakespeare's Dane in grisaille, but not totally, for there's the faintest hint of alizarin crimson on a velvet waistcoat peeking out from under a heavy cape. Looking at the face, I am at once drawn to eyes wide with curiosity and the familiarity of the bone structure causes me to wonder who he used as a model. My Hamlet is young, clean-shaven and with a somewhat feminine aspect. As always, Charles's use of chiaroscuro and sfumato create a figure so life-like he appears to breathe.

To get the most enjoyment out of a painting, I often need to pause and refresh my eyes, much like the gourmet who may sip at water or wine to refresh his palate. In the kitchen, I plug in the kettle and wait for the water to come to a boil. Kora follows, running to her empty bowl where she does her pre-dinner dance, twirling on her silent paws. I pop a tea bag into a china mug and drown it with boiling water, before filling her bowl with kibble and returning to my painting.

Cup in hand, I stand before the mantel in silent admiration. I can hardly believe that Charles has given me such a gift and with my nose inches from the painting, I examine each brush stroke, noting the fine use of oil glazes. Checking for Charles's signature, I discover that he has written something in tiny letters just below it. Although I squint as tight as I can, it's impossible to read. I bring the painting near the light of the picture window but soon realise a magnifying glass is the only answer and retrieve one from the top drawer of a battered oak desk that had once belonged to my father. Through the glass I read, "Act I, scene v." How strange. I'd never seen this kind of notation on any of his other work. I look again at the face of Hamlet and seeing eyes that betray shock more than inquisitiveness, I follow his gaze across the stone wall. There sculpted as a relief in the background rock, is another face. Who is this?

It's been years since I'd read the play. I could understand why Charles had given Rupert a painting of Socrates with his student, but how was Hamlet related to me? From my overstuffed bookcase I retrieve a tattered copy of the *Complete Works of Shakespeare*. Cradling the volume in one hand, I guide my thumb along the pages, letting them fall until I find "Hamlet, Prince of Denmark," Act 1, scene v.

On a remote part of the platform at Elsinore Castle, Shakespeare's tenebrous words play gravely and I begin to feel a sense of dread. It is the scene where the ghost, Hamlet's father, tells his son of a murder most foul. I raise my eyes to the painting, concentrating on the face etched into the stone wall. My heart pounds, my knees weaken. It's a self-portrait. It's Charles.

"O God!" I echo Hamlet's words. Charles, is this painting your ghost, carrying a message to me? Were you poisoned by someone close to you, someone you trusted? The thought overwhelms me and for a moment, I feel faint. Quickly, I lower my head below my knees. I'd never fainted before and with sheer determination I would not faint now. When it feels safe to raise my head, I allow myself a few minutes to simply breathe. Then I begin to read, from the beginning, "Hamlet, Prince of Denmark."

A dismembered head floats in front of my face, its lips mouthing the word revenge. I turn to run but I have no legs. I awake with the sweat clinging to my body and my breath coming in short gasps. God what a night! I raise my head then let it fall back on the pillow, in confusion I wonder if

I have even slept. But I did sleep and perchance did dream. Though, as with so many dreams, it all but evaporates like the sweat on my brow. One image remains intact, that of Charles walking on the balcony of Casa Loma, the only castle-like building I've ever visited. He was carrying a brush and painting on the stone walls.

The painting! I leap out of bed with a vigour fuelled not by energy but by panic and rush into the living room. There it is, safely perched on the mantel. I need some help to sort through my thoughts and while the water drips over the coffee grounds to perform its magic, I go back to the bedroom to dress, choosing a pair of well-worn jeans and a recently purchased sweatshirt. Perhaps its cosy fleece will dispel the chill of the dream. On the floor next to the bed, I retrieve my book and carry it to the table, where I can sit with a view of Charles's painting. After pouring a cup of coffee, I set a writing pad and pen next to my copy of Shakespeare's plays.

Hamlet had doubted the words of the ghost, and I too have my suspicions. I write the sentence, 'Charles bequeathed me a painting of Hamlet because...' then I write the following endings and rebuttals.

1. He liked me and wanted me to have a piece of his work; the choice was random.

Unlikely. I hadn't seen Charles in months and although he didn't seem to dislike me, our relationship had been tainted

-24-

after I found his father and inadvertently destroyed his long-held paternal fantasy. I remember the day I confirmed I had indeed found Lt. Philips. Charles had picked me up off the ground in the grandest of hugs. Whirling me round, he kept repeating, "You did it, oh thank you, you clever, clever girl." And as quickly as he had risen to a pinnacle of bliss, he crashed in despair when I revealed his father's condition. The man he had wanted to know for so many years was now incapable of knowing anyone. The hurt was too heavy for Charles to bear. I didn't mind shouldering some of the blame, if it relieved him of some of the pain.

2. Charles never felt he had properly recompensed me for finding his father.

No. I recall being quite happy with the money Charles had paid me for my time and effort and he never said anything to suggest he felt otherwise.

3. Charles appreciated my curiosity and my ability to ferret out the truth. The painting is just what it appears to be. Charles is asking me to find his killer.

Possible. Charles could have been poisoned. Zarina said he had flu-like symptoms and he was taken to the hospital after Rupert found him unconscious. But, if he thought he was being poisoned, wouldn't he do something more than create six paintings? Maybe he tried but failed. Maybe, he didn't really believe it but began the paintings just in case it was true and he found out too late. Maybe he was delusional and actually died of natural causes, as Alissa had said.

As my first two alternates were false, I would continue on the likelihood that the third was true. Either he was murdered or he died of natural causes while under the misguided belief that he was being poisoned. I sincerely hoped it was the latter, because if it was the former, I may recently have been in the company of a murderer.

I consider calling the hospital and inquiring about the autopsy but I'm not a relative so I'd need a good story. I have to discuss this with someone. Uncle Sid seemed the obvious choice but, I don't even know if there's a case and if there is, he might keep me behind the desk and investigate it himself.

I decide to call my friend, Finella. We'd met years ago in one of Charles's classes and when she retired from selling real estate, she left Toronto for a small village east of the city.

"Finella, it's Maud, how are you?"

"Fine Maud, good to hear your voice. What are you up to?"

"Well, there's something I'd like to show you and I need to talk to you."

"Show me? I hope it's something you can bring to me. I'm without a vehicle at present and I doubt these old legs of mine could handle a bike ride to Toronto."

"Yes of course," I assure her. "I could be there around two this afternoon, if that's okay?"

"Sure, pack your jammies and stay the night, or as long as you like, for that matter."

"One night would be great. I'll see you soon."

I close the call with renewed feelings of optimism. Finella has enviable commonsense and the wisdom gleaned through intelligence plus experience. I don't expect her to have all the answers but she usually asks the right questions.

I take a long shower and eat a short breakfast, which, according to my watch is, in reality, lunch. The shower and the final emergence of the June sun warm my day, so I trade the sweatshirt for a short-sleeved cotton T, but re-don the favoured jeans. After packing a small overnight bag, I stuff the *Complete Works of Shakespeare* and my notes on top, and put down extra food and water for Kora. I also lock her cat door. The door allows her access to the fire escape and the backyard but since I'm going to be away overnight, I prefer to keep her in the apartment. She hates the car so taking her with me would be a misery for both of us.

Charles's painting is carefully placed in my leather portfolio and by one o'clock, I'm standing at the door ready to go. Well, almost ready. I make one more trip to the bathroom then double-check that I've turned everything off that needs turning off. There's a part of me that hates to leave home. It's not agoraphobia but rather an irrational fear that I've neglected something and the place will flood or burn in my absence.

Finally, on the road with a full tank of gas, I battle the traffic to get out of the city. Within an hour and a half, I'm past the last major centre and can lower my shoulders from my earlobes. Forty minutes later, I'm pulling up the dirt road to Finella's log house. Hidden among the trees, it's a beautiful site. Many of the art students questioned her move to the boonies, but one visit would remove all doubt. I see her working in the garden as I pull up to the garage, and when I exit the car she strolls over to see me.

"Welcome," she says, slipping off her gardening gloves to give me a hug.

"Gosh it's good to see you." I hug her back, her tiny frame easily enveloped in my arms. Inhaling a lung-full of fresh country air I add, "It smells so good here. Must be your garden."

"That or the breath of the trees." Offering a hand she asks, "Can I help you with your case?"

"If you don't mind. I just have to get my portfolio out of the trunk."

Seeing the large black carrying case she says, "So you brought a painting to show me. Is it one of yours?"

"Yes and no."

"Ah, very mysterious. Come on in and let's have a look."

Finella holds the door and I walk into an entry that offers a view of the kitchen, with natural pine cupboards and a wood stove; the dining area, with matching pine table-and-chairs and a spacious living room, complete with stone fireplace. The large picture window frames a spectacular view of the garden, pond and surrounding trees.

"Look, I can't contain my curiosity. Why don't you sit down and I'll make you a cup of tea."

"That would be great." I rest the portfolio against an overstuffed armchair before dropping into it. "Your garden looks terrific. I love those red poppies."

"Looks like we're finally getting some warm weather so things should really start blooming, which will also be good advertising for me."

"Advertising?" I ask.

"Yes, right. Since I moved out here, I've taken a serious interest in horticulture. Joined the local club and now have three customers I garden for."

"You really are amazing." She hands me a cup and I take a slow sip of my favourite beverage. "Delicious, thanks. So you're keeping busy, eh?"

"Yes indeed. I've got lots of reasons to get out of bed in the morning. But what about you? If you don't mind my saying so, I sense more than the usual tension for a city girl. What's up?" Her eyes focus on my portfolio. "Or should I say, what's new?"

"First of all, I guess you heard about Charles."

"It was in the Toronto paper. You know, from the perspective of a senior citizen, he was far too young for a heart attack. Is there something more than what was reported in the news?"

I tell Finella about the letter, lunch with Zarina, the meeting at the lawyers and that each of us received a painting. I don't tell her the names of the other works but do let her know mine was called 'Hamlet, Prince of Denmark' and that beneath his signature, Charles had written the words, "Act I Scene v." I reach for the portfolio and carefully remove the painting.

"Ah," she sighs as I prop it up against the table. She continues to peruse it for a few more minutes before saying, "He was a marvellous painter, wasn't he?"

"He certainly was."

"I'll just get my copy of the play. It's been some time since I read it."

"I have a copy here in my bag," I say, passing it to her. "It starts where I've put the bookmark."

As she reads, she occasionally glances up at the painting. "I see the face in the stone wall. That must be King Hamlet; his brother Claudius poisoned him. You know, I think Charles painted himself as the king, which rather begs the question, did Charles have a brother?"

"No." I could see where her thoughts were going. "So you think he was trying to tell me he was poisoned?"

"It certainly looks that way."

"I wonder who modelled for the young Hamlet? He looks kind of familiar."

"I'm not surprised," says Finella. "To my eyes, I'd say he has more than a passing resemblance to you.

Chapter 3

"Oh my God, it is me isn't it! Not exactly though or surely I would have noticed." I turn to Finella, my eyes begging agreement.

"Right," she says, pursing her lips. "Charles would have painted you from memory. The face is in shadow and of course the hair and the clothes are definitely not you. However, I do think we can agree that he is sending you a desperate message. What can you tell me about the paintings Charles bestowed upon his nearest and dearest?"

"Rather than trust my memory, I'll get my voice recorder from the car. We'll need some paper for notes, if you don't mind." I run out to grab the recorder off the dashboard and when I return, I find a notebook and a plate of home-baked cookies on the table.

Finella calls to me from the kitchen, "I baked those this morning. You go ahead, I'll just brew a fresh pot of tea."

While the kettle boils, I listen to my voice re-corder, take notes and eat two cookies—maybe three. "These are heavenly."

"Why thank you little lady." She mimics a Southern drawl as she strolls in with a tray and places it next to me on the table. "This is ginger spice tea, I think you'll like it." Glancing over my notes, she asks, "Now what have you got?"

"Here's the list of the people at the reading and, opposite, I've added the name of the painting each one received, best as I could remember them anyway. Mr. Evelyn Baer, affectionately known as Teddy, was Charles's agent. Did you ever meet him?"

Finella shakes her head. "Well, he's about six foot four, built like a football player and the last person you would expect to be called Evelyn. What were his parents thinking? Somewhere along the way, he got the nickname Teddy and it stuck. Suits him too. He's like a huge teddy bear. His painting is 'Nero and Britannicus' and at the reading, the lawyer read Charles's words, 'to my emperor of an agent.' I figured that was the connection. Come to think of it, Nero wasn't a particularly good emperor was he?"

"No, he wasn't. He was said to have fiddled while Rome burned, and has even been accused of starting the fire that destroyed his city. I'm not sure who Britannicus was so let's search the Net. I'll get my laptop."

"You have a laptop?"

She narrows her eyes and mumbles something about it being the 21st century, before disappearing into her bedroom. When she returns with the computer, she sets it on the table and without hesitation, flips it open and plugs in the phone line.

"Really Maud, I may be old but I'm not a Luddite and you know, this was a valuable tool when I was in real estate. Only dial-up I'm afraid, but it will get the job done. Shall I start with Nero and Britannicus? I prefer Google, unless you have an alternate suggestion."

She obviously has things under control so I sit back and watch her type away at the keyboard, wondering if I suffer from ageism.

"Right," she says bringing me back to the task at hand. "I have a reference here to Britannicus being a rival to Nero and subsequently poisoned to clear the way for him to become emperor."

"Okay, murder by poison. Rather fits with my Hamlet, doesn't it?" She agrees. "How about Leona's? It was Theseus and Med-something."

"I think it might be quicker to use my *Bulfinch's Mythology* for that one," she says.

I look down at my notes. "While we're connected, how about Socrates and Melita, for Rupert?"

Within a few minutes, Finella finds a related site. "According to this, and it's Meletus not Melita, he was the one who brought accusations against Socrates. Accusations that ultimately resulted in his death when he drank hemlock."

"Poison again." I add this information to my notes. "There's a deadly pattern developing here."

"It certainly looks that way. I'll get my *Bulfinch's*." It's a few minutes before she returns with the book. "I'm having a golden moment here. Who was I going to look up in this?"

"Theseus and Med-something and don't be so hard on yourself—these are hardly household names."

There are numerous entries for Theseus but she finally finds it. "Right, but it's Medea and she was a sorceress who contrived to have Theseus presented with a cup of..." She pauses allowing me time to finish the sentence.

"Poison." I shudder. "I think I know where we're going with Alissa's painting of Hercules and Dejera but you better look it up too."

She flips back to the index and quickly finds the entry. "Right. It's Deianira, by the way. She was married to Hercules and according to this," she adds, scanning the page, "she feared she had lost his affections to another and attempted a love-spell to get him back. She was more than a little shocked," Finella glances at me over the rim of her glasses, "but I'm sure you won't be, when she discovered that she had inadvertently poisoned him."

"Nasty. Okay." I peek at the page, "I want to get this down correctly. What's the spelling for Hercules's wife?" She pointed at the entry. "Now, the last one is Zarina's painting of Guinevere and Sir Gawain."

"We're in luck with that one. I'm well versed in the legends of King Arthur, sort of a hobby really." Finella continues, "A jealous squire put poison in an apple he expected Guinevere to give to Sir Gawain. The plan failed when she presented it to a visiting knight. He ate it, writhed in pain, fell senseless and subsequently died. Another victim of poison."

"Gosh."

"Gosh, indeed," she echoes. "You mentioned that when the lawyer read Charles's words regarding the painting for his agent, he said 'to my emperor of an agent.' Do you remember the phrasing for the other bequests?"

I look at her as if she has just spoken to me in Arabic.

"I know this is painful Maud. But, for example, can you remember what the lawyer read in reference to Alissa?"

"I think he just said 'to my wife.' Of course, I did think it odd that having left her everything, the painting was kept apart and given to her at the reading."

"But it ensured that you would know about it and would, therefore, include her in your list of suspects."

"They are all suspects, aren't they?" I say. "I had really hoped Charles died of natural causes."

"That's possible, I suppose," muses Finella. "However, it would appear that Charles thought otherwise."

"If he knew about the poison, wouldn't he do something?"

"What could he have done? Prepared all of his meals, using only fresh ingredients? It is also possible that the poison was not in his food. Was there anything else about the reading of the will that struck you as noteworthy?"

I try to recreate the scene in my mind, slowly sifting through the events. "No," I say, feeling defeated. "I can't think of anything."

"Right, I'd say we've done enough for now. Why don't we pause for sustenance?" She shuts down the laptop and pushes back her chair. "I prepared a salad after you called this morning and thought we might barbecue hamburgers."

"I can do that."

"Thanks. You'll find the burgers in the refrigerator. It's such a beautiful evening; I thought we might eat on the patio. I just have to set the table and bring out the wine, salad and condiments."

With our individual assignments, we soon have dinner on the table. We keep the conversation light, chatting about the garden and life in the village, but over a dessert of fresh fruit and cream, Finella asks, "Why would anyone want to kill Charles?"

Although I'd been trying to push them away, these same words keep rising to the surface of my mind like rocks in a farmer's field. Murder is a shock at any time, but an almost unbearable one when it happens to someone you know and care about. I stare at my empty plate, but barely focus on it. "If Charles was not delusional then you're right and someone wanted him dead," I admit, before lifting my eyes to meet hers. "But I can't figure out why, not that knowing would make me feel any less angry. What a disgusting species we are."

Finella reaches out and touches my hand. "I understand how you feel. However, if you are going to respond to Charles's plea to 'revenge his foul and most unnatural murder', you must try to detach yourself. Hamlet was unable to and it cost him his life. As you know, exposing a murderer is dangerous business."

"You're right, again. But for now I'm just an armchair detective, safe in the Ontario countryside. Since there's no concrete evidence, I'll proceed on the possibility that Charles was poisoned. Which leads us back to motive. There are, I think, only a few basic motives for premeditated murder. Money is a popular one and then there's power, revenge, jealousy, and malice."

"As far as money is concerned, I would have thought that he was worth more alive than dead. Dead men don't create paintings."

"That may be true Finella, but, dead men's paintings are worth a whole lot more. If Van Gogh was still alive, no one would have paid millions for those darned sunflowers. So, money is still a possibility and so is jealousy, if what Zarina hinted at regarding Charles's amours is true. Somehow Alissa doesn't strike me as the type capable of murder."

"I know what you mean. She's so, so . . . delicate. Even so, we must not forget the method—poison. And poison is considered a woman's weapon."

"It may not have the surety of a knife or a bullet but it does allow someone to murder from a distance."

"What a macabre thought." She pushes back from the table. "More wine or would you like a cup of coffee?"

"I don't want to be a demanding guest but if you have decaf, I'd love a cup. Otherwise could I have tea?" I rise and begin stacking the dishes on a nearby tray.

"Decaf it is and if you'll leave those dishes on the counter in the kitchen, I'll pop them into the dishwasher. And Maud, I think the insects will soon begin biting in earnest, so perhaps we should have our coffee indoors."

I carry in the first tray, then return to the patio and bring in the rest of the dishes. "You know, Charles has given us clear indication of the method of his murder. Maybe, he's provided some clues as to motive in the stories behind the paintings. Alissa's painting of Hercules and Deianira depicts a woman afraid of losing her husband's affections even though the potion aimed at getting him back was deadly. Could be that Charles suspected Alissa's plan was to make him need her, you know, incapacitate him, not kill him."

"Perhaps. And what of the gallery owner, Leona? Her painting suggests a sorceress very definitely setting out to murder. What do you know about her?"

"Very little," I admit. "I saw her for the first time at the reading of the will. She's attractive, but too well-dressed for my taste—very A-type personality if you know what I mean. Actually, Zarina told me she reminded her of Charles's aunt, Theo. Did you ever meet her?

Placing two china mugs on the counter, Finella pours a little cream into each one before filling them with coffee. "Yes, I certainly remember her—a feisty old doll—went to all of Charles's shows. Didn't she send him to Italy to study art?"

I pick up one of the mugs and carry it into the living room. "Is that what he told you?"

"I guess he must have." She sits down in the chair opposite me. "Was he colouring the truth just a tad?" I hesitate and she adds, "You know Maud, the man is dead. It might be important."

I tell her what I know of Charles's past and the difficult relationship he had with his aunt.

"Is she still alive?"

"As far as I know. I wouldn't be surprised to hear she's still in her own home on Manor Road. But, I would think that someone like Theophilus Venable would satisfy her vengeance by making the poor fellow's life a living hell, rather than giving him a speedy demise." I smile at the image forming in my head. "If Leona was the lover scorned, as Zarina suggested, she may have resorted to murder."

My hostess offers me an after dinner mint. "Speaking of Zarina, she could get off on a plea of insanity."

"Oh Finella."

"Really Maud, you must admit, she knits with only one needle."

"Yes, I know, but her painting suggests that if she poisoned Charles, it was accidental."

"Or without full use of her faculties," she insists.

"And what about Teddy and Rupert? Teddy replacing Charles as emperor and Rupert ridding the youth of corruption. I don't get it."

"Yes," she agrees. "Those two demand more information. When you finish your coffee, why not take a rest from these cares and worries and have a lovely bath. I have some scented oils that promise to transport you to another world, or so they say on the commercial."

"Thanks. It's worth a try."

"It's almost time for my favourite television show. I'll amuse myself with that, while you have a soak. There are a few magazines in the rack by the tub. They might offer a pleasant diversion."

The over-sized tub takes a little longer to fill but it's worth the wait as I sink myself into the warm silky water. Within ten minutes my muscles relax but not even an attempt to meditate by focusing on each breath puts my mind to rest. I can't seem to stop the mental images of each suspect, smiling hideously while pouring poison on Charles's food. Our research gave us some answers but it raised even more questions. I need to figure out how to get the autopsy report, surely there must have been one. I decide to call Zarina when I get home and sign up for one of Rupert's classes.

In need of a distraction, I reach over the side of the tub for one of the magazines on landscape architecture. The pictures are beautiful and I amuse myself by studying the flowers and deciding what colours I would mix to get the right value, hue and chroma. It was Charles who taught me that every colour has these three qualities. "Though blue is the hue, it's not just blue," he'd remind us in painting class. "How light is it? How dark is it? That's the value. How dull is it? How bright is it? That's the chroma."

I force myself to read an article on garden follies with the knowledge that I'm not absorbing anything except water. I toss the magazine on the floor, lift myself from the tub, side-stepping the magazine to avoid dripping on it as I towel off.

Slipping into a night-shirt, I join Finella in the living room. Not wanting to disturb the remaining few minutes of her show, I wander over to the bookcase to check out her extensive collection. My best hope is to read myself to sleep.

"Looking for something in particular?" Finella asks from her chair in front of the TV.

"A book to sleep by. But don't let me interrupt your show."

"You're only interrupting another bloody commercial. Good heavens, they're tedious. I'm inclined to boycott any product advertised on television." She joins me at the bookcase. "As to reading material, I do my best to avoid buying anything soporific, but I'm sure this is exactly what you're looking for tonight. The best I can offer is a compilation of short stories so you can read as few or as many as needed to help lull you into sleep."

"Thanks," I say, taking the book. "I guess I'll turn in now. And thanks for all your help today."

"You're very welcome. I'm sure we will both have a good night's sleep and awake tomorrow refreshed and with some inspired insights." As I open the door of the spare room she adds, "Oh Maud, I forgot to tell you that I put a feather mattress on the bed since you were last here. Hope you like it."

When I ease myself between the covers, I'm pleasantly surprised. The feather bed receives the contours and mass of my body and makes me feel weightless. After reading for less than thirty minutes I turn off the light and let myself fall blissfully into the arms of Morpheus. Of course, I would rather have fallen blissfully into the arms of Cary Grant but he only lives on old celluloid.

I awake the next morning at eight-thirty and as Finella predicted, feel refreshed, though unaware of any inspired insights. Padding into the kitchen, I breathe in the unmistakable aroma of freshly brewed coffee.

Finella looks up from her newspaper. "Did you sleep well?"

"I did. It must be that feather bed."

"That and the country air. Would you like breakfast now or do you prefer to wait awhile?"

"I usually don't eat breakfast." I pour myself a cup of coffee. "But I would like to take you to that restaurant in the village. We could have breakfast, brunch or lunch, whichever you prefer."

"Well, I usually do eat breakfast, though I am willing to compromise and go for brunch. I did put together a fresh fruit cocktail if you're interested."

I have to admit the colourful bowl of strawberries, orange and banana slices looks irresistible

"See what the country does for you. You eat better, sleep soundly and if I can get you to spend some time in the garden, you'll find your spirit will benefit too."

"I'm willing," I tell her. "But be warned, I don't have a good track record with plants."

"I don't want you to do anything with the plants. I want you to get rid of the weeds."

We spend the better part of the morning removing the dreaded weeds from her garden and, by eleven, we're happily settled at the Inn, a delightful country brunch spread before us.

"Thank you, Maud. I'm enjoying this."

"It's the least I could do after all you've done for me. I feel more than ready to face what lies ahead."

"Do you indeed, and what does lie ahead?" she asks.

"First, I want to find out the details of Charles's autopsy report. I had thought of a visit to the hospital where he died, but it might be easier to get some information from Charles's aunt Theo. Then, I'll call Zarina and sign up for a painting class. Essentially, I hope to find out what I can about Charles's last days."

"I want you to promise me that you will be very, very careful. You must know that each of the suspects is aware of the painting you received from Charles. To those who are innocent it will mean little but to the guilty it will trigger a potent warning."

"What do you mean?"

"What I mean, Maud, is if the killer unravels the meaning behind your painting of Hamlet, he or she will be watching you. Watching to see if you respond to Charles's plea to revenge his foul and unnatural murder. By taking a class, you are entering the scene of the crime and there is one individual who will do whatever is necessary to keep you from uncovering the truth."

Chapter 4

I arrive back at my apartment just after five and find Kora waiting at the door like an impatient mother. If she owned a wristwatch, she would have been tapping it with her paw. I reach down to pet her, but she twirls away from me, swishing her tail. "Come on now my little fur face. It was just one night." I scoop her up and carry her into the kitchen, giving her nuzzles and pets until she purrs her forgiveness.

"That's better. Now let's get you some dinner." Leaving her to her kibble, I unzip my portfolio and return the painting to the mantel. Though its message is clear, I'm not. Charles, I wonder, am I up to the task you've given me?

As I stand, preoccupied by self-doubt, the painting suddenly falls from its perch and lands face up on the floor. Every hair on my body bristles as I rush to check its condition. Thankfully, it's unharmed. Had I propped it so carelessly or was some other force at work? In recognition that there are more things in heaven and earth than are dreamt of in Horatio's, and my philosophy, I make a promise, "All right Charles, I'll do my best."

Too uncomfortable to put it back on the mantel and not ready to hang it on the wall, I place the painting into the portfolio and slide it under my bed. I'm a solitary soul but my uncle's an occasional visitor and I don't want to explain this treasure. I do, however, want to make that call to Zarina. Kora curls into a doughnut on my lap.

"Zarina, it's Maud," I get in quickly.

"Ah yes Miss G., calling to sign up for Rupert's painting class are we?"

"How did you know?"

"I expected you to be inspired by Charles's wonderful painting."

"Did you see it?"

"I didn't need to. All Charles's paintings are wonderful. Don't you agree?"

I know every great artist produces the odd mediocre work, but I'm certainly not going to suggest this to Zarina. She's completely biased where Charles is concerned.

"So, painting is Tuesday evening? We expect you at your easel and ready to begin promptly at seven."

"Fine, I'll be there." I thank her and return the phone to its cradle. Lifting Kora from my lap, I offer to open the cat door for her to have a prowl. Rubbing the side of her body against my calf before following me into the kitchen, she chooses to stay close to her Mom.

It's hard to be inspired when cooking for one, but as Zarina so ingenuously reminded me, "you are what you eat." It may not be fancy but it would be healthy. I choose a tuna melt on rye, carrot sticks and a cup of ginger tea and while the meal is tasty, the television fare is bland. After a couple of hours I give up and go to bed. Kora generally sleeps, well, anywhere she wants to, but on this occasion, she curls up next to my feet and is still there when I wake up before six the following morning.

My Uncle Sid shows obvious surprise when I open the office door at seven forty-five. "You're here early." I hear the pleasure in his voice.

"Yes, you too." Since the death of my Aunt Emma last year, I had begun to suspect that my uncle has a hidden closet and Murphy bed somewhere in his office. "Spent a night in the country with a friend from art school. She's got this great featherbed—you know, I think I should get one. Anyway, I have some paperwork from last week so I'm here to finish it up, unless there's something else you want done?"

"No, no that's fine. You just carry on as usual. Good to hear you had a nice weekend." He glances at his watch. "Look, I have to get to Brampton by nine. It's not likely, but if you need me I've got my cell phone. Oh, and Al was doing surveillance last night so don't expect to see him." He grabs a file folder off the desk, gives me a wave and is out the door.

The computer occupies most of my morning, but I can't stop my mind from drawing images of Charles's studio. How will Rupert, who seldom strings four words together, give instruction to a class of avid students? Will I be watched with suspicion or will my investigation go unnoticed? And what am I investigating anyway? Half my brain deals with these questions, and the other half gets me through the day. When I finally arrive home that night, I'm still trying to decide if I'm taking the right approach. By the end of the evening, the mental track circling in my brain has worn me out and I fall asleep.

Tuesday is business as usual and by six o'clock, I feel surprisingly relaxed. Zarina had said to be there at seven and although it means an apple and a muffin for dinner, I intend to be prompt. I retain this confidence until my travel paint box breaks open on the way to my car, spilling its contents across the gravel drive. I take a deep breath and entertain the possibility of at least getting to the studio by seven.

When I open the studio door, familiar smells of paint and turpentine prepare me to see Charles standing next to the raised platform, anxious to explain how the folds in drapery tell the story of its material. But it won't be Charles teaching me tonight and tiptoeing into the room, I suffer Zarina's glare as she begins addressing the class at exactly seven o'clock.

I scan the room for a vacant drawing horse—an uncomfortable apparatus that one is expected to straddle, as if on horseback, while propping a drawing board or stretched canvas against its "neck." Presumably, dedication and concentration can be measured by the length of time one can ignore lower body discomfort and reduced blood circulation to the feet. Finding a spot near the door I sit, side-saddle, resting my paint box on my lap.

I hear Zarina giving a short history of the studio and recall Charles's pride when he moved from the cramped digs of a former chiropractic office to this reclaimed factory space. It had once housed a ceramics manufacturer and when he rented the ground floor, Charles drew up a floor plan for an office area next to a kitchen and a small sitting room next to a bathroom. With Rupert's help, the walls were erected, leaving the largest area, where eight large windows conveyed a steady stream of light, as a studio and classroom. For evening work, Charles installed a combination of fluorescent and incandescent fixtures, best suited to mimic natural light.

Glancing toward the west wall, I'm surprised to see an unfinished mural until I remember Zarina telling me that Rupert was finishing Charles's commission from MetLife. Unframed and hanging above the mural, is an exquisite painting Charles had done of Toronto's Old City Hall. In the far corner stands his over-sized easel, and against the back wall, his taboret and drafting table. A work in progress rests on the easel—a young woman of pale and haunting beauty tenderly emerging from the canvas. Soft blonde ringlets frame a fairy-princess face. Tucked behind the easel, I see the heavy red curtain and remember a conversation from another time.

"Do you sew?" Charles had asked me.

"I'm not sure how to answer that Charles, but if you're asking me if I have a sewing machine, the answer is yes and if you're asking me if I can whip you up a designer suit or a dress shirt with french cuffs, the answer is no."

"I want curtains. Can you make curtains?" I told him I could handle curtains.

"That's great then. You see, I have this red material and I'm going to run a rod in a semicircle around my easel—keep out prying eyes."

I'd made him the curtains and seeing them now, I want to wrap them around his solitary easel.

An involuntary sigh brings me back to the present and I'm instantly aware of an unnatural stillness. Zarina has paused in her talk to the class and is waiting for my attention. I lower my eyes to the floor in apology and she continues.

"As I was saying, I'm sure most of you are aware of the dangers of solvents in unventilated areas. The amount used during the process of oil painting is, I believe, negligible. However, we do take every precaution with open windows and fans. Be aware also that many oil paints are highly toxic and should not be ingested, so keep your supplies away from young children and pets. The earth colours, that is, the ochres, umbers, siennas and earth reds are of minimal risk but the cobalts are particularly poisonous."

My spine straightens involuntarily.

"And now, as this is the first class of the summer semester and for some of you, your first visit to the studio, I would like to introduce Mr. Rupert Jaynes. He apprenticed with our maestro, Mr. Charles Venable, and has thankfully agreed to carry on the wonderful tradition begun by our sorely missed master." She waves her hand theatrically in his direction and he walks to the front of the room.

Slight of build and an inch or two shorter than average, Rupert's boyish appearance has charm but lacks presence. Although I expect bashful incoherence, he approaches the class with confidence.

"Welcome to you all," he says, then pivots his head, casting a smile across the room. "For our first class I have set a rather simple exercise. I trust you are ready for it." He pauses, as if asking for agreement and is rewarded with several nodding heads. "Simple in its subject matter," he continues, "deceptively difficult in its execution. We have on the stand behind me a goose egg placed in front of a glass vase holding two large white feathers and for the background a simple piece of black mat board. The drawing horses have been arranged to allow an interesting vantage point for everyone but feel free, within reason of course, to rearrange your position. For those who wish to stand, the drawing horse may be turned on its end to form an easel. I'll turn on the spot light and you'll see the wonderful cast shadow and the beautiful modulations of tone." Rupert reaches above his head and turns on the light.

"I expect each of you to render this lovely still life in grisaille, beginning of course with a cartoon, in pencil, on tracing paper. When your drawing has been approved, you will transfer it to the canvas. We have, I think, four newcomers, and I will meet with you at the back of the class for a preliminary lesson. The rest of you have some experience and can begin your drawings." He gestures to the back wall. "You will find drawing boards on the far wall and knitting needles, for measuring, in the jar on the bookcase. You can also purchase paper, pencils and erasers from Zarina, if you did not bring your own. I will allow you to erase, for that which is imperfect will not be allowed to stand. Now everyone, you may proceed to lay an egg."

There is a smattering of laughter at his little joke and as the beginners collect at the back of the room, the rest of us head over to retrieve a drawing board. I queue with a few of my classmates to buy paper from Zarina. When it's my turn, she smirks at me like Frans Hals's 'Laughing Cavalier.' "Nice to see you here, Maudy, and almost on time."

"Thank you, Zarina. I need to buy a pad of tracing paper."

I'm deciding between two sizes of paper when the studio door bursts open and Alissa struts into the room. The look of shock on Zarina's face tells me Charles's widow is the last person she expected to see. I pay for the paper and discreetly return to my drawing horse.

Reaching Zarina, Alissa stands next to her, arms akimbo, waiting for the students to finish with their purchases. When the two women withdraw to the office, I consider moving to a drawing horse within earshot and begin to gather my belongings.

"Aren't you staying for the class?" It's a soft feminine voice and turning, I see a face that parallels it perfectly. Standing next to her drawing horse, her denim shorts and halter-top reveal the slim figure of a fashion model.

"Oh, yes of course," I tell her. "I'm just read-justing my view of the still life."

"My name is Grace," she whispers, in defer-ence to the students working nearby.

"I'm Maud," I whisper back, noting her warm grey eyes and unnaturally long lashes. Like a clas-sic ballerina, her fair hair is pulled back from her face and accentuates her elegant neck.

She extends a small delicate hand toward mine. "It's a pleasure to meet you, Maud. Is this your first visit to the studio?"

"I attended the studio years ago, but this is my first class with Rupert."

"Oh, you knew Charles," she says with child-like expectation. "Did you know him well?"

"Fairly well, I guess, although I hadn't seen much of him recently. How about you?"

"I've been coming here for over a year. Charles was instrumental in changing my life."

I'll bet he was. It was a cynical thought and I'm not proud of it, but for my former instructor, this fresh beauty would have been irresistible. "Was Charles very ill before he died?" I ask innocently.

"He seemed fine to me. I mean, really fine," she nods her head for emphasis. "I had an assign-ment the week before he died so I didn't see him, you know, just before."

"And how are you two getting along?" Rupert steps into the gap between us. His question is addressed to us both but his attention is focused on Grace.

"We're fine," she tells him, avoiding eye contact.

He hovers around her like a hummingbird near a hibiscus and finally seats himself at her drawing horse, making a frame with his outstretched hands. "I see you have a nice view here, Grace. Are you intending to use sight-size? If you are, your subject will be rather small."

"No, I hadn't intended to, Rupert." Her tone is telling him to take a hike but if he has any awareness of it, he chooses not to notice.

"What's sight-size?" I ask, hoping to divert his attention.

With careful enunciation of each word, he says, "I will be explaining that shortly." He rises from the drawing horse and continues on to an examination of the next student's work.

Grace sits at her drawing horse and with the familiar knitting needle, begins taking measurements for her drawing.

"You don't like him much, do you?" I mouth, inclining my head in Rupert's direction.

"When we... that is, when Charles was alive, I got along with Rupert. It was easy. He was so, so . . ." she struggles to find the right word. "Distant," she concludes. "I mean he was there but not there. Now, he's too much here. Sorry, it's hard to explain."

As though hearing his name, I see Rupert turn in our direction. Fortunately, a waving hand signals for help and he strides off in the other direction. After a quick word, and a few deft pencil strokes, he steps to the front of the room. "I think it is time for a lesson on sight-size. This is a technique that Charles first encountered during a visit to an art school in Italy but one I can't wholeheartedly recommend, as I feel it can be too restricting. The basic procedure of measurement remains the same but the need for comparing ratios is eliminated, which does provide a shortcut. However, what I consider to be problematic is that the size of the drawing is identical to the size of your view. Allow me to demonstrate."

Rupert begins an illustration as he talks about accurate measurement and academic drawing, most of which is already familiar to me, though the information regarding sight-size is new. Traditionally, artists hold up their pencils or brushes to take measurements, which will then be used as ratios. Charles had favoured the metal knitting needle because of its narrow diameter. After the artist makes an arbitrary decision, for example, like the size of the head if drawing a portrait, the knitting needle is held vertically, at arm's length, and key measurements are made for the placement of eyes, nose, mouth, and ears. The artist then transfers these measurements to paper, using ratios and proportions.

In summing up, Rupert explains that the only difference with sight-size is that the measurements are transferred to the drawing paper exactly as seen. Both methods require attention to measurement, but I agree that the traditional approach afforded maximum control.

His lesson over, the students settle down to their work. The room is too quiet to allow even a whispered conversation with Grace. I want to know more about her relationship with Charles and what she knew about his final illness, but will have to wait until the break. I also don't want to raise undue curiosity by appearing too inquisitive so I turn my attention to my drawing and begin laying in the necessary shapes.

Drawing is a right-brained activity and even though it holds its own set of frustrations, I find it a relaxing break from a culture that over-uses my left brain. I feel time evaporate while I bask in complete concentration. After my initial anxiety about coming to the class, I find I'm enjoying myself, and the basic outline plus most of the shadow shapes magically appear under my pencil before Rupert's voice enters my consciousness.

"That's the halfway mark. Why don't we all take a break?"

I pull myself from my picture and glance over at Grace's drawing. Good God, it's a tangle of discordant lines and faulty proportions. I'm even more convinced Charles was not interested in her artistic ability. When she sees me checking out her drawing, I can't pretend otherwise. "So, Grace, well, um, you got quite a bit done there."

"Oh yes." Enthusiasm fills her voice. "I really get into it you know and Charles was always so encouraging."

"Was he? Speaking of Charles . . ." Before I can pursue my line of questioning, Rupert is back like a mosquito bearing down on bare flesh.

"How are we doing?" he asks, a hand on each knee, his neck practically touches her shoulder as he bends to look at her drawing. I think the vision before him steals his voice but it's temporary.

"Well, well, well. You've made an excellent start there, Grace," he coos. I see his nose grow a centimetre but what the hell; it's not my place to intervene. If others are blinded by Grace's beauty, she's developed her own blind spots in response.

"Thank you Rupert. Excuse me, I need a glass of water."

I expect little attention from my love-struck instructor, so I rise to follow her, but before I take two steps, the door to Zarina's office bursts open. Alissa stomps out like an angry Tinkerbell, then turns abruptly and walks back into the room. We can no longer see her but her voice is clearly audible. "This studio now belongs to me and it would be in your best interests to remember that." She re-emerges, plants both feet in front of Rupert and declares, "That goes for you too." Strutting toward the front door, she pauses to add a closing comment. "I'll be back."

When the door slams behind her, the tension in the room is palpable. Finally, one of the students murmurs, "Was that Arnold Schwarzenegger?" and the room erupts in nervous laughter.

There are two people who are not amused. Rupert, who's fixated on the closed door and Zarina, standing just outside the office, her arms crossed firmly over her midriff.

"We will have to be patient with Mrs. Venable," Zarina says, when the room is quiet. "As we all know, she is crazed with grief at the loss of her dear husband." Insincerity permeates her voice but a smile sweetens her lips as she walks toward the kitchen. "I'll have some tea and decaffeinated coffee ready in just a few minutes."

A few students collect their cigarettes and head for the street, while others huddle in small groups, chatting quietly. I stroll over to Charles's easel to have a closer look at the painting. The colours are clean and the glow of multiple glazes adds to the fine detail of the work. I feel it's a little sappy, which is unusual for Charles, for he seldom romanticised his subjects. Though unfinished, I make a futile check for a signature.

"What do you think?"

I involuntarily elevate from the floor. "Rupert, you startled me."

"Sorry." His stare tells me he's impatient for an answer.

"I think it's lovely," I tell him.

"Thank you."

"You painted this?" I can't stop the rising inflection.

"You needn't sound so surprised."

"No, no, it's not that. It's just that, it's on Charles's easel so I assumed, well you know."

"Charles doesn't need this easel anymore." He leaves me watching his back as he approaches a group of students.

When the break ends, I resume my drawing and return to my pocket of timelessness. Sadly, the right moment never presents itself for a continued conversation with Grace. I hope she might linger at the end of class but at the stroke of nine, she packs up her work. When she pauses at the door to wave me a cheery good-bye, her loosened hair falls in soft ringlets to her shoulders and I look back at the portrait emerging on Charles's easel.

Chapter 5

"Do you think Charles was having an affair with her?"

"It's a good possibility."

"How old did you say she was?"

"I'm guessing twenty, twenty-one."

"That's a difference of over thirty years." The thought of thirty years caused a momentary silence. I'd called Finella from the office to update her on the events of the previous evening.

"And you're sure it was Grace's portrait on Charles's easel?" she asks.

"Yes, though I admit I didn't see the likeness until she let her hair down."

"So Rupert is using Charles's easel. Do you think she posed for him, Maud?"

"Somehow I doubt it. She did her best to avoid all his attentiveness and I can't imagine she would want to be alone with him, even if it meant having her portrait painted. And they practically ignored one another when Charles was alive."

"Interesting. And imagine Alissa barging in like that. I guess there's no doubt she said the studio belonged to her?"

"No doubt. In fact it was a proclamation for all to hear."

"Do you think she was referring to the business or the whole building?"

"Oh, well, I thought she was talking about the studio. It didn't occur to me that she might mean the entire building. From what I remember, Charles was a tenant, but that was years ago and I suppose things could have changed."

"It might be a good idea to check with the land registry office. They keep records of all the properties and for a small fee, you can get a printout that will tell you who owns the property. It will give you some insight into Charles's financial situation, which could lead to another possible motive for Alissa."

"I was thinking of calling the bereaved widow. Thought I might feign concern for her outburst from last night."

"Ah, good idea. Now, what about the gallery owner and the agent?" she asks.

"Leona and Teddy. I plan to drop by Leona's gallery. I'd like to have a look at some of Charles's paintings, and chat to her for a bit, though I don't hold out much hope. From our brief meeting at the lawyers and from what Zarina said, Leona is a gate-keeper, unlikely to share any information."

"Didn't Zarina compare her to Charles's aunt Theo?"

"She did and now that you've mentioned his aunt, I intend to pay her a visit too. She might be able to tell me something about Charles's final days and whether or not there was an autopsy. I'd considered going to the hospital, but as I'm no relation, they probably wouldn't tell me anything. As far as Teddy is concerned, I'll need some reason to seek him out."

Finella clears her throat. "I have an idea for that."

"I'm all ears."

"He's an artists' agent right?"

"Yes."

"And Maud, you're an artist."

"No."

"You're painting, aren't you?"

"Finella, I'm working on a goose egg and a couple of feathers."

She sighs. "As I recall from our lessons with Charles, you were becoming a fine portrait artist."

"Gee, thanks."

"Just stating the facts, Maud. You really should start doing portraits again. Don't you think?" When I don't respond she continues. "Anyhow, you could go to Teddy and tell him you're considering a career change. Say you need his help to make a smooth transition, you know, out of the office and into the studio. Art school provided little information about the business side of the arts."

"I get your drift. I'll pose as a passionate artist whose interest is rekindled after the death of her famous teacher."

"That's the idea! And who knows, you might even come to believe it."

I'm not convinced, but it gives me a good reason to meet with Teddy. "I'll keep you posted," I promise before withdrawing the receiver from my ear.

"And Maud," I hear Finella call out.

I pull the phone back to my ear. "Yes?"

"Be careful!"

"Don't worry. I'll call you tomorrow."

I have a half hour before my uncle is due back at the office. Enough time to organise all the necessary telephone numbers and maybe make a call or two. I don't want to be in the middle of a conversation when he returns. Reaching for the phonebook, I quickly find the listing for Theo Venable and transcribe it on a piece of scrap paper. Next, I copy down Alissa's number and finally, I locate a number for Teddy in the yellow pages under "Artists' Managers and Agents." I consider calling Theo first but she might not remember me and that will be awkward. I decide to approach her in person. I stare at Alissa's number and chicken out. That conversation needs planning. The thought of talking to Teddy raises the least anxiety, so I make the call. Prepared to hear his voice I hesitate when a young woman answers but do my best to sound business-like when she says hello for a second time. "May I please speak to Mr. Evelyn Baer?"

"He's not here right now. This is his daughter speaking. Can I help you?"

"Oh, I, well . . ." I didn't know he had a daughter. "I don't suppose he has a cell phone number I could call?" I hear myself sounding pushy so I add, "Or not."

"He hates cell phones but he did leave a number where he could be reached. May I ask who's calling?"

"My name is Maud Gibbons and I know your father through Charles Venable. I wanted to ask him about the business. That is, the business side of the art world and about being an agent."

"Do you want to be an agent?"

"No, no. I want to hire him."

"I see, well this is where you can reach him."

I'm sure she gave me the number just to get rid of me. I recite it back to her and before hanging up realise it has a familiar ring to it. My eyes scan the other numbers on the page and stop at Alissa's. It's the same number Teddy's daughter has just given. Damn, should I call him at Alissa's? My decision is made for me by the early return of my uncle. Grabbing the scrap of paper, I shove it unobtrusively into my pocket.

"Hi Sweets. How are things going?" He's in a good mood.

"Just fine. Mrs. Willoughby called about her deadbeat hubby—still no cheque for child support. Guess you're not too surprised. She wants to know if we've had any luck tracing him."

"Call her back and let her know that I went to his last place of employment. Naturally, he doesn't work there anymore, but I do have a good lead. I'll be following it up first thing tomorrow morning."

"Okay. Is there anything else?" I ask.

He narrows his eyes. "You got something you want to do?"

"Nothing really pressing." I stack the files on my desk.

"All right, you can get out of here—after you talk to her."

I snatch up the phone and call Mrs. Willoughby while Uncle Sid rummages through the files I just tidied.

"Where's that paperwork for Mainstay Insurance?" he asks, when I close the call.

"I filed it."

He winks at me. "You're nothing if not organised, my darling niece."

"Years of art training and cat ownership, *mon oncle*."

"Speaking of art, how was the course last night with the new teacher?"

He asked the question but as he is now browsing through the filing cabinet, I don't think he's all that interested in the answer. "It was fine," I tell him, rising from my chair. "Just one little mishap when Vincent shot himself in the stomach."

"That's nice dear. Well, you tootle along now and we'll see you tomorrow at nine."

Retrieving my purse from the small closet next to the door, I turn to find my uncle sitting at my desk, leafing through the file. "Bye for now," I say, leaning over and kissing his bald head.

"Maud?" he calls out just as I leave the office.

"Yes?"

"Van Gogh should never have packed a pistol in his paint box."

I sign a thumbs-up before closing the door. My plan is to go home and make the phone calls but I decide on a detour to Charles's aunt Theo's. Depending on the traffic, I might get there for tea-time, assuming of course she still adheres to this English tradition.

I've no problem locating the red brick house on Manor Road but finding a parking spot would challenge Percival. These old homes were built before our love affair with the automobile and not one of them sports a driveway. With street parking at a premium, I travel a couple of blocks before finding space.

The only time I have truly aced parallel parking was sixteen years ago, when I did my driver's test. Since then, the whole procedure causes me profuse sweating and intense swearing. I'm convinced I have some kind of mental block but no amount of positive self-talk alleviates the situation. Maybe I should include a phrase like, "I am good at parallel parking" in my morning affirmations and if I ever get around to doing morning affirmations, it will be first on the list. By the time I make the walk to the front door, the sweat has evaporated, and the swearing abated. When Miss Theo Venable opens the door, I'm ready. "I'm sorry to bother you, Miss Venable. My name is Maud Gibbons and I was a student and friend of your nephew, Charles. We met when . . ."

"No bother and no need for further introduction. I remember you. Come in." She takes a step back and pulls open the door.

It's been a few years since our last meeting and I hope my facial expression doesn't betray the shock I feel. Although she still wears her silver hair piled on top of her head like one of the Gibson Girls from the nineteen twenties, her Rubenesque figure has been redone as a Modigliani and the loose fitting skirt and blouse, dyed the colour of a cold winter sky, make her seem ghost-like.

Her voice tremulous, she says, "I was just having tea. Would you like to join me?" I tell her I would and follow her measured steps through the kitchen to a sunny, enclosed veranda. With a gesture toward the chair on my left, she says, "Make yourself comfortable. I'll just get you a cup."

From what I remember of Theo Venable, an offer of help would be insulting so I simply sit down in the white wicker chair and become enveloped in its high back and plump gingham seat cushion. On a matching wicker table with a glass top sits a silver tea service, complete with a plate of buttered scones. Theo returns, her arthritic fingers clutching a bone china cup and saucer. She puts the saucer down first and after two attempts manages to right the cup. "Forgive me. My hands are uncooperative. Milk and sugar?"

"Just milk, thank you. I hope you don't mind my dropping in on you?"

"No, no. It's a pleasure to see you again, Miss Gibbons." She gestured toward the scones. "Please help yourself. Or perhaps you would like something else, a sandwich, a piece of fruit? I serve a very minimal tea these days."

I thank her and reach for a scone. She seems much more approachable than I remember.

"I suppose, Miss Gibbons, you've noticed that I have mellowed in my dotage," she says, expressing my thoughts.

Empty compliments are likely to be unappreciated so I agree with her and add, "Please call me Maud."

"I shall be happy to, if you will call me Theo." Watching my face she adds, "I know what you're thinking. There was a time when that would have rankled but that time has gone. I've lost all my friends, either through death or bad feelings. And now that my beloved nephew is no longer with me, I have shed my former persona, at least as much as I am able at this late stage. My constant regret is that I did not make the effort when he was alive."

"I was so sorry to hear of Charles's passing. It must be difficult for you."

She clasped one hand over the other, her knuckles whitening. "Yes, I admit to an outpouring of anger. I was angry with God for taking my nephew. And I was angry with Charles for not taking care of himself, and for not confiding in me. Finally, I was angry with myself." She loosened her grip, forcing her fingers to relax. "But I now know the destructive force of internalised anger. With what little strength I have remaining, I intend to conquer this demon."

"You're certainly to be commended Miss Venable—Theo, but I'm afraid the information I bring you may test that resolve. I'm here because Charles bequeathed me a painting. I'll tell you about it, but first would you mind answering a few questions?"

"Lay on MacDuff."

"Was Charles ill before he died?"

"He wasn't ill exactly but he had what I would call bouts of illness. It was his habit to visit me—check up on me is probably more accurate—on Thursdays. Often we would go out for dinner. But that began to change."

"Change in what way?" I ask.

"In the few months before he died, he arrived too tired to go out. I didn't question it at the time. I assumed he was working hard and to be honest I was just happy to have him visit his old auntie. Then I noticed he was losing weight. When I mentioned it, he said Alissa had him on a diet. Not that he was ever fat," she adds. I shook my head in agreement. "About a month before he died, he arrived looking particularly pale and complained of stomach cramps. I wanted to call a doctor but he insisted that if he just went to bed, he'd be fine in the morning. And that's what he did. Sure enough, he was up bright and early and off to the studio."

"What was the cause of death?"

"The autopsy cited heart failure, with complications of liver disease."

"Had Charles been drinking heavily?"

"Never in front of me, but what he did privately, I couldn't say. Certainly that wife of his would drive anyone to drink." I hear the voice of the Theo Venable she was trying so hard to overcome. "I see by your face that I've backslid in character. It sounds harsh but Alissa did put enormous demands on Charles and even when he met them, there was no respite."

"Do you mind telling me what sort of demands?"

"Most of them involved money but in the last few years she could hear her biological clock ticking. She was desperate for a child. Of course, she's considerably younger than Charles, part of the reason she had him on that ridiculous diet, but he was over fifty and not interested in child rearing. Now my dear, will you tell me about the painting Charles left you?"

"Yes of course. It's a wonderful depiction of Hamlet on the rampart of Elsinore Castle. As much as I appreciate the gift, I couldn't understand why Charles left me a painting or why he left me that particular painting. Then I saw he had written "Act I, scene v" under his signature. I'm afraid he suspected . . ."

"Murder most foul," Theo interrupts me, her eyes wide and intense. "My nephew was a man of strong character and prodigious talent. I have no doubt that he had enemies, but murder?"

"Yes." I look at this frail, elderly lady. Tears pool in my eyes and though I will them not to, they find passage down my cheeks. Theo reaches for a box of tissues and offers it to me. "I'm so sorry to tell you this, and after all you've suffered." I dab at my tears.

"That's all right dear." She places a comforting hand on my arm. "What you are telling me is Charles suspected that he was being poisoned. As was his custom," she removes her hand and her voice trails off to a whisper, "he did not confide in me."

"I understand."

We sit in silence. I see her slumped shoulders and bowed head, wishing I had words of comfort, knowing I only have words of pain.

Her eyes meet mine. "There was no suspicion of foul play, you see. And therefore, no need to pursue further investigation. However," she sighs before continuing, "in light of what you're telling me, things may not have been what they seemed. I'll need some time to further construct his last days. Thank God, my memory continues to be quite reliable. Is there anything else?"

I tell her about the reading of the will and the other bequests. "There is also the possibility that Charles was, well . . . I hesitate, searching for the right way to tell her that her nephew may have been delusional.

"Yes?" Theo prompts.

"Perhaps he just imagined he was being poisoned."

"Are you suggesting he was mentally unstable?"

"No! Well, maybe."

Raising her chin and dropping her shoulders she says, "There is one thing I can be quite sure of Maud. Charles was in full use of his faculties." My vigorous nod seems to soften her defences and she agrees quietly that we had best take Charles's message seriously. "Now, as to the possible culprits," her voice gains strength, "all of these people received a painting from Charles, not really as gifts from him but as clues for you, right?" Before I can respond she adds, "I had but a passing acquaintance with most of them. Could you go over the list again?"

I start but she stops me to retrieve a pad of paper and a pen. "I think it would be best if you write them down and leave a little space after each so I can add any thoughts that might help you," she says.

The list complete, I hand it to her.

"Oh my dear, I need my glasses. Would you mind, they're on the kitchen counter."

I get them for her and she studies the list. "Oh not Teddy. He's such a dear man—it just couldn't be Teddy. You are already aware of my feelings toward Alissa—temperamental, with expensive tastes but capable of murder? I don't know. However, I'm now very suspicious of that diet she had him on. I don't know what to say about the others. The one constant, given what you've told me about the paintings, appears to be the element of poison." She removes her glasses. "You know, my dear it is a terrible thought but I could demand to have Charles's body exhumed for further tests."

"I've thought of that and I suppose it's inevitable but would you give me a little time to follow Charles's request. An exhumation may prove the existence of poison but is unlikely to give us clues to the murderer. Involving the police will alert a killer who may at the moment think he or she has committed the perfect crime."

"I will agree, provided you will not put yourself in danger and you will keep me abreast of your findings."

Unwilling to make promises I can't keep, I tell her I'll do my best. I rise from my chair but feelings of remorse make me reluctant to leave her. The poor old thing had finally come to terms with her loss and I'd provided her with a new and even more painful set of circumstances. When I try to express these sentiments, she tenderly wraps her hands around mine, reassuring me that, even though the manner of his passing had changed, she had come to a place of peace with regards to his death and nothing I could say would destroy that.

After making plans to visit her in a couple of days, I leave her with my phone number, the list and her thoughts.

Steering my car south on Mount Pleasant, I take a detour that will lead me past Alissa's. I admit to being directionally challenged and it's been a long time since I visited Charles and Alissa's home in the Beaches but I know it's south of Queen Street and close to the water treatment plant. As I tour the narrow streets, I watch for a Tudor-style brick house with a memorable front door. Recalling my first visit, I hear Charles's deep baritone. "So, Maud, how about this door! It's a high chroma cadmium red, value scale number 5, right out of the tube. I'm not all that partial to the colour but Alissa likes it. Small concession eh?"

As I drive up the fourth street I see that unforgettable door, my eyes scan to the house and finally to the car in the driveway—a champagne Mercedes.

Chapter 6

There may be a perfectly innocent reason for Teddy's car to remain parked in Alissa's driveway. Perhaps they're intimate friends. Then again, perhaps they're just intimate. I consider finding a sheltered spot for an all-night surveillance but, knowing I've fallen asleep during many an exciting movie, my hopes of staying awake watching a stationary object are nil. Better to get up early and take the long way to the office. If his car is still sitting in Alissa's driveway at seven tomorrow morning, well, who would take a cab when he owns a perfectly good Mercedes.

I arrive home just after six and find one message on my answering machine—Leona Tellman telling me to drop by the gallery before one o'clock the following day. I call her back to confirm but leave my own message as the gallery's closed. I'm not sure why she wants to see me but assume my newly acquired "Venable" is the likely reason. At least I don't have to fabricate a motive to meet with her. I'm deep into an imaginary conversation in which I get her to reveal her affair with Charles, when the ringing of the phone interrupts my thoughts.

"Maudlin, it's Zarina. I'm calling to let you know that we have space for one more at Thursday night's class. Are you interested?" Before I can answer she adds, "You will progress much more quickly, you know, if you enrol in two classes a week."

Knowing it will give me greater opportunity for investigation, more credibility in convincing Teddy of my ardent need for a career change, and the fact that I truly enjoyed myself on Tuesday evening, I agree. "Is it seven on Thursday, as well?"

"Yes, Matts and do try to be prompt this time."

She hangs up before I can respond. Her concern for my progress likely hides a monetary interest but it doesn't matter. It is a good idea. With so much to do, I need a good night's sleep.

After a leisurely bath, Kora and I climb into bed before ten. She busies herself with ritual grooming while I have a hot cup of chamomile tea and spend a half hour on a crossword puzzle. I'm ready for sleep when I turn off my bedside lamp at twenty after ten but it does not remain a peaceful repose. I plunge from one nightmare into another, with each one featuring Charles's aunt Theo rubbing her gnarled arthritic hands until she finally uses them to wring my neck. I awake with a start, very relieved to find that she's not actually in my bedroom.

Dreams, some say, are a waste product of the mind. The refuse of our thoughts gets sifted, sorted and disposed of while we sleep. I know my dreams are motivated by guilt. Theo had wounds that were only partially healed when I came along to pour on the proverbial salt. I couldn't blame her if she wanted to strangle me.

On the positive side of a nightmarish night, I was up with plenty of time for my 'drive-by-spy' at Alissa's. I find my way easily and am only a little surprised to see the Mercedes sitting cosily in her driveway. Presumably, Teddy was cosy as well. Zarina had said Alissa may have found another shoulder to cry on and though she hadn't put a nod toward Teddy, his shoulders were very broad indeed.

Arriving at the office before nine meant I could accomplish the morning's work in ample time for my meeting at Leona's gallery. I feel calm when I leave the office, but after stopping for lunch, I find I can't eat the sandwich I've ordered. I leave the café wishing Leona's message had explained her reason for wanting to see me. With a few deep breaths, I reassure myself that I can handle whatever she might say.

No one greets me when I enter the gallery and I wander alone through the three lavishly renovated rooms, keenly aware of the sound of my shoes hitting the gleaming hardwood floors. Warm white walls display exquisite oils and watercolours, hanging as testament to Leona's excellent judgement in the visual arts. Each painting, whether representational or abstract, reveals a technical expertise and creative ability I'm sure most people can appreciate. The work is by contemporary artists but I'm disappointed by the absence of Venables. I'd hoped to get some idea of Charles's finances by the price tag on his paintings.

"See anything you like?"

I turn in the direction of the voice and receive a well-practised smile from Leona Tellman.

"Almost everything." She approaches and we shake hands. Elegantly dressed in what is likely one of her many designer suits, I marvel at the perfect alignment of her hair. How does she do that?

"Each work is of a consistently high quality. I'm very impressed, Leona." I feel her smile change to one of genuine warmth and although my comments help smooth our introduction, I am sincere. "My only disappointment is in not seeing any of Charles's work."

"That's what I want to talk to you about," she coos. "I'm planning a retrospective and memorial to his artistic genius and although I have many of his paintings here at the gallery, presently in storage, I would like to gather as much of his work as possible. I'd appreciate it if you would lend us your painting." My body language must indicate how protective I feel toward my 'Hamlet' because she adds, "Don't worry. It will be quite safe."

"When would you want it?"

She flattens a non-existent wrinkle in her skirt. "Actually, I began the initial plans for the show shortly after Charles passed away and as I have already made contact with many collectors, it's just a matter of getting his most recent work. I'll let you know in ample time when to bring it in. It's Hamlet isn't it?"

"Um . . ." I want to lie but that would be foolish. "Yes it is," I admit.

"Charles enjoyed the plays of Shakespeare and painting portraits, so it doesn't seem too surprising that he would have combined the two. Do you have a special interest in Hamlet?"

"Oh yes!" Deception springs quickly to my lips. "I was in a high school presentation and it was an episode in my life I told Charles about."

"Did you play Hamlet?"

Is she asking an honest question or is she toying with me? Either way I created my own dilemma. Having told a little fib, I was now committed to telling a bigger one. What role could I say I'd played? I rack my brain for a minor female part and come up blank. In desperation, I finally blurt out that I'd been Rosencrantz. Great, I manage to choose one of the major liars in the play. It's a response that would make Freud proud.

She straightens an already perfectly aligned painting. "Interesting," she says, her voice trailing in disinterest. Turning to face me, she asks again, "Will you lend the gallery your painting?"

"I guess it would be okay."

"Wonderful! You're welcome to look around for as long as you like. I have some work I must attend to. I will soon be calling you about the show." With the Queen's wave she turns and leaves the room.

I find I'm clenching my teeth so hard my jaw aches. She's so, so patronising! And why drag me all the way to the gallery to ask me something I could so easily have answered over the phone? I want to run after her and demand that she show me all of Charles's paintings. I want to quiz her about their relationship. I want to wring a confession out of her and haul her off to jail. Damn! I take two deep breaths and count to ten. It's a missed opportunity but there's little point in jeopardising another by a show of temper.

It seems a wasted trip until I realise I'm in the vicinity of the land registry office on Dundas Street—only a minor detour on my way back to the office. I find it with relative ease and once inside step up to the front counter. The kindness of the woman who offers to assist me helps dispel some of my pent up anger.

Apparently, Toronto had recently gone electronic and everything is on the computer. For a small fee, I'm given a pin number for the address of Charles's studio and that in turn gives me a copy of the pertinent information for that property. Not only did Charles own the building; he owned it outright, no mortgage, no encumbrance. While I'm there, I decide to see if he had a mortgage on his home—another small fee and another printout. As I suspected, he had owned that free and clear as well. So, the monetary gain for Alissa was quite substantial.

With this information in hand, I'm anxious to return to the office and call Finella. Adhering to my Protestant work ethic, I finish all the paperwork before making the call.

"Hi Maud. Your timing is impeccable. I just got in from tending to a customer's garden and have some time to chat."

"Great. There have been some developments I want to talk to you about." I tell her about my visit to Charles's aunt Theo and vent my anger at the wasted trip to the Tellman Gallery.

"Leona wants your painting? That could be dangerous, Maud. She's aware of the subject, right?"

"Yes. But she said something about Charles liking both Shakespeare and portraits so I told her it was in recognition of my having acted in the play in high school."

"You were in *Hamlet*?"

"No, I lied about that bit."

She responds with more than a hint of sarcasm. "Terrific. What part did you say you played?"

"Rosencrantz."

"Rosencrantz! Maud, you didn't!"

"I know, I know. But I couldn't think of anyone else and it just popped out."

"Well, what's done is done. Let's hope she believed you. Now you must be even more vigilant. If Leona is the murderer, she'll figure out the message of your painting."

"I don't think so, Finella. She was so nonchalant about it, not a hint of curiosity."

"I'm not convinced. But it sounds like you had a good meeting with Charles's aunt, Theo. She will be a valuable ally. Did you manage to find out anything about the studio property?"

"Oh yeah, I forgot. I went to the land registry office and Charles owned both the studio building and his home, outright. Incredible eh? He was more successful than I gave him credit for."

"Yes and it strengthens Alissa's motive."

"It may be that Alissa had an accomplice." I tell Finella about Teddy's car and presumably Teddy, spending the night with Charles's widow.

"I assume this means you haven't talked to him yet?"

"No, with any luck I can reach him at his office tomorrow. I've got a few things to finish up for Uncle Sid, so I'll call you again in a couple of days." I rush her off the phone before she has the chance to give me another warning.

En route to my apartment, I stop for a take-out meal and eat most of it in the car. When I get home, I feed Kora and after a second walk-through to check the well-being of my apartment, I load my art supplies into the car. I'm determined to get to class early and arrive at quarter to seven. The studio appears empty but I can hear voices from inside the office, and confirm that one of the speakers is Zarina when she loudly proclaims, "Fraternising, that's what it is and don't try to deny it."

"I'm merely trying to be an attentive teacher, like Charles," is the reply I'm sure comes from Rupert.

Zarina raises her voice again. "Like Charles! You are nothing like Charles and never will be. In fact, you are ridiculous. It is obvious that she does not welcome your attentions and equally obvious that you are a fool. I would strongly suggest that you . . ." Before she can finish her sentence, three students enter the studio, their laughter and jovial chatter masking her words. As Zarina leaves the office, I fall in behind them, hoping she will assume I've just arrived.

Within the next few minutes, the studio fills and we're sitting on our respective drawing horses. I survey the room for Grace and although she's not there, I do see one empty place and so expect her to arrive shortly. I'm taken aback when Zarina, wearing an electric blue artist's smock, picks up a drawing board and sits at the available horse.

When Rupert trudges to the front of the classroom, his shoulders are slightly stooped, his head is down and I know he's not shaken the effects of Zarina's tongue-lashing. His smile reveals more pain than pleasure when he says, "This evening we will be working from a, um, a live model, as this is after all life drawing. I would like to review, for those of you familiar with it and introduce, for those of you who are not, the mannequin. Now here on the blackboard," he directs our gaze to the wall on his right, "you will see that I have drawn a figure. The human adult is approximately eight heads in height. In this drawing you will note that the moveable parts, that is, the neck, shoulder joints, elbows, wrists, midriff, hip joints, knees and ankles have been omitted. Likewise, the joints of the fingers and toes." Using a pointer, Rupert taps gently at each of the areas mentioned. "In your initial drawing of the model, I want you to omit these parts of the anatomy. The body is made up of rectangles and the first thing to place on your paper is the rectangle representing the head. Make sure you place it to allow enough room to complete your drawing. You don't want the feet falling off the end of the page." Rupert looks toward the back of the class. "Ah, I see our model is ready now. As she takes a simple pose, I'll do a demonstration drawing on the blackboard, according to the instructions I've just given you."

Wearing a shapeless pink robe with her hair loosely tied at the nape of her neck, my jaw drops involuntarily as Grace walks toward the stage. Stepping up on the platform, she pauses to whisper something to Rupert. After muttering an apology, he dashes to the back of the class, picks up a small padded armchair and carries it awkwardly around the semicircle of drawing horses before heaving it onto the platform next to her. He then asks Grace to begin with a simple standing pose.

She slips out of her robe, draping it casually over the chair, and with one hand on the back of the chair and the other on her hip, tilts her head toward Rupert. "Is this okay?"

He gives her a nod before addressing the students. "We'll assume I'm working on a piece of paper that is thirty inches long. Allowing at least an inch at the top of the page and two inches at the bottom, I have twenty-seven inches for the figure. Therefore, I'm going to draw my rectangle to accommodate a three-inch head." Rupert deftly renders the pose, pausing as he completes each of the representative rectangles with further explanation of the procedure. Convinced that we now have the necessary knowledge to continue, our instructor turns to Grace. "Let's begin with a few more simple poses of about ten minutes." To the class he adds, "These poses will be short so there's no time for detail. I want you to capture the essence of each pose. Which foot carries the weight, where are the arms, what is the tilt of the head? Look for the active and passive side of each pose and watch out for foreshortening." He steps from the stage. "Okay let's begin."

I marvel at the nude figure in front of me. She is aptly named as she so gracefully takes a pose and her well-proportioned body is a delight to draw. With good musculature she's able to hold the position. Shaky models are a student's bane. Admiring Grace's elegance and stamina, I'm reminded of her antithesis from another art school and another time.

Next to his shabby robe, dropped carelessly on the floor, was a brown paper bag. It contained a liquid snack he must have enjoyed liberally before class began because when it came time to pose, our model was so unsteady he draped himself awkwardly over an uncomfortable metal easel. When he failed to remain upright for more than three minutes, the instructor suggested he lounge on a divan and only when he had fallen into a stupor, did any of us get a chance to execute a decent drawing.

After a half dozen poses Rupert suggests we take a break and Grace slips back into her robe. I approach her as she steps daintily from the stage. "I just want to thank you Grace. You're a very good model."

"Oh, you're welcome Maud but the real credit should go to Charles."

"Yes?"

"I'm sorry, perhaps we can talk after class. I need to make a phone call. Will you excuse me?"

As Grace makes her way into the office, I walk over to Rupert and sensing that he's in need of a kind word, praise him for his enlightening demonstration of the mannequin.

"Ah, well, thank you Maud," he says, a shy smile playing at his lips. "Shall we have a look at your drawing?"

I lead the way to my drawing horse, standing back to give him a clear view of the work. "Oh I say, Maud. Have you been practising your drawing lately?"

"Not really and I miss it. That's why I've come back for classes."

"After the break we'll have one long pose and if the students agree, we could continue it next week as well. I think you could turn out something quite impressive."

"Thanks, but it also helps to have a good model and Grace is excellent."

"Yes."

"I guess she's modelled for you before." I nod toward the painting on Charles's easel.

"No. This is the first time I've hired her."

"But your portrait?"

"Oh, that was done a while ago." He dismisses the subject so quickly I'm convinced there's something clandestine about it. I follow his gaze and see Zarina staring at us but when I smile at her, she looks away.

"So, did you paint it from memory?" I ask.

"Not exactly." Turning away from me, Rupert addresses the class. "Let's get back to work, shall we. Where's Grace?"

"I'm right here." She's sitting on the stage directly in front of him.

"Sorry. Okay, let's have one long pose. Grace you can take a break when you get tired."

"Was there any particular pose you wanted?" she asks.

"What? No, um, no, anything comfortable. Wait. Remember that one you did for Charles? You were sitting on the chair with your arm, your left I think, bent at the elbow and resting on the back of the chair, while the other arm crossed in front of your body and rested on your left thigh. And could you let your hair down?"

Grace pulls the elastic from her hair and assumes the pose. Again, I appreciate her lithesome beauty and plan my drawing with attention to accuracy and eloquence of line. Oblivious to the passage of time, I'm returned to the present when Rupert's voice breaks the stillness.

"Grace are you sure you don't need a break?"

"I'm fine Rupert."

She keeps the pose for the remaining hour, an amazing accomplishment. At the end of class I begin packing up my supplies, while Grace gets dressed. She reappears in her street clothes, and I ask if she has time to join me for a drink and a chat. She agrees but as we turn to go Zarina stops us at the door.

"Thank you Grace, good work as usual. And Maudlin we'll be seeing you soon I trust."

"Sure," I tell her, wondering what she means by "soon."

Once outside Grace says, "Maudlin? I don't mean to be rude but that can't be your real name."

"No, it isn't. I think it's just Zarina's idea of a joke."

"Really? I doubt Zarina has a sense of humour."

We make our way to a little café close to the studio. "Is this place all right?" I ask.

"This is fine." Grace scans the small room with its tiny circular tables. "I hope they serve herbal tea, if I drink coffee this late, I'll be up all night."

I recognise a couple of students from the class, but the tables are so small I'm sure they won't invite us to sit with them. The café offers a variety of herbal teas and after placing our order I ask Grace about her reference to Charles, and why she credited him for her modelling ability.

"I had asthma as a child and was consequently inactive and overweight. A few years ago, my doctor suggested I get a hobby so I started taking drawing lessons. It got me out of the house and away from the television. I wasn't very good and would have quit but then I found out about Charles's studio and started going there. He was so patient with me, even though it was obvious I had no talent."

I consider voicing a denial, but it was true and she didn't seem to harbour any false hope.

"One night," she continues, "the model he'd booked for portrait painting class didn't show up and he asked me if I would pose. As long as I didn't have to take my clothes off, I didn't mind. It turned out I was rather good at it and Charles got me more work at other art studios."

"You're great to draw—you have good muscle definition."

"I do now. Thanks to Charles, I started feeling better about myself. I watched my diet and found I could exercise without the asthma bothering me. It's been months since I had an attack. Before

Charles died, he helped me put together a portfolio for fashion modelling and I've been getting some lucrative jobs." Grace looks at me over the rim of her cup, her long lashes casting a shadow on her cheeks. "That's what I meant when I said that Charles had changed my life."

"I have to admit, I thought it meant something quite different."

She giggles. "Don't worry about it, so did everybody.

"What do you mean everybody?"

"Oh, Rupert, Zarina, Alissa. You see in the months before his death, Charles and I spent a lot of time together, but it was business, not romance. He found me a great photographer and used to accompany me to the shoots. He refused to explain the circumstances to anybody. Of course, I wanted to clarify things, at least to his wife, but I hardly knew her and Charles said it would make things worse. There was only one person who resented the time he spent with me."

"And that was . . .?"

She allows an uncomfortable pause before saying, "Leona Tellman."

"Do you think he wanted her to believe you two were having an affair?"

"Maybe. It was like he wanted her to get mad at him, but I don't know why."

She's got me thinking about the possible reasons Charles might want to upset Leona. If they were involved and he'd tired of her, then why not simply end it? But then, men are often cowards in relationships and it's not unusual for them to provoke a break-up. However, he also had a business relationship with her and that added an extra complication.

"Grace, did the Tellman Gallery have exclusive rights to Charles's work?"

"Can they do that, galleries I mean?"

"Yes they can. Do you know if Charles showed his paintings in any other gallery besides Leona's?"

She thought for a moment before answering. "No, I'm sure he didn't."

"Well, maybe that was it. Maybe he was trying to get out of a contract."

"I guess." Her voice trails off but she adds, "Does it matter?"

"No, no," I assure her. "It's not important."

I switch the topic back to her modelling career and she's happy to dwell on that while we finish our drinks. Exiting the café I feel like there's something else I should ask her but it refuses to come into focus. We say our good-byes and as we're headed in opposite directions, I walk back to the car alone. I'm unlocking the door when I feel a hand grab my shoulder. Folding my arm I make a swift jab with my elbow, then spin around ready to belt the assailant with my backpack. Zarina lays crumpled against the side of my car.

"For cryin' out loud, Maudy," she groans. "What did you do that for?"

Chapter 7

"Damn, Zarina, why did you sneak up on me like that?" I put a hand under her arm and help her to her feet.

"Like what? I barely touched your shoulder. Really Maud, I think you have a problem! You could have seriously wounded me." Her concern for her person transfers to her clothing and she skims the palm of her hand repeatedly across the front of her madras skirt.

I'm momentarily speechless, not only because of what she's said but because she's just used my proper name. She's upset and she's got me on the defensive. "Listen Zarina, it's dark. It's late and I'm alone. Suddenly there's a hand on my shoulder and how the hell was I supposed to know it was your hand?"

"Well really!" She crosses her arms over her chest and stares at me.

"What?" I ask, feeling more than a little exasperated.

Looking down her nose, with equal emphasis on each word, she says, "I await your apology."

I blurt out, "Oh, for Christ's sake!" but her glare doesn't falter. "Okay, okay, I'm sorry I elbowed you. Next time, give me a little warning."

"Consider yourself warned." She pivots on her heels like a Nazi commandant and storms off.

I could run after her but it's late, I'm tired and she's obviously lost interest in speaking to me. Unlocking my car and climbing in, I secure the doors then sit perfectly still until I feel calm enough to drive home and once there, I practically fall into bed. That's enough fun for one day.

I awake happy in the knowledge that I slept soundly and roll over to see Kora, a calico crescent next to my pillow. "So, my darling cat, are we ready for another day?" The phone rings as I'm about to step into the shower.

"Maud, it's Theo, Theo Venable. Did I wake you?"

"No Theo."

"I'm sorry my dear. I called last evening but your machine came on."

"I forgot to check it. Did you leave a message?"

"Maud, I never know what to say on those things, that's why I'm calling you now. I won't keep you but could you come by later today, around tea time?"

"Sure. Is everything all right?"

"Oh yes, I just want to talk to you."

I arrive at work to find myself in the midst of a minor crisis. Al is hovering next to a woman whose identity is hidden by the handkerchief she'd sobbing into. His facial expression tells me, 'Thank God you're here' and as he gently turns the distraught woman in my direction, he says, "I don't have time for this, I have to be, . . . somewhere." He's talking to the back of her head when he says, almost as quickly, "Mrs. Willoughby, this is Miss Gibbons. She'll help you." Then he grabs his briefcase and runs from the office.

As she dabs at her tears, I gently cup her elbow with my right hand and steer her to the nearest chair. In a hoarse whisper she tells me, "The landlord is threatening to throw us out, my three young children—no money—I don't know what to do."

"What did they tell you at Social Services?" I ask.

"Where?"

I don't know enough about applying for assistance to give an adequate explanation, and I'm sure we're both relieved when Uncle Sid arrives. His smile says 'I'll handle this' and as he bends over Mrs. Willoughby he places one hand on her shoulder. "Dear lady, I was just at your apartment. It'll be all right now. I have some money for you. Come into my office and we'll get things sorted out."

She stands to follow him, pausing to thank me before going through the door. A short time later, a smiling Mrs. Willoughby accompanied by my uncle, comes into the reception area. "I'm so relieved. I can't thank you enough, Mr. Gibbons."

"No, no dear lady, that's what I'm here for. You go on home and try to get some rest. We'll have a support system in place so this kind of thing won't happen again."

After closing the door behind her, he turns to me. "She didn't disclose the seriousness of her financial condition. It should never have come to this. That poor woman married a man who is filling a necessary void."

"You found him though, right?"

"Yeah, but he could get unfound by tomorrow." Although disgust is evident in his voice, his tone softens when he says, "So, Sweets, I need you to go to the court house and pick up a file for me. Ask for Jenny when you get there, she'll have it ready. After that, you can call it a day."

Uncle Sid usually lets me leave early on Friday afternoons. I suppose it's his contribution to my love life and though I seldom have a date on Friday night, he's ever hopeful.

"You got any plans for this evening?"

"I'm having dinner with a friend."

"You know I think you spend too much time alone but on the other hand, I hope you're using good judgement, Maud. There's some real scum out there."

I suppress a smile. "Don't worry it's a feline friend."

His eyes narrow. "You're talking about your cat aren't you?"

"You're quick, Unc, you're quick."

He paws the air. "Get out of here."

"Okay, I'll see you later." I grab my purse, ready to battle the city traffic, not only on my way to and from the court house, but again on my way to Theo's.

During the drive into town my foot spends more time on the brake pedal than the gas but there's less traffic on the return trip. By the time I reach the office I remember that during the summer months many city folk leave work early on Friday afternoon. It's cottage time, but I don't know why they do it—all that tension getting out of the city, one day of relaxation and a traffic crawl Sunday evening getting back. My drive to Theo's is like a car commercial. I even find a nice wide parking space right in front of her house. God bless those cottagers.

Theo answers the door, and I take an involuntary step backwards. She's done her hair and dressed for tea, but nothing could hide the dark circles under her eyes or her fatigue as she supports her weight with the door frame.

"Theo, you don't look well." I slip my hand under her elbow and help her to one of the wicker chairs in the sun-room.

"Really, my dear, I'm fine."

Perching on the adjacent chair I tell her, "You don't look fine. You look exhausted."

"It's true. I haven't been sleeping very well. I keep going over the list, making notes and thinking about Charles's last days. There's something I know is important but I can't bring it to mind. That's why I thought if I talked to you it might help resurrect a memory."

"What do you remember most vividly about those final days?" I ask.

"Charles in my library."

"Pardon?"

"Oh, I'm sorry my dear, that does sound grand, doesn't it. Actually, I have a small room off the dining area where I had bookcases built. I'm a bit of a bibliophile, you know. Would you like to see it?"

"Yes, but let's rest a bit. You just sat down."

"No, really, I'm fine." Pushing herself up from the chair, her pained expression says otherwise, as she consciously places one foot in front of the other on her way down the hall. I follow, bracing myself to catch her if she topples over.

Entering the library, I see immediately that she is more than just 'a bit' of a bibliophile. The room is lined with shelves, floor to ceiling and there's barely a gap between the volumes. An elegant mahogany, leather-topped table accompanied by two mahogany chairs sits in the centre of the room. I'm not that familiar with antiques, but the set looks valuable.

Theo follows my gaze. "I see you are admiring the furniture. It was a gift from Charles. The chairs are Regency carvers and the table is a William IV library table. Both are from the early 1800s."

"They're beautiful! And look at all these wonderful books. This is truly a place filled with knowledge and ideas." My hand involuntarily dances along a row of leather spines. "You said Charles spent a lot of time in here. Was he reading for pleasure or doing research?"

"He had asked me about my books on Greek and Roman myths and," she pauses in mid-sentence. "Now I remember! It was the book on poison! That's what has been haunting me. One day, after he'd left, I came in here and found a book about common poisons on the table. I remember thinking that he must have pulled it off the shelf by mistake, but from what we now know, it was surely a deliberate choice."

"Can you show it to me?"

"Yes, dear, it's the only book I have on the subject." She retrieves it from the shelf and hands it to me. I note a piece of paper marking a page and turning to it quickly find a chapter heading that reads, "Arsenic."

"Oh, I think we need to take a closer look at this." We sit at the antique table and I prop open the book. After scanning through the first bit on chemical structure, I turn to the second page where a couple of sentences have been underlined. Seeing these marks in the book, Theo says, "Charles must have done that, I never write in my books."

The first sentence is about the use of arsenic in weed killer, rat killer and in the production of pigments and enamels. The second underlined sentence heads a paragraph on the symptoms of arsenic poisoning. These include a metallic aftertaste, garlicky smelling breath, abdominal pain, nausea, vomiting and diarrhoea.

"Theo, may I borrow this? I'd like to check it thoroughly."

"Of course, my dear."

As I pick up the book, a scrap of paper flutters to the floor. Even before I pick it up I see something written by hand across the middle of the page. "Theo, the name Madeleine Smith is written here. Does that mean anything to you?"

"No, I don't think so. May I see it?" She pulls her glasses from the pocket of her skirt. "I can tell you that it was written by Charles. He has—had—a very unusual script. But, I don't think I know anyone named Madeleine Smith."

"Okay, I'll see what I can find out."

"Are we finished in here my dear?" Theo stands up. "These chairs are lovely but they're not the most comfortable for my old bones. Let us retire back to the sun-room. I made some iced tea earlier and if you wouldn't mind, Maud, it's in the pitcher in the icebox." She giggles. "Listen to me, I sincerely doubt that anyone these days has an icebox."

"It's okay, I know what you mean. Have a seat and I'll get us each a glass."

Returning with the tray, I place it on the glass-topped table before pulling up a footstool for Theo.

"My dear, I'm fine, don't you fuss. Now, I have something for you." She reaches into her pocket and pulls out a sheet of paper. "This is the list you wrote out for me of those who were at the reading of the will. I've tried to think of possible motives but I'm afraid I'm not much help."

She taps at the paper with a crooked finger. "As you see, I would eliminate Teddy. I just don't believe Teddy could hurt anyone. As for Zarina, she was extremely, almost pathologically, dedicated to Charles and it's because of the element of pathology that I can't quite eliminate her. My prime suspect would have to be Alissa, but then I am biased." She pauses to take a sip of her iced tea. "I hardly know Rupert; he's a quiet chap. I do know that Charles thought very highly of him. Leona is a complete unknown. I've met her because of the shows she's had for Charles and although she was always very gracious, that means nothing. Here you are," she hands me the paper, "you can read it for yourself."

I unfold the page, anticipating a few clues but find her handwriting almost illegible. For a while I'm lost in the art of deciphering but when I look up to ask about a particularly difficult passage, her head is slumped against the back of the chair, her jaw slack. She seems so lifeless, I place my hand close to her mouth, relaxing only when I feel the warmth of her breath. Lifting a knitted afghan from the back of another chair, I place it gently over her legs, then fold the paper, tuck it inside the book on poisons and tiptoe to the front door, letting myself out.

On my way home I stop at the mall for frozen pizza, expensive cat food and treats, popcorn, and a bottle of Pinot Noir. In no mood to risk television disappointment, I also rent the movie, *Arsenic and Old Lace*. Seems a bit macabre, but hey, it's Cary Grant.

Kora and I enjoy our dinner and movie. She's more enthusiastic about the food, but then she's already seen the film. I bring the book on poisons to bed with me but as soon as my head hits the pillow I know I'm too tired to read it. In the middle of the night, I awake to the sounds of a terrific thunderstorm—a real Ride of the Valkyries event. Turning on my bedside lamp, I pick up the book.

I re-read the first sentence Charles had underlined on the uses of arsenic in weedkiller, rat poison, pigments and enamels. Would that include artist's oil paints, I wonder? Knowing sleep will escape me until I find out, I turn on my computer and search the web for references to arsenic in artist's oils. Now replaced with other substances, it was once in common usage, especially in the cobalt colours. I remember Zarina saying that the cobalts, the blues and violets were extremely poisonous but how could the murderer induce Charles to ingest paint?

I make a mental note to find out what happened to all of Charles's art supplies. Rupert is using his easel; is he also using his paints? Alissa might be able to answer that question. I decide to call her in the morning and go back to bed.

I manage to make up for my nocturnal activities by sleeping in till after nine. I may have slept even later had Kora not roused me with her penetrating cat stare. I fill her bowl with kibble and after two cups of coffee feel ready to phone Alissa, hoping to catch her before she makes plans for the day. As Leona was unlikely to be one of her favourite people, I'd use her request for my painting as the reason for my call. Once we get through the usual niceties, I tell Alissa about my visit to the Tellman Gallery and my concerns with regards to lending the painting. She commiserates with me on the demanding nature of Miss Tellman and sensing the moment, I ask if we might get together. She hesitates for only a minute before inviting me for lunch.

Halfway there, I decide it would be rude of me to arrive empty handed. I'm sure there's a bakery on Queen Street but it takes me fifteen minutes to find it. I buy some lovely pastries that I now hope will make up for my tardiness and once more I'm on my way.

Alissa, a vision in black spandex, welcomes me at the front door. Always petite, her curves have become angles—perhaps the stress of recent months. She ushers me into the living room where a wonderful example of a Venable building hangs above the marble fireplace. Charles may have been an architect in a previous life—so much delight was visible in his portraits of unusual buildings, or usual buildings from unusual angles. Although he'd sold most of them, he had kept this one of the Gooderham Building. Erected at the turn of the last century and also known as the Flatiron building, it looked like a brick sailing ship gone aground at the junction of Toronto's Front and Wellington Streets.

Turning my gaze from the painting to the room's interior, Charles's painting seems to be the sole survivor of his expression in this room. It had once housed antique furniture, lovely old tapestries and 16th century Italian art, but now it's ultramodern. The Persian rugs have been replaced with cold colours in geometric form. A black leather sofa and love seat, their severe contours suggesting cost more than comfort, supplant French Provençal and glass topped metal tables replace solid walnut. I feel that if Alissa wasn't guilty of murder she should be incarcerated for her decorating crimes.

"It's nice to see you Maud," says my hostess, glancing at her watch.

"You too, Alissa. I'm sorry I'm a little late. I stopped at the bakery for a dessert." She looks at the box but doesn't take it from me.

"Have a seat. You mentioned that you have some concerns about lending your painting to the Tellman Gallery?"

I perch on the edge of her leather sofa, cradling the pastries. "Yes. Leona got me down to the gallery and almost demanded that I lend her the painting. I don't know much about her and I wanted to check with you."

"I'm sure it will be quite safe. It's a reputable gallery. But of course, the final decision is yours. If you don't feel good about lending it, don't."

"I did say she could borrow it, but would she give me a hard time if I changed my mind?"

Before replying, Alissa pushed herself back into her stiff looking leather club chair, bent one leg at the knee and hugged it close to her chest. "I doubt it. Leona will have plenty of Charles's paintings for her show. If you don't want the confrontation, don't answer her calls. She's unlikely to show up at your door."

"That's good to know. Maybe I don't want to deal with her because I just don't like the woman." I hope my candidness will prompt Alissa to share her own feelings.

"I don't like her either, but for reasons other than her stunning personality."

"Yes?" I try not to sound too curious.

"Would you like a cup of coffee? I just brewed some."

I agree to the coffee and follow her into the kitchen, another ultramodern room filled with chrome and glass. I set the box of pastries on the counter and watch her pour the coffee into china mugs, nodding to her offer of cream. "I've started taking classes with Rupert." Did she notice me there the night of her outburst, I wonder?

"Oh, really?"

Apparently, not.

"Yes, I was there last Tuesday night. I don't want to pry," I lie, "but you seemed very upset. Is Zarina giving you a hard time?" She studies me with a look of indecision, strolls over to the kitchen table and sits down, gesturing for me to do the same.

"Goddamn it, I feel as though I'm being left out again." Her bottom lip protrudes slightly but she quickly straightens her spine in an effort to remain calm. With a noticeable sigh she continues, "When Charles first opened the new studio we had big plans. It was supposed to be a partnership. It soon became apparent to me that although my money was welcome, my presence was not. He wanted me to stay home and look after all his needs here while he hired Zarina to look after the studio. Initially, he persuaded me that involvement in the studio and the home would be too much work but I came to realise that he had his own selfish motives and merely wanted independence to carry on as he pleased."

"You said your money was welcome. Did you invest in the studio?"

"I guess you could say that. I paid for the building."

I force my jaw shut with the heel of my hand. "You bought the building?"

"Oh yes," she continues, "I inherited enough money to buy the studio and pay off the mortgage on the house."

"And did you have joint ownership for both?" I already know the answer to that but I want to know why.

"No. In deference to Charles's inflated ego, he was sole owner. In retrospect, I was incredibly stupid. The more I gave, the more he took and the worse he treated me. The one thing I really wanted was a child, but when his interest in sex diminished and then finally disappeared over the last year, I knew that was never going to happen."

"He lost interest in sex? Was he impotent? Sorry, forget I asked that."

"It's okay, but I can't answer you. He stopped even trying to be intimate. I thought he might have been having an affair but I never had any proof. Charles was an exceptionally selfish man. The fact that his aloofness was causing me great pain and destroying our relationship didn't seem to affect him. If he hadn't died, I was planning to file for divorce. Are you ready for lunch?"

It takes me a minute to comprehend her question. "Sure. Can I do anything?"

"No, it's just soup and sandwiches. I hope that's all right?"

"It's perfect. I'm grateful for your hospitality." I'm left with my thoughts while Alissa busies around the kitchen. If she intended to divorce him, why commit murder? And would she tell me about her unhappy marriage if she thought she might be a suspect?

"So, are you going to get more involved in the running of the studio?" I ask.

She ladles the soup into our bowls, putting about two tablespoons into her own, and sets the pot back on the stove. "I'd like to but I'm not sure what role to take. Right now I'm just the landlady." She removes the cling-wrap from a plate of sandwiches she's just taken from the fridge and places them on the table. "You have your choice of tuna or ham."

"Thanks, I like them both. What about classes? Are you still painting?"

"I no longer work in oils. I prefer pastels now. This is mushroom soup, I hope that's okay?"

"That's great. Maybe you could teach a class in pastels. It would involve you in the studio."

"That's something to think about, I guess." She seems uncertain about the idea. Maybe it's a lack of self-confidence. "Can I get you anything else?"

I glance down at the table. "A spoon for the soup perhaps?"

"Oh, I'm sorry. How stupid of me." She rises from her chair and gets each of us a spoon. Mine is a dessertspoon, but never mind.

"So, what happened to Charles's art supplies?" I ask, casually.

"I don't know." By the way she says it, I don't think she cares either. "Since he's finishing Charles's commissions, I would imagine that Rupert must be using them."

I eat a second sandwich; she nibbles on her first, and an uncomfortable silence falls between us. Looking around the room, I wonder where she might have hung the painting she received from Charles. I hadn't seen it in the living room and cer- tainly, it wasn't in the kitchen.

"Do you know anyone named Madeleine Smith?" I ask between tiny mouthfuls of soup.

"No, why? Was she a friend of Charles's?" The emphasis on 'friend' suggests an alternate meaning.

"I don't know. I saw it written somewhere and thought maybe she was a student."

Alissa sets her spoon down next to her empty bowl. "If you want any information about students, you'd best ask Zarina."

Abruptly, she stands and begins clearing the dishes. It would appear that lunch is over. I quickly finish my soup and shove the last morsel of bread into my mouth. While I look longingly at the box of pastries, Alissa looks at her watch. I must be keeping her from something.

"Alissa, do you mind if I use your washroom before I go?"

"No, not at all. It's just down there, first door on your left." She points me in the direction of the hall.

I check the walls as I walk hoping to see the painting. There are four framed pictures but they're floral pastels. I see a door on my right that might lead to a bedroom and tentatively turned toward it.

"Maud!"

I pull my hand from the knob as if it's on fire. Alissa is watching me from the end of the hall.

"I said the door on your left."

I raise my hands in apology before following her directions and closing the bathroom door behind me. I wish I'd made a casual reference to the painting when we were sitting in the living room. Now it's too late. I wash my hands and as I exit the room, I see her watching for me from the kitchen. I thank her for lunch and her suggestions in dealing with Leona before feeling like I get the bum's rush out the door.

As I back out of the driveway, a child runs into the street to retrieve a carelessly thrown ball. I reverse the car close to the curb and watch him pick it up and return safely to his own yard. I barely have time to take my foot off the brake, when a champagne Mercedes pulls into Alissa's driveway. Well, at least Teddy will enjoy those pastries.

Chapter 8

Arriving home just before two, I can't shake the frustration I feel for bungling my attempt to see Alissa's painting. I decide to redirect my negative energy into some therapeutic time on my apartment, vacuuming, scrubbing, spraying and scouring. I also reorganise my bedroom closet, and give Kora a brushing, collecting almost enough fur to make another cat or a very small sweater. She isn't impressed, but she looks beautiful.

Hunger pulls me to the kitchen. I make a peanut butter sandwich and munch on it while considering my studio. I don't have a separate room, just a bamboo divider to cordon off a section of the living room. It's been too long since I last worked on a painting at home and the divider is crunched up against my easel like a shield. I pull it back and turn a bookcase perpendicular to the wall to create the illusion of a separate space. In emptying my taboret, I find hardened tubes of paint and thickened medium. These go in the garbage and I make up a shopping list. I'm ruthless with my brushes, discarding any with splayed hairs and caked ferrules. Before going to bed I organise my travel art box.

Sunday morning I go through my photographs and choose a particularly good one of Kora. Not only did she deserve to be immortalised in paint, Finella suggested I return to portraiture and it seemed a good place to begin. Feeling organised and motivated, I drive to my favourite art supply store.

I sometimes feel like Sisyphus when shopping for groceries—I'm forever loading up the cart only to have it emptied again, but shopping for art supplies gives me the boost of adrenaline I imagine some women get from looking at a rack of shoes.

Although oil paint can be almost as expensive, I tend to restrict my palette to the earth colours, so my pennies go further.

During one of Charles's colour courses, he stood at the front of the class with three tubes of paint in one hand and two in the other. "In an ideal world," he'd said, "these are all the hues you will ever need." He raised the tubes of paint above his head. "Theoretically, the three primaries plus black and white can be mixed to create every known colour, tint and shade." "But," he lowered his arms,

"It's not an ideal world and we don't have perfect primary colours, so you have some decisions to make. You will need some of the cadmiums—yellow and red, as well as ultramarine blue but I recommend a reliance on the earth colours. They are inexpensive yet expressive, and they're versatile, especially in portraiture."

No Charles, I thought, it definitely is not an ideal world, but thanks to your instruction, I can mix a plethora of hues. What I save on paint, I splurge on brushes. Cheap brushes can ruin a painting experience. I'm deciding on three new sables and two made from skunk hair, when I see Rupert at the end of the aisle.

"Hi Maud. Stocking up on supplies?" He responds to my smile.

"I spent yesterday taking inventory and a few of my paints had hardened in the tube."

Grabbing something off the shelf, he walks over to me. "Have you tried this brand?" He hands me a tube of yellow ochre.

"No. Is it good?"

"Yes, and it's cheaper than what you've got in your basket. Although some of the less expensive brands reduce the ratio of pigment to oil, this one is high quality and nice to work with."

"Okay, I'll give it a try." I say and begin exchanging what I'd already chosen for those of his recommendation.

He alternates his weight from one foot to the other. "Um . . . maybe you want to try just one tube of this new stuff. You might not like it."

"But you just recommended it."

"You trust me then do you?" He smiles at me and it's an attractive smile.

"You're the teacher," I remind him.

"Yes, well, I hope you like it."

"Me too, I'm going to start a painting of my cat."

"Your cat?" He seems interested.

"Yes, I named her Kora, after the goddess of painting. She's a beautiful longhaired calico. You know, three colours, white, orange and black. Did you know that calicos have three colours of fur because they have an extra X chromosome and because of that they are almost always female?"

The gaze he directs over my left shoulder suggests he's not all that interested.

"Really? Okay then, I'm here to get some canvas, so I'll see you later." With a slight nod, he walks toward the back of the store.

Okay so not everybody loves cats. I direct my attention to the brushes I need and wander around the store finding all the supplies on my list, plus some that aren't but I have to have. At the checkout counter I give the cashier a substantial portion of my week's salary and tote everything out to the car. I'm stowing my purchases in the trunk when

Rupert comes out of the store carrying a large roll of heavy canvas.

I call to him and when he strolls over offer to give him a ride home.

"Thanks Maud, I'd appreciate that." He loads his canvas into the back-seat.

"You know Rupert, it's just about lunch time and there's a great little restaurant nearby if you'd like to join me?"

He hesitates with a throaty "um" but I sigh audibly and add, "Oh well, if you're too busy." He looks down at the concrete of the parking lot as if it will help him make a decision. "I guess it would be okay," he says finally, and with a shrug, "yeah, sure, why not."

His response seems rather insulting but maybe it's just shyness. I don't even try to make conversation during the short drive to the restaurant but after the waiter brings menus to our table on the patio, I make a few recommendations. Rupert quickly decides on a burger, and after placing his order, just as quickly focuses his attention on something or someone behind my right shoulder. I casually drop my napkin and when I bend down to pick it up, I note that the object of his attention seems to be a large maple tree. I'm beginning to wish I'd brought a book. With little else to do I scan my mental index cards, searching for a subject that might prompt a conversation.

"So, Rupert, do you like teaching?"

"It's okay." Anyone watching us will think he's talking to the tree.

I try again. "How are the commissions going?"

"Good."

I need a question that can't be answered in one or two words. I sip my iced tea. "I had lunch with Zarina last month." Finally, he makes eye contact. "You know, I don't think she's made any progress in the sanity department. Is she as bossy with you as she once was with Charles?"

His gaze shifts from me to his glass of beer but he responds to the question. "I just try to ignore her, most of the time."

"That works then, does it?"

"No, not really," he admits. "But I never noticed her bossing Charles around."

"She wouldn't have been obvious about it and I think Charles would have dealt with her by being passive-aggressive."

"What's passive-aggressive?" he asks. At last I have his full attention.

"Well, Charles would agree with her and then quietly do whatever he wanted. I think it's more important to Zarina to feel heard than to be heeded. Do you know what I mean?"

"You're saying I should listen to her, agree with her and then ignore her."

"More or less. You don't need to ignore every-thing she says though. She has some good ideas. She's the one who suggested I come back and take classes. I know losing Charles has caused her a lot of pain yet at the studio she seems in control."

"Yeah, she's in control all right." His shoulders slump and we lose eye contact.

"That passive-aggressive thing might have worked for Charles but I doubt it will work for me."

"It's best to introduce it gradually. Charles probably let her feel she was running the show but he had the final say. Now that he's gone, Alissa's in charge, isn't she?"

He looks up, his raised eyebrows making his forehead wrinkle. "I guess so."

The waiter brings our lunch and conversation stalls between mouthfuls, though Rupert does reas-sure me that it's a good burger and finishes it while I'm halfway through my spinach salad. After he or-ders and receives a second glass of beer, I ask him about Charles.

"It was hard at first but it's a little easier now," he tells me, his eyes returning to the safety of the tree.

"Well, that's good. Still, it must be difficult, especially being at the studio, you know with the constant reminders."

"Oh, yeah, right."

"Had Charles been ill for long?"

"Off and on. Some days were worse than others."

"Zarina told me that Charles insisted it was just the flu. Is that what he told you?"

"He didn't really talk about it."

"But Rupert, you're the one who found him unconscious, right? That must have been frightening."

"Yes, I did and it was. He'd been sick and there was puke everywhere."

"Oh dear, and you had to clean him up?"

"Of course not! I called 911."

"I'm sorry, I didn't mean to upset you."

He runs a hand through his long hair and I couldn't swear to it but I think his upper lip quivers. "Well, why are you asking me about this?"

"Morbid curiosity, I guess. It doesn't matter. There is one other thing I'd like to ask you though." His sigh is audible but I forge ahead. "I saw a book at the studio about Pietro Annigoni. I'd like to know where I could get a copy."

"He's one of my favourites!"

"Me too. He did wonderful modelling of the flesh."

"Oh yes, and his technical expertise was outstanding." Rupert puts both elbows on the table and hunches closer to me. "In 1956, he was commissioned by the Fishmonger's Society to paint what became one of his most famous portraits, Queen Elizabeth II just after her coronation. The image was then exploited throughout the Commonwealth on prints and postage stamps and Annigoni didn't get a cent in royalties. After that he painted a portrait of Prince Philip and in the lower right-hand corner he painted a man carrying a fish over his back."

"Really?"

"Oh yeah, I think it was to show how he'd been duped. Apparently, the copyright laws were different in England than in Italy. He thought the artist always retained copyright, but different country, different laws. I don't know if he had an agent but if he did, the guy screwed up royally."

"Speaking of agents, what do you think of Teddy?"

"He's okay."

"Is he your agent?" I ask.

"I don't have an agent."

"Why not?"

"Well, you need a good body of original work. Once I have that, then I'll look for an agent."

"Would you consider hiring Teddy?"

"I doubt it. He's past it, I think." Rupert emptied his glass.

"He can't be that old," I counter.

"Close to sixty, but it's not just age, it's also attitude."

"What's wrong with his attitude? He did well by Charles, though I heard they had quite an argument just before Charles died."

"I know anger was building between the two of them. Another reason I wouldn't want him as an agent. I mean they'd been friends for years and maybe Charles was being unreasonable but that was no reason for Ted to threaten him."

"Teddy threatened Charles?"

"Yeah, he wanted to sign with another gallery and the contract Ted had arranged with Leona was going to be tough to get out of. Could be he was also going to set everything up without the use of an agent which would mean old Ted could lose a lot of money. So," he tips his chin toward me, "who told you about this argument?"

"Zarina."

"That Zarina is just a wealth of misinformation isn't she?"

"What do you mean, misinformation? She was right about Teddy and Charles."

"She's not always right and as you know, she likes to talk." He squeezes his lips into a thin line, indicating that he doesn't.

I have one more question that might loosen his jaw. "Do you know where I can get that book on Annigoni?"

"You might be able to get one in the bookshop at the Art Gallery of Ontario. If not, try one of the online bookstores. In the meantime, want to borrow my copy for a couple of days?"

"Could I? That would be great."

"Sure, if you want to drive me home now, I live in the building next to the studio, I'll run in while you wait and get it for you."

I offer to pay for his lunch, but that seems to threaten his masculinity so we agree on separate bills. Rupert directs me to the driveway between the studio and his apartment building.

"You can't really park here, but I'm sure you'll be okay while I run up and get the book. I just need to get my canvas from the back seat." He has the book when he returns. "I know you'll take good care of it. Could you bring it back on Thursday evening, when you come in for class? Just put it in the bookcase at the studio."

"Yes, I'll do that," I promise.

Arriving home, I unpack my supplies and as I put my paints in colour wheel order, I see a mental image of my finished painting of Kora. Most artists are visual learners and I'm no exception, but having a mental image of the painting before I get started is a great motivator. I don't own a light box so when I need to draw an accurate outline of the shadow shapes of a photograph, I tape the picture to a sunny window. Over the photo of Kora, I tape a piece of tracing paper and very quickly have my outline. This is re-taped to a piece of graph paper which allows me to enlarge the image to any size I choose. It's a tedious but reliable method that's been used by artists for centuries. I make the image about half life-size and have just finished when Finella calls.

"So Maud, how are things going? Any new developments?"

"Well, for one thing, Charles was not having an affair with Grace. He was helping her establish a modelling career. But get this, he deliberately kept that a secret and seemed to want some people to believe they were romantically involved."

"Let me guess. Those 'some people' would be his wife and his girlfriend, assuming Leona qualifies as his girlfriend."

"Yes, I think so and from what I can glean from Rupert, Charles was trying to get out of a contract he had with Leona."

"Rupert? When were you talking to him?"

"Oh, we met by chance at the art supply store this morning and I invited him for lunch."

"Oh yes, so?"

"So, Teddy is somehow involved in this contract. Well, I guess he would be as the agent, but anyway, Teddy didn't want Charles to break it. Rupert said he even threatened Charles but I don't know exactly what was said."

"Ah, your gentle Baer has a temper after all."

"So it would seem," I agree. "I also went to see Theo again and she is vehement in her opinion that Teddy could never hurt anyone. Which reminds me, Theo told me that Charles was researching poisons and she lent me the book he was using. According to this information, arsenic was used in the preparation of paint. Although I can't imagine how anyone would get Charles to eat his own paint."

"That would be difficult."

"One other thing, Finella. In the book, there was a piece of paper on which Charles had written the name Madeleine Smith. Ever heard of her?"

"Madeleine Smith, I don't think so. Was she a student?"

"Not that I know of but I could ask Zarina."

"Anything else of interest from your lunch with Rupert?"

"Not really," I confess. "Though, he seems to be someone in search of a personality."

"Which means?"

"Well, he can be socially inept but at the same time he has a certain charm. In general conversation, I'd call him terse, but ask him about Pietro Annigoni and he'll become positively loquacious. He even lent me a book about him."

"Rupert always seemed to be somewhat guarded but maybe you're right and he's just shy. How does he get along with the lovely Zarina?"

"Not too well, I gather. I told him to try the passive-aggressive approach."

"You mean the way Charles used to handle her?"

"You noticed that too, eh? Oh, I almost forgot. I think I can just about erase Alissa from the list of suspects." I tell Finella about my meeting with Charles's widow and how her money paid for the studio and house, how she planned to divorce Charles and that Teddy had pulled into Alissa's driveway shortly after I pulled out.

"It looks like those two are pretty tight. You know, divorce laws being what they are, Alissa would likely get half of everything, but as a widow—she gets it all."

"You've got a point there." I agree. "I also found out that their house and the studio were in Charles's name."

"Really! I thought you said they were bought with Alissa's money."

"They were but she let him hold the title."

"You're kidding, what century is this woman living in?"

"I know what you mean."

"So Maud, this is fuel for a lengthy conversation. See how your week goes, I'd love for you to visit next weekend. We can chat, weed and maybe enjoy another barbecue if the weather co-operates."

I voice my agreement and tell her I'll call a couple of days in advance.

Returning to my cartoon of Kora, I apply charcoal to the back of the drawing and retrace it onto my stretched canvas. I use diluted India ink to go over the charcoal lines and darken the shadow shapes, essentially turning the line drawing into a mass drawing. The ink dries almost immediately so I'm able to apply a veil of diluted oil colour. A warm underpainting suits my subject so I combine yellow ochre with light red plus enough medium and thinner to get a soupy mixture. When brushing it over the entire canvas, it's thin enough to allow the inked drawing to show through. I prefer to use distilled turpentine and actually like its pungent odour. After rinsing my brush in mineral spirits, I wash it with detergent and warm water. While squeezing out the moisture with a paper towel, I admire my burgeoning painting before curling up on the couch with the Annigoni book and my faithful feline.

Opening the front cover, I notice a solid black line in the upper right hand corner of the title page. Under it is written, Property of Rupert Jaynes. Going over to the window, I open the page and hold it up to the light. The black marker is concealing something that appears to be a capital C and a U or a V. Of course, it had once read, C. Venable. This was Charles's book. Like his easel, Rupert obviously figured Charles had no further use for it.

Carting it back to the couch, I spend the first half hour looking at all the beautiful reproductions. That man could paint! When I find an interesting section on his tempera technique, I take the time to read through the procedure. Annigoni enjoyed his wine and according to the text, he also mixed it into his tempera, which would help the mixture from developing the nasty smell of rotten eggs. I continue reading until my eyes are so heavy they refuse to remain open. When I'm jarred awake by the ringing of the phone, I find myself in darkness, and grope around for the light.

"Maud, it's Finella. Sorry to disturb you, but on a whim, I got on the computer and searched for Madeleine Smith. Thought you might be interested to know the result."

"You found her on the Internet?"

"It's an unusual spelling for her first name so that helped. The Madeleine Smith I discovered was accused of poisoning her lover. She was tried for murder in 1857 in Glasgow, Scotland, and the poison of choice was arsenic."

"What happened?" I'm wide-awake now.

"Despite lots of incriminating evidence, she was acquitted. According to the text from the trial, her lover, Emile L'Angelier, suffered from stomach cramps, nausea and vomiting. His landlady testified that he had three separate bouts of illness. After the third attack, he died. The autopsy found that his body contained large amounts of arsenic."

"Those symptoms sound much like what Charles suffered. Perhaps he recognised the similarity between himself and Madeleine's lover." More questions occur to me. "I wonder how he heard about the case? And why write her name on a scrap of paper? If he was leaving it as a clue, how could he be sure I would find it?"

"Right, but you did find it," she says with emphasis. "Now, is he pointing a finger at Leona, if indeed she was his lover?"

"That's a possibility. Maybe something happened after he did the paintings to make him think she was a more likely suspect but she's an ice maiden and won't drop her guard. I feel like I'm not getting anywhere."

"But you are, Maud. You've just found more incriminating evidence about Leona and you said that Theo is absolutely convinced that Teddy couldn't have done it. Why don't you try to meet with him and see if Theo might be right?"

"Okay, I'll try. Maybe I can see him tomorrow. And by the way, Theo is also convinced that Alissa is the murderer." After reassuring Finella that I will be careful, I hang up the phone and pick up the book on Annigoni. Before my unscheduled nap, I'd been reading about the artist's use of wine in his tempera. I knew that Charles had used oily tempera in combination with his oils and wondered if he too would have added wine to his egg and oil medium. From my own experience, I'd learned that oily tempera could be kept for months in the refrigerator. With any luck, Charles's tempera mix would still be in the studio fridge.

Chapter 9

By eleven-thirty Monday morning, I'd made a four o'clock appointment to see Mr. T. Baer. Teddy has an office in his home and his home is in the Rosedale area of Toronto—very nice. My uncle is away from the office for the day and by three I'm ready to set the answering machine and lock the doors.

Driving across a city like Toronto makes it challenging to pursue an accurate arrival time, but today traffic is light and I find myself parked outside Teddy's red brick, three storey house with twenty minutes to spare. I hate waiting and wish I kept a paperback in the glove box for times like this.

I note Teddy's lovely convertible parked in his driveway and imagine an open country road, a clear cerulean sky and me, my hair dancing in the wind, behind the wheel. I'm engrossed in my daydream when a second champagne Mercedes convertible pulls into the driveway and I watch with intense interest as a young woman gets out of the car and walks up to the front steps. Hopping out of my vehicle, I get to the door just as she closes it. It's quickly reopened in response to my knock.

"Hi. My name is Maud Gibbons. I'm a little early but I have a meeting with Teddy, uh, Mr. Baer."

"Hello. I'm Evelyn, Teddy's daughter." She's tall with the dark hair and eyes of her father.

I look over my shoulder at the driveway. "You have a car just like your Dad's," I tell her, as if she didn't already know this.

"Yes," she says politely. "It was my mother's. She and Dad thought it was cute to have twin cars. My sister Christine and I inherited it when she died a few years ago."

"Oh. Well, that's nice. No, it's not nice that you lost your mother, but it is a nice car."

"It gets us from A to B. I'll tell my Dad you're here." She disappears down the hall. So, two identical cars. Which one spent the night in Alissa's driveway? It must have been Teddy's because his daughter gave me Alissa's number when I wanted to reach him.

Evelyn returns. "Miss Gibbons, my father will see you now. His office is this way." I follow her along the wide central hall, slowing as I pass a large room on my left. Seeing the spectacular tapestry on the far wall brings me to a complete stop and I note two fine portraits, 16th century Italian, on the adjoining wall, and on the floor, an exquisite Persian rug.

"Miss Gibbons?" Evelyn walks back toward me.

"Sorry, I'm coming. I was just admiring the antiques in the drawing room. The portraits look familiar."

"My Dad bought them and the tapestry and rug from Alissa Venable. Do you know her?"

"Yes, I do. I studied with her husband."

"Alissa is a good friend of mine. So, are you coming in to see Dad?"

I follow her to the back of the house, and into an office off the kitchen. Teddy stands to meet me as I enter.

"Maud, how are you? I know we saw each other at the reading of Charles's will but that was not the place for conversation." He shakes my hand and it disappears in his grasp. Smiling, he gestures toward a winged armchair opposite his desk. "Here, sit, make yourself comfortable." Sitting across from me in an over-sized black leather office chair, he asks, "Now, what can I do for you?"

"Thanks so much for taking the time to see me. I wanted to talk to you about the art business. I'm thinking of a career change."

"Are you still working for your uncle?"

"Yes, but I'm hoping to reduce my time at the office and spend more time on my painting."

"I see. Good for you. Chose 'to be' rather than 'not to be,' right?"

His reference to Hamlet could be coincidence but it causes me to stare at him for longer than what would be considered polite in most circles. "I'm sorry?"

"What I mean is, don't hide your talent. It's hard to put one's work on display, to risk those slings and arrows, but I think the alternative's worse."

"Show the magic before I leave the stage, right?"

"Exactly. Now, the first thing you need is an inventory. And it goes without saying that your work must show a high level of expertise. So if you feel you don't have it yet, keep working until you do. There's far too much mediocrity in the market place. What are you working on presently?"

I tell him I'm working on an oil painting of my calico cat.

"If pets are your passion and it shows in your work, you will find a market in pet portraiture."

"I hadn't thought of that. This will be my first animal portrait. What about regular portraits, people not pets?"

Leaning his elbows on his desk, he continues, "Portraiture is a specialised genre. I advise you to do some sample portraits, preferably of recognisable faces, like celebrities so potential clients can be assured of your ability to capture a likeness. I think it best to keep them rather conservative, with appeal to the CEO and his wife or her husband, if you know what I mean. You know, Maud, the children's market is another potentially lucrative area. Do a few particularly charming paintings of children. Whatever you decide, I can get the word out and help get your work into suitable galleries. If you have the financial wherewithal you can advertise in the right magazines." He gestures apologetically before adding, "Though that can get rather pricey."

I lean forward in my chair and admit that I don't have that kind of money. Teddy raises one hand in a gesture that indicates he has an answer for that problem. "Are you familiar with the life of Pietro Annigoni?" he asks.

"Strange you should mention him. I just borrowed a book from Rupert, but I've only had time to look at the pictures."

"As you know, Annigoni is famous for his portraits. He did not however, begin his career that way. One of the first exhibits to bring him recognition was held in London, England, and the subject matter of his work was landscape. You might consider a couple of shows to get your name known and then focus your attention on portraiture." He pauses and smiles at me. "It's just a suggestion, of course."

"I think it's a very good suggestion, Teddy. Thank you."

"Well, Maud, see how it goes. Whatever your subject matter, you'll need twelve to fifteen paintings of your highest calibre. When you have those, and give yourself at least a year to do this, come back to see me and I'll help you find the best venue for your work."

He also explains the possibilities of government grants, artist-in-residence programs, lectures, workshops and the print and Internet market and gives me a booklist and a couple of pamphlets on grants and funding resources. "Have a look at these. There's some helpful information in them. Now can I offer you something to drink?"

"Thanks, but only if you're having something."

"This time of the day I enjoy a glass of white wine. Sets the palate up for dinner. Would you like one?"

I agree to a small glass and when he leaves the office, I pick up a picture frame that's resting on his desk. It's photo of an attractive red haired woman sitting between two young girls, one brunette with dark brown eyes; the other, redheaded like her mother. I put the picture back just as Teddy returns with a tray.

"Evelyn did up some cheese and crackers for us before heading back to Alissa's," he says as he places the tray on the desk.

"Back to Alissa's?" I echo.

"Yes, she's been staying with Alissa off and on since Charles died. Speaking from experience, the death of a spouse is pretty hard to cope with. Evie says she's over the worst of it. Also, my daughter is an investment counsellor and she's been helping Alissa organise her finances."

"Was it Evelyn I spoke to when I called last week? She gave me a number to reach you but I recognised it as Alissa's and didn't want to disturb you."

"No, you were talking to Christine. Evie was probably on her way to Alissa's. You could have called though. I was only there to pick up a couple of paintings."

"I saw them in the living room. I gather you bought the tapestry and the rug too. I thought they looked familiar. This is very nice wine, by the way." I take another sip. "Charles liked his wine didn't he?" I watch Teddy's face closely, figuring that if he poisoned Charles's wine the guilt might show on his face.

His only reaction is to chuckle softly. "Yes. He was a bit too fond of it, I think."

"I hadn't realised he had the kind of drinking problem that could result in cirrhosis."

"No, I didn't either. I guess you never know." He shrugs his broad shoulders.

"Perhaps he had a weak liver and it succumbed to disease with only a minor drinking problem."

I'm approaching sensitive ground and he could send me packing but I press on. "You two were very close. You must miss him."

"I do miss him. Sure, he could be stubborn and moody but he was a good friend. We shared a working relationship as well as a friendship." Teddy holds the wine bottle up, offering me more, but I shake my head. He pours himself half a glass and relaxes into his chair.

"You know how Zarina likes to talk." A slight tilt of his head indicates agreement.

"Well, she said you and Charles had a very serious argument."

"Did she indeed?" He leans toward me. I feel the tension and brace myself, but then he settles back into his chair, the tension drains. "Well she speaks the truth. And you know what Maud, I may never forgive myself for walking out on him and letting my anger create a silence that will last forever."

Fingers of compassion tug at my heart when his eyes fill with tears. "You never got the chance to resolve things?"

With a deep breath he admits, "No and there were things I said that I should have apologised for."

"I guess you were very angry."

"Yes, but that's no excuse. He was a great artist and in my fury I lied to him. My last words before slamming out of the studio were to tell him

he'd be finished. Prophetic, I know, but I was referring to his career. He wanted to break an exclusive
contract with Leona Tellman. She has more power
than he was willing to admit and the contract was
only in effect for another year. As usual Charles
was impatient and once he'd made up his mind it
was impossible to get him to see otherwise. He was
his own worst enemy." His voice drifts off and he
stares down at his hands, their fingers clasped and
resting on the desk.

I give him a mental hug, wishing I knew him
well enough to make it real. I make an attempt
to shake off the cloud that's descended upon us.
"Leona called and asked me to stop by the gallery. I
have to say, she has excellent taste in art."

"Oh, she knows her stuff all right," he agrees.
"Why did she want you at the gallery?"

"I wasn't there for long but I'm guessing that
Leona is not an easy person to get to know."

"Well, I'll tell you this. You don't want Leona
Tellman as an enemy."

"Hi Daddy." We both look toward the door.

"Maud, I'd like you to meet my youngest
daughter, Christine. Chris, honey, this is Maud
Gibbons."

"I think I spoke with you on the phone." She
enters the office with her hand outstretched. At
twenty-something, she looked just like the woman
in the photograph.

"It's a pleasure to meet you. You certainly take after your mother." I nod toward the picture on Teddy's desk.

"Yes, Mom and Dad replicated their genes quite nicely. Bit of a screw up though. Evie should have been a boy."

"But we like her just the way she is, don't we, darling." Teddy laughs warmly and rises to embrace his daughter.

I rise and both father and daughter look toward me. "I want to thank you for your time, Teddy. You've been very helpful." I extend my hand and it's engulfed once more.

"Anytime Maud." Pointing to his left he adds, "You needn't go back through the house. There's a door here." He turns and opens it for me. "This walkway will take you back to the street. Now you let me know how you get along with your painting. I'd be happy to come and see your work when you're ready."

"I almost forgot. What do I owe you?"

"Nothing. I'll get a commission from the paintings you're going to sell."

"Thank you for those encouraging words, and for your time and information."

Stepping onto the walkway I turn to wave good-bye. "Thanks again."

"Anytime, Maud."

During my drive home I consider the possibility that Theo was right. Teddy didn't seem the type to hurt anyone, let alone commit murder.

I call Finella when I get in and tell her about the twin Mercedes' and the likelihood of Teddy's innocence.

"You're definite about this are you?"

"Maybe not definite. Let's say ninety percent sure and if you had been there Finella, I think you would agree with me. I met Teddy a couple of times because of Charles's shows but I never spent any time talking to him. He's truly a warm, kind and generous man."

"You almost sound smitten."

"He does strike me as someone a girl could feel safe with."

"You know, Maud, he is old enough to be your father."

"But they say age is irrelevant."

"Yes, so they say. But what I want to say, is that until you have found Charles's killer, be on your guard. For now, why not just take Teddy off the A list."

"I hear you Finella."

"I know you hear me but are you listening?"

"Yes, my five suspects are all guilty until proven innocent, okay?"

"Okay. And call me soon, I worry about you."

In some cases when someone else carries your burden of worry it can be a freeing experience but this time it wasn't happening for me. I know Finella means well but her concern gnaws at my self-confidence. I return to my notes and my computer looking for some certainty in a sea of questions.

The painting Charles bequeathed to Teddy is 'Nero and Britannicus.' The suspicion had been that Britannicus was murdered to clear the way for Nero to become sole emperor. Initially, I thought Teddy's motive to kill Charles had been his desire for Alissa. With what I now knew, this seemed a remote possibility. There had been an argument between Charles and Teddy and Charles had refused to follow Teddy's advice but that hardly constituted a motive for murder. Was I missing something? Searching the web, I find more information to indicate that the poisoning of Britannicus had been the idea of Nero's mother, Agrippina. Furthermore, the actual poisoner had been an early Roman version of the hit-man, in this case a professional assassin named Jocosta.

When the situation demanded it, Charles was a thorough researcher. One of his first commercial commissions had been a mural for the Hudson's Bay Company. They'd requested a historical depiction for their head office and Charles had spent hours researching the landscape, modes of transportation and general appearance of the early traders. However, for the paintings he bequeathed, he must have believed his time was limited. Not knowing how deeply he delved into the information behind each painting meant that I ran the risk of my research being counterproductive. Knowing too much could take me in the wrong direction so it would be a balancing act and I only hope my awareness of the dangers will help protect me from them.

So, was Charles telling me Teddy poisoned him out of a need to eliminate a threat and take his place "in the kingdom"? Or, as in the case with Nero, was a woman the real killer and had she hired someone else to do the deed? Teddy may not have known about the plan and if there was a woman behind the scenes manipulating the outcome, who was she? Alissa? Leona? Zarina?

Alissa wanted Charles out of her life and divorce would seem the most reasonable option. Although she insisted that was her plan, just how reasonable a person is Alissa? Her painting depicts Hercules with his wife, Deianira, who in jealous desperation tried a love potion that went terribly wrong.

With further research, I discover that the potion came from the blood of a Centaur named Nessus. According to the myth, Nessus collected a fee for carrying travellers across a river. While on a journey, Hercules forded the river but Deianira was carried by Nessus. When the centaur decided to kidnap her, Hercules heard her screams and shot him with an arrow. As Nessus lay dying he told Deianira to take some of his blood for if she ever feared the loss of her husband's affection it could be used to make a love potion.

It was a short time later and following one of his many conquests, that Hercules seemed smitten with a young maiden, and Deianira saw this as an opportunity to use the Centaur's charm. She applied it to her husband's cloak, but its poison caused him intense agony.

This painting would suggest Alissa had unwittingly given Charles poison. Could it also suggest, she'd been beguiled by an evil Centaur?

Finella had been quite thorough with her information about 'Guinevere and Sir Gawain,' Zarina's painting. Someone with a vendetta against Sir Gawain had put poison in an apple of fine appearance expecting the Queen to present it to him, as he held a position of great dignity. However, a visiting Knight was seated next to Guinevere and she presented him with the apple. He died but it had been without her intent. Was Charles trying to indicate that although he suspected Zarina, she hadn't really meant to poison him?

The same thing could be said of the painting presented to Rupert, that of Socrates and Meletus. Meletus may have been responsible for the charges brought against Socrates, but death by hemlock was not his decision and the philosopher drank the potion himself.

As far as Leona's 'Theseus and Medea,' my notes indicate that Medea contrived to have Theseus presented with a cup of poison. Although she was present when the poison was offered, she did not present the fatal dose.

I continue to search multiple web sites, but after restarting my old computer twice, I give up and call it a night, resolving to leave work early and check at the library before Tuesday night's class.

My day at the office is business as usual but my resolve evaporates when my uncle asks me to stay for a delivery. The library will have to wait but I manage to gauge my time correctly for class and impress Zarina when I enter the studio. She makes an impression on me too. Her vivid vermilion curls are now straightened and dyed an inky black. They match the full-length shift she's wearing. Maybe it was just the contrast, but her skin looks so pale I consider checking her wrist for a pulse.

"So Zarina, a new look."

"Ah, Maudlin, thank you for noticing." She turns and floats toward the office. You'd have thought I'd picked up on a change in lipstick.

I retrieve a drawing board from the stack next to the painting rack and carry it over to the area in the room where the view from the drawing horse matches the cartoon I'd drawn. By the time I have my equipment organised, most of the students have arrived. I'm watching for Grace and feel pleased when she glides onto an adjacent horse just before Rupert makes his way to the front of the class.

"Welcome everyone, to our second session on this still life." With shoulders back and chin up, Rupert seems to have regained his composure since our previous class.

"Before leaving last week," he continues, "I used masking tape to outline the position of each drawing horse. Look on the floor and you'll see that I also wrote each of your names on a piece of the tape, in case you couldn't remember where you were sitting." We follow his instructions like a group of synchronised swimmers and I marvel at his keen memory and powers of observation.

"Are there any questions before we get started?" He flashes a toothy smile in Grace's direction before slicing his fingers through his long brown hair. "Okay, let us begin. Remember to draw what you see and not what you think you see." Rupert reaches over and turns on the light above the still life. Winding his way toward the back of the class, he hovers over Grace and while he seems to be hoping for a sign of recognition, she keeps her eyes on her drawing. He looks like a dog who realises he's not accompanying his owner and I can't help thinking that it wouldn't hurt her just to give him a smile.

When he's out of ear shot I lean close to Grace, keep my voice at a whisper, and let her know I'm happy to see her.

"It's good to see you too, Maud."

"I couldn't help noticing that Rupert was trying to get your attention."

"I know. I could feel him standing next to me," she murmurs. "I don't want to appear rude but at the same time, I don't want to encourage him. If I so much as smile in his direction he might take it as a sign of my undying love." She shivers, showing her discomfort at the very thought. "I don't hate him or anything, I just wish he could be, I don't know, ambivalent."

"I see your point. I was thinking that it couldn't hurt to smile at him, but maybe you're right. Would you like me to say something?"

"No, it's okay, he'll get the message eventually."

Our conversation is interrupted by the arrival of Alissa. When the door opens, all eyes looked in her direction. I'm sure no one has forgotten her last visit to the studio.

"I'm sorry, I didn't mean to interrupt." Her smile is as false as her words. "Please carry on."

Rupert rushes to her side, there's a short exchange before he gallops to the kitchen and pours her a cup of coffee. When she joins him there, I'm so curious to know what they're saying it makes my skin itch. I turn my head to give my ears full advantage but my hearing is not acute enough to pick up anything other than the odd word and the occasional giggle from Alissa.

I turn back to my drawing, and quickly bring it to the point where it's ready to be transferred to the canvas. After Rupert's suggestion that we transfer only perfect drawings, I look around for him, hoping to get the okay to continue. He's still hovering near Alissa, but they've moved next to a drafting table in the far corner of the room. When I catch his eye and signal with a short wave for him to join me, he raises his forefinger telling me he needs another minute. His hair intertwines with Alissa's as he bends over her and I turn away feeling like I just opened their bedroom door.

"Yes Maud?" Rupert suddenly materialises next to me.

"Oh, um, could you check my drawing? I'd like to transfer it to the canvas."

He gives it a cursory glance. "It looks fine. Go ahead and transfer it."

Was I to be offended or complimented? "Rupert, are you sure?"

"Yes." He checks his watch. "Okay everyone, we're at the halfway point. You're welcome to take a fifteen minute break."

While a few students leave for a quick smoke outside, the non-smokers prefer coffee in the kitchen. With Zarina sequestered in the office and Rupert busy with Alissa, it looks like the perfect time to search in the refrigerator for the egg tempera.

I pause next to Grace as she continues to work on her drawing. "Can I get you some tea?"

"Sure, if you're making some for yourself."

I plug in the kettle and not wanting to become involved in the conversation of my fellow students, make the refrigerator my focus. I'm excited to see a small bottle of tempera tucked into a shelf in the door. The egg and oil have separated telling me that it's sat there for quite some time. I pocket the bottle with my left hand while reaching for the milk with my right.

"What do you think you're doing?"

As I swing round, my hand and the milk hit the counter. I involuntarily release the container and the milk sprays across the floor and the unfortunate students in its path. Mouth agape, I stare into the ashen face of Zarina.

"Miss Gibbons, I always make the tea."

"Well Zarina, as the kettle has yet to reach a boil you still can." I step over the spilt milk and I return to my drawing horse. "The tea will be ready in a couple of minutes," I tell Grace after surreptitiously slipping the bottle of tempera into my purse.

She looks toward the kitchen. "Maud, Zarina is standing in the door of the kitchen with a scary look on her face."

"She took umbrage at my making my own tea."

The students begin returning to their places and I cover the back of my drawing with charcoal before transferring it to the canvas. We never do get our tea. Zarina went back into the office, presumably after cleaning up the milk. In the remaining hour I carefully apply the India ink to canvas. I've decided to take it home and apply the veil when Rupert arrives to peer over my shoulder. He seems to have remembered that he has students and is 'doing' the room.

"That's really very good, Maud." I hear an element of surprise in his voice. "Might I borrow it for a moment?"

"Sure, I guess."

"Excuse me class. I'd like to show you Maud's picture. You see, she finished the drawing, properly referred to as a cartoon and has transferred it, using charcoal, onto a piece of stretched canvas. Here on the canvas you will see that she has used a mix of India ink and water to create a mass drawing. Over this, she will apply a thin layer of paint, called a veil. In this case, a grey, at a value of 5 would be most suitable. Thank you Maud," he says, handing me back my canvas.

"Many of you will be ready to progress to this stage next week so be sure to bring the necessary supplies. I've made a list of what you will need and you can pick it up before you leave. Thanks for working so hard, and I'll see you next week."

I pack up my supplies and turn to say good-bye to Grace. "I'll see you Thursday. I just want to apologise to Zarina before I leave." I haul my portfolio and paint-box over to the office, knock once and open the door slightly. I didn't plan to go in, I merely wanted to make amends for the mess and be on my way.

"Zarina, I just wanted to say sorry for spilling the milk and leaving you to clean it up."

"Maudy, I need to speak to you. Come in for a few minutes?"

Damn.

Chapter 10

Leaving my art supplies just outside the door, I step into the office. Zarina is sitting at her desk looking like a stern vice-principal. I expect the strap at best and expulsion at worst.

She nods and with a smile that doesn't reach her eyes, gestures me into the room.

"Matty, do come in and make yourself comfortable." I take one step toward the chair opposite her desk when the smile fades and she orders me to close the door.

Like an obedient pupil I obey her command, remaining upright and with my back against the door.

"Zarina, I really am sorry about the milk and I didn't know I wasn't allowed to make tea."

With her fingernails, she taps out a monotonous beat on the top of the desk. "Don't worry about that now. That's not what I want to talk to you about. I want to know if you are lending your painting of Hamlet to that witch, Leona?"

"Oh. Well, I . . ."

Zarina continues without letting me finish. "She wants mine too of course. But I know what she's up to. I've given this a lot of thought and I've made some notes." She stops tapping to gesture toward the drawer of her desk. "I think Leona was in some way responsible for Charles's death. She knew he was pressing the delete button and she didn't like it. What do you think?"

"Oh. Well, I . . ."

"Yes, yes, we're all suspects, as far as you're concerned, but you've got to be considering that iceberg Tellman as number one, right?" I open my mouth but close it again when she keeps on talking. "Given the evidence, I figure our dear maestro was poisoned. He told me it was the flu. I should have seen through that." She stands up to emphasise the point, then sits down. "In all the years I'd known him, he never once suffered from the flu or anything serious, for that matter. So, as far as I can tell, that should rule out the quack's autopsy report of liver disease too. I know he liked his wine and that may have damaged his liver, but I just can't believe it would have killed him. What do you think?"

She stares at me, her face flushed. "Well?" she demands.

I shift my weight from one foot to the other. "Oh, I'm sorry. What was your question?"

"Really, Matts. And would you please sit down, I'm getting a kink in my neck." I sit. Zarina continues, "Considering the group who received a painting, you are an outsider. I thought something untoward had occurred between you two and Charles was commemorating an amour, but Hamlet is hardly a love story." She's been speaking quickly, but suddenly she pauses, pushes her face toward me and carefully enunciates, "So, I'm asking you if you believe Charles was poisoned?"

She's weird, but I'm beginning to think she's not a murderer. "Yes," I tell her, "I believe he was poisoned."

"And what do you think of Leona? She is definitely hiding something."

"I don't know Zarina." I massage the back of my neck, trying to ward off a burgeoning headache. "She got me down to the gallery to ask about borrowing my painting but she didn't give me any opportunity to speak to her. And I don't really know her or anything about her relationship with Charles. What do you think she plans to do with our paintings?"

"Destroy them of course."

"Destroy them!"

"Think about it Maudy. They are the only evidence we have that Charles was poisoned.

Eliminate the paintings and she has committed the perfect crime. Right?"

"Possibly."

"Not possibly, surely. Unless of course, your investigation has revealed some alternatives."

"Unfortunately, my investigation has turned up very little."

"Look at me Maud. Are you being evasive?" She contracts the muscles around her eyes. "You must have learned something?"

"All right Zarina. I have talked to Charles's aunt Theo. She is adamant in her belief that Teddy couldn't kill anyone and I think I agree with her. We part company, though, when it comes to her suspicions of Alissa."

"Alissa? The little sprite's got a temper, but if Charles was poisoned, we're talking premeditation. I see our merry widow as the crime of passion type. Still, I do concede, she's a possibility and so is Rupert, for that matter. However, myself excepted, he had the most to lose with the death of our dear Maestro. Besides, I'm not sure he's clever enough to carry it off."

"Well, I don't know about that. He seems smart enough but is he capable of murder?"

Zarina sits back in her chair, head held high. "Maudlin, we are all capable of murder." A light rap at the door interrupts us and while I have a startled response, Zarina calls out a calm invitation to enter.

The door opens slightly and Rupert peers around it. "We're leaving now, Zarina."

"We?"

"Oh, Alissa and I."

"Alissa? I didn't know she was here."

"Yes, she was working at the drafting table." He sounds apologetic. "She's considering teaching a . . ." he breaks off as the door is pushed completely open and Alissa brushes past him. She does a quick scan of the room.

"Oh, hi Maud. I didn't know you were in here." She sounds like she doesn't care either.

Although she isn't asking for an explanation, I feel compelled to give one. "I just came in to apologise to Zarina for spilling some milk in the kitchen. I'm leaving now."

"Don't go on my account. Besides, you may like to know, I decided to follow your suggestion and teach a class on pastels. Rupert's been kind enough to help me with the course outline." Turning to Zarina, she continues, "We also designed a mock up brochure for advertising and I'd appreciate it if you would do it up on the computer." She places some papers on Zarina's desk.

I can feel the tension and wonder how Zarina will handle this request, especially after last week's outburst. She surprises me when she smiles sweetly and murmurs, "Don't you worry Lissa, I'll take care of you." With an abrupt turn to me she adds, "Your apology is accepted."

As I am now dismissed, I say my good-byes, pick up my portfolio and supplies, carry them out to my car and load them into the trunk. I'd found a parking spot right in front of the studio and as I check in my rear-view mirror before driving away, I see Rupert getting into Alissa's car.

I intend to call Finella but it's well after eleven when I get home. Physically exhausted but mentally wired I try to force the energy into constructive thought. It doesn't work and I've no idea how much time I spend with my mind going in cerebral circles. When I finally doze off, I sleep right through the alarm and it's a frenzied rush to get out the door. I need to get to the office on time, but I also want to stop off at the lab with a sample of the tempera I've borrowed from the studio.

The chemist, a friend of my uncle's, obligingly puts a rush on the analysis. He can't say exactly when it will be completed so I'm pleased when he calls the office shortly before five, ready to fax me his report. Along with the expected tempera ingredients of egg, water, damar, and stand oil, he had also isolated the components of wine; grape juice, pectin enzyme, dextrose, citric acid and finally a substantial amount of arsenic.

I'm impatient to get home and call Finella, and when I hear the phone ring as I unlock my front door, I rush to answer it. Kora crosses my path at the wrong time and in trying to avoid her, I hit my taboret with my knee and send my paints and brushes careening across the floor. I manage to remain upright, grab the phone and answer with a breathy 'hello.'

"Hello?"

"Yes, hello," I repeat, choosing to sit on the floor and give Kora access for a body rub.

"Maud?"

"Yes."

"It's Theo speaking. I'm sorry my dear, it didn't sound like you. I thought I had misdialed."

"No Theo, it's me. Just a little accident on my way to the phone."

"Are you all right? Do you want to call me back?"

"No, no, just bumped my knee. How's everything with you?"

"I'm well. I've been sleeping much better since the last time I saw you. And by the way, I apologise for dozing while you were here. That was very rude of me."

"There's nothing to apologise for. You were exhausted and it was good to see you getting some rest," I tell her.

"Thank you, my dear. I called to inquire as to how your investigation is going and to invite you for tea tomorrow."

"I'm sorry Theo, I have a painting class right after work tomorrow."

"I see. Well how's Friday?"

"Actually, I'm going to visit a friend who lives in the country. It's east of the city so I could drop in on my way out of town."

"You no doubt intended to get an early departure to avoid the traffic. If you come to me you will forfeit that opportunity."

"I don't mind, but what about tonight? I could be at your place by six and take you out for dinner. Would you like that?"

"Yes indeed, but with one condition," Theo says firmly. "You must allow me to pay for the meal."

Few people argue successfully with Theo Venable. "Thank you that's very generous. I'll feed my cat and be right over." I replace the receiver and hobble into the kitchen, Kora in tow. While she munches on her favourite cat food, I have a look at my knee. A little red and likely to bruise but the pain is beginning to subside.

Returning to the living room, I right my taboret, throwing the tubes of paint and brushes back into it. There's no time to recreate the perfect order I'd only recently established. After a double check to see that all electrical appliances are off, I'm on my way, arriving at Theo's just before six. She's waiting on her front doorstep.

"Hello Maud." She waves as I climb from the car. "Don't get out, I can manage."

I return to the driver's seat and reach across to push open the passenger door.

"Thank you, my dear," she says. "How is your knee?"

"Oh, it's fine. Nothing to worry about."

"I'm glad to hear it. Now, there's a little restaurant just a few blocks from here. I'll direct you." Within a couple of minutes, we're pulling into the parking lot of a charming little Italian restaurant.

"Here we are," she says, reminding me of a little girl on her first picnic. "I haven't dined out in some time. This is a treat!"

"Then I'm glad we thought of it."

A smartly dressed gentleman with silver hair greets us when we enter the foyer.

"Miss Venable, a pleasure to see you. Almost a year, I think."

"That long, Mr. Bellini?"

"Maria and I were so sorry to hear about your nephew. Such a loss! He will be much missed by us all. You have our sympathy, *caro* lady."

"You're very kind." Turning toward me she says, "I'd like you to meet my friend Miss Maud Gibbons. She was a student and a friend of my nephew's. And Maud, Mr. Bellini is the proprietor of this fine establishment."

"A pleasure to meet you." He bows slightly and smiles warmly before sandwiching my hand between his. "Now Miss Venable, I think your favourite table is available. If you don't mind to wait, I will check."

When he scurries off, Theo remarks, "Sorry Maud. I neglected to ask if you like Italian food." I assure her I do. Mr. Bellini returns and leads us to a circular table near french doors. They open to a small courtyard where roses, in crimson and pink, bloom in fragrant abundance.

Breathing deeply, I say, "I can understand why this is your favourite table."

"It is enchanting, isn't it? Of course this was Charles's favourite as well."

"Did the two of you come here often?"

"Occasionally, but Charles dined here more frequently than I."

"Alone?"

"I don't know but I think Mr. Bellini will. You may ask him, he's very cordial."

As if on cue, he returns to our table.

"Ladies I have brought you your menus. It would be my honour to serve you tonight. Can I bring something to drink?"

"Perhaps a half-litre of your excellent house red. Is that agreeable to you, Maud?"

In response to my nod he says, "I shall return uno momento."

"Maud," Theo peers at me over her reading glasses and the top edge of her menu. "I just thought I'd mention that I've tried every dish on this menu and they are all delicious. My personal favourite is the Chicken Marsala, with the stuffed artichokes making a delightful appetiser."

"All right then," I agree. "And how about the Chocolate Tartufo for dessert?"

"Yes, let's have a special treat." Theo places the menu on the table, avoiding the cutlery and beams at me. I find myself ruing the fact that I waited so long to invite her out for dinner. She is clearly enjoying herself. Mr. Bellini returns with our wine and we are ready to give him our order. He leaves and we chat about beauty and how important it is to one's quality of life.

I note the red of the roses are two parts alizarin crimson to one part cadmium red. Pulling the air through my nostrils I savour the scent that defies colour.

"The Dutch have an expression, 'If you have only two pennies, buy bread with one and flowers with the other.' You can tell how old that saying is by the fact that you could actually buy either of those things for a penny."

"Absolutely. I don't know if it's true in the Holland of today, but there was a time when almost every household owned at least one original oil painting. That seems to me a more lasting purchase."

"You have a point," I agree.

Mr. Bellini returns, places a plate in front of each of us and sets the platter of stuffed artichokes in the centre of the table.

"Excuse me Mr. Bellini, Miss Venable has just been telling me that her nephew used to dine here quite often."

"Oh yes," he says.

" Alone?"

The restaurateur looks questioningly at Theo. "It's fine," she reassures him. "Miss Gibbons has a good reason for asking."

"When we first opened he would bring his lovely wife but I think over the last few years things are maybe not so good between them. So, sometimes he would dine alone but he was most frequently accompanied by Miss Tellman, the same one who owns the gallery."

"Was it always an amiable date?"

"Sorry?"

"Did they seem to get along well?"

"Oh, yes. But not too well, you understand. No, how shall I say, displays. They talk, they are good at conversation together, you see?"

"Like good friends?"

"Si, yes. Like good friends."

We sip our wine and split the appetiser between us. It's delicious, and sets the palate nicely for the entrée. Theo savours each mouthful and our conversation focuses on the joys of eating. After a short pause she says, "It is good to know that Charles had someone to talk to. It pains me that I could not fulfil that role."

"Don't be too hard on yourself Theo. You were his aunt and his guardian. You supported him in many ways. No one can be everything to one person."

"You're right of course. For example, I have often lamented that the expectations within a marriage far exceed their capabilities."

"You know, it seems weird to me that Charles's confidant would be Leona. I had quite an interesting exchange with Zarina last night."

"That fruit cake."

The seriousness of her remark causes me to giggle. "Yes, I know what you mean. She is quite eccentric and that does interfere with her credibility."

Theo raises her forefinger and presses it against her lips. "Hmm, I don't know that I would call her eccentric. I think eccentrics are in full knowledge of their behaviour and there is something reassuring in their choice to be peculiar. People like Zarina are frightening because they think they're perfectly normal. That aside, what did she have to say for herself?"

"She was adamant that Leona poisoned Charles. In fact, she believes Leona is orchestrating the retrospective as a ruse."

"A ruse, why?"

"She's convinced her intent is to acquire each of our paintings in order to destroy them."

Theo drops her fork. "For heaven's sake, why would she want to do that?"

"Zarina's theory is that the paintings are the only evidence we have that Charles was murdered."

"Foolish girl," Theo says with disdain. "She should know that there is much evidence to be gained from an exhumation which may indeed reveal the presence of poison."

I tell her about the results of the analysis of the tempera I took from the studio fridge.

"I imagine there is no doubt in your mind that this was the tempera Charles had been using?"

I shake my head. "No, no doubt."

"So, along with the usual ingredients, his tempera contained wine and arsenic." Her comment is a statement but I know she's asking for confirmation.

"That's right." I pause, allowing her to draw her own conclusions.

"As I am certain that Charles would not be ingesting the tempera, I therefore conclude that someone put poison in the wine."

"My thought exactly. Apparently, the artist Annigoni used to add wine to his tempera, presumably to control the odour. I think we can assume that Charles did the same. Before we take that step of exhumation, however, I'd like to try to meet with Leona again. As a possible confidant to Charles, she may have some vital information. By the way, I met with Teddy and like you, I believe in his innocence."

She smiles warmly, "Oh, I am so glad to hear that."

"I also have information about Alissa."

"Really?"

"I had a quick lunch with her the other day." I'm understating the event as I picture myself bolting down the soup before she cleared the bowl. "She told me that she had plans to divorce Charles."

"Well, easy enough for her to say that now," Theo counters.

"I know. She also told me that the house and studio were bought with her money, an inheritance actually."

"Charles, as you know, was quite successful. If anything, the house and studio may have been paid off with Alissa's inheritance, but I'm sure Charles made the initial purchase."

I had understood Alissa to mean that it was her money and hers alone. Perhaps she deliberately mislead me. "If she divorced Charles, Alissa would have received half of everything."

"The Alissa I know has never been good at sharing."

I knew that my attitude toward Alissa was based more on a feeling in my gut than on tangible evidence but it was something I couldn't explain to Theo. "This chicken is excellent. Thank you for recommending it."

"I'm glad you like it, Maud. I thoroughly enjoy a good meal. Unfortunately, I detest cooking one."

"Did Charles like to cook?" I ask.

"Oh, yes. His speciality was Italian cooking. But then, he spent a great deal of time in Italy. As you no doubt read in the notes I gave you during your last visit, Charles went to Italy for the last time, as it turned out, about six months before he died."

"Ah, right." I can't admit I didn't actually decode that bit. "Did Alissa go with him?"

"No no, as I recall he said it was a business trip and he was travelling with a colleague."

"Rupert?"

"My dear, Charles would not consider Rupert to be a colleague."

"You don't suppose it was Leona?"

Before she can answer, Mr. Bellini returns to our table. "Are you ladies ready for your Tartufo?"

Theo looks at my empty plate before giving her confirmation. "The dinner was delicious, as always." She places her knife and fork across the plate, and leaning back into the chair, she signals our host to clear the dishes.

When Mr. Bellini returns with the decadent-looking dessert, he pauses, bends slightly at the waist and in hushed tones says, "The woman of whom we spoke earlier, she is at the table across from here." We both looked to the other side of the room and there in a suit the colour of fresh moss, sits Leona Tellman.

Chapter 11

Theo looks inquiringly in my direction.

"Shall we ask her to join us?"

"I don't know Theo, what will we say?"

"You leave that to me my dear." Her conspiratorial smile is followed by a wink. Mr. Bellini had stepped respectfully away from our table and Theo now motions him back with a slight nod of her head.

"Could you please ask Miss Tellman to join us?"

"Yes of course," he replies, his voice just above a whisper.

I watch surreptitiously as he approaches her table. When I see her nod in agreement, I turn back to Theo.

"Are you sure about this?"

"It'll be fine," she says through closed lips, her eyes on Leona as she walks toward us. Mr. Bellini, a chair at the ready, guides her close to the table.

"Is there something I can get for you, Miss Tellman?"

"Yes, Paulo. I'll have a Bloody Mary."

"So lovely to see you Miss Tellman." Theo's smile looks sincere. "And so nice of you to agree to join us."

"Thank you for inviting me and please, call me Leona," she mirrors Theo's smile, then tilts her head toward me, "Very nice to see you too, Maud."

"Oh, and you too, Leona," I lie.

She directs her attention back to Theo, for which I'm exceedingly grateful.

"Miss Venable, I haven't seen you since the funeral. Please forgive me for not speaking to you at that time." She lowers her eyes and actually seems to be struggling with her emotions. Not quite the ice maiden I'd judged her to be.

"No need to apologise, Leona," Theo reassures her. "It was quite an emotional time and there were so many people in attendance."

"You weren't there were you Maud."

I'm not sure if it's a statement or a question, but it feels like an accusation. I resist my desire to ask her if she really cares and certainly I can't tell her the truth, and confess to having panic attacks at funerals. Thank God, I'll be dead for my own. Instead, I say, "No I'm afraid I had lost touch with Charles and Alissa. I felt that since I hadn't been there for him when he was alive, there was little point being there after his death."

"You are now though, aren't you?" She sits back, her look of self-possession reminding me of Raphael's Veiled Woman.

Before I can respond, Mr. Bellini returns with her drink and although he places it on the table, she has it to her lips before the ice has settled. In advance of suffering oxygen deprivation she lowers the tumbler and addresses Theo. "So Miss Venable, how have you been?"

"Tonight I have been thoroughly enjoying myself." She inclines her head toward me.

"And it was so kind of Maud to invite me out to dinner. This restaurant is one of my favourites, and Charles and I used to dine here frequently. I understand you and he did as well."

Her startled expression belies a ruffling of her perfect feathers and prompts another long swallow of her drink. Placing the glass on the table, but with her hand still cradling it she admits, "Oh, well, yes we did."

Like a kindly village spinster, Theo pats Leona's hand.

"I am so glad Charles had someone to talk to."

In response, our guest lets her shoulders relax.

"I think Charles would agree that he and I were good companions."

"Is that why he took you to Italy on what was to be his last trip abroad?"

Her shoulders snapped back up to her ears. "It was a business trip!"

Theo's eyebrows raise and with one look she tells the lovely Leona to behave. The gallery owner clears her throat and continues in honeyed tones.

"We went to meet a friend of mine who owns a very prestigious gallery in Rome. He was interested in mounting a show for Charles. It would have given him great exposure in Europe as my friend has many lucrative connections."

Although Leona contrives to appear composed, she's clutching her hands so tightly I can see the flesh whiten on the top of her knuckles.

"Maud tells me you're orchestrating a retrospective of Charles's work," Theo says.

"Yes, I am. The invitations should have been mailed last week, so I'm shocked that you haven't received yours. I'll have a word with my assistant but if it isn't delivered in the next day or two, let me know and I'll have one couriered to you. The opening will be a week from Saturday, from three to nine. You will attend, I hope?"

Theo pulls a small monthly planner from her purse and writes down the information on the appropriate date.

"Unless I need the invitation to get through the door, I have everything I need."

"You will be an honoured guest, Miss Venable." Leona returns her attention to her quickly diminishing beverage, taking several sips before turning to me.

"I intended to call you tomorrow, Maud. Could you bring in your painting of Hamlet on the Thursday before the show? That will provide ample time for hanging."

"Will you be collecting all of the paintings that Charles bequeathed?"

"I hope to, and since we are on this topic, Miss Venable, if you have any of your nephew's work that you would be willing to loan the gallery, it would be much appreciated."

"I will consider your request and let you know," says Theo.

This was not the answer Leona anticipated. The colour rises in her cheeks but she's spared further comment when Mr. Bellini returns to our table.

"Are you ready now for tea or coffee?" he shifts his gaze between Theo and me.

"I would prefer decaffeinated coffee if you have it. Maud?"

"I'll have the same, thank you."

Leona hands him her empty glass. "And Paulo, bring me another." It would appear that Leona and Charles shared an interest in alcohol as well as art.

Perhaps to impress Theo, Leona says, "I expect the show will be the event of the season."

"Yes, I'm sure it will be very well attended."

Our host returns with the drinks. "Would you like now to order some dinner, Miss Tellman?"

"No, I'm meeting someone shortly."

Theo stirs her coffee. "So, was your trip to Italy a success?"

"Indeed. My friend truly appreciated the work." Leona raises her glass, seems to have another thought and returns it to the table.

"I also know of someone who is interested in writing a biography of Charles. Theo, would you agree to be interviewed? It shouldn't be too demanding."

With Leona's use of her given name, Theo's neck straightens and her eyebrows arch.

"That is a possibility, Miss Tellman. Of course, I would like to meet the writer before I give my consent."

"Oh, yes, of course. It may be a while, before she contacts you. I think she's presently finishing a novel."

"I shouldn't think it would be wise to wait too long," Theo adds.

"Why? Are you going somewhere?"

"One never knows."

Although the alcohol is making her more relaxed, it's also slowing down her mental processes. Leona finally seems to clue into the possibility that Theo is referring to her life expectancy as a deep blush darkens her cheeks, and she opens her mouth but no words exit. Saving her from further embarrassment, Theo picks up her purse from the floor.

"Maud dear, are you ready to go?"

As I push back my chair, Mr. Bellini appears, ready to assist.

"Could we please have the bill?"

"No no, *mia bella*." He raises his palms toward us. Gesturing toward his surroundings he continues. "This meal, on the house."

"No, no. You're too kind," argues Theo.

"I insist. Now we talk no more about it. Only you promise to come back and see us soon." He steps behind her and helps her from her chair.

I pick up my purse and stand beside the table, offering my thanks and complimenting him on the meal.

"You are most welcome. Please bring our Miss Venable back soon."

I agree before turning to say good-bye to Leona, who is standing, drink in hand, ready to return to her original table.

"I'll be calling you Maud and it was a pleasure to see you again Miss Venable."

"I will consider your requests regarding both the paintings and the biography and let you know my decision. Maud?"

"I'm ready, Theo." I take her arm and we walk out to the car, but as I help her into the passenger's seat, I spot a young woman entering the restaurant and note jet-black hair cascading over an eye-catching, multi-coloured, full-length vest. Could that be . . .?

"Theo, I just want to check something, I'll be right back." Before crossing the threshold, I fall behind a group of patrons and they provide me with a sheltered venue. Looking toward Leona's table, I see Zarina. Her face, a deathly pale next to the black hair, is dotted with deep colour on each cheekbone—an application of too much blush or a sense of high excitement?

Back to the car and slipping into the driver's seat, I turn to Theo, "Guess who Leona's dinner companion is?"

"Rupert?"

"No. Zarina."

"Do you suppose she's, what do they call it, pursuing leads?"

"Probably Theo, but jeez, I don't have a good feeling about this." As I wait for an opening to drive from the parking lot I ask Theo why she guessed Rupert.

"Well, he has replaced Charles at the studio, I thought he might also be ready to get his work into a gallery."

It's a short trip to the house and once I park, thrilled to find a wide space in front of her door, Theo invites me in, leading the way to her sun-room.

"Would you care for a small brandy?" she asks, when I sit down.

"Brandy? I've never actually tasted brandy so I don't know."

"Well, my dear I'll get you a small glass and you can see what you think."

As Theo walks in the direction of her dining room, I'm pleased to see the steadiness of her step. She returns carrying a tray with two small crystal glasses.

"You enjoyed yourself tonight, didn't you?" I accept the deep amber liquid.

"I must confess Maud, I did. I feel better than I have in a long while."

"And," I look into her twinkling eyes, "I think you've shed ten years."

"Not ten but certainly a few. Try your brandy."

"My grandmother used to keep brandy on hand. She said it was good for the heart." I raise the glass in a toast and take a sip. Instantly my taste buds go on red alert and my eyes fill with tears. "My God! That's terrible. No wonder Granny kept this stuff around. It could revive the dead."

"You don't like it then."

I stare at her wide-eyed and she stifles a giggle.

"Forgive me, Maud. I don't think I've ever seen quite that reaction. Is there something else I can get for you?"

"Do you have a mint?" I squeak.

After a cascade of laughter, she says, "I'm sorry but I don't have any mints. How about some sweets for the sweet? I think I have some butter-scotch whatsits." Before she can get up I rise from my seat.

"You stay there. I'll get them, if you just tell me where they are."

"There are some on the coffee table, in the living room. In a china bowl with red flowers on it."

"I'll find them." It's my first opportunity to enter Theo's living room and what a splendid room it is. The furnishings are stylish but it's the walls that capture my attention. The area to my left is devoted to framed drawings and watercolours. With closer examination and seeing that some were dated, I realise they would have been completed when Charles was a child. I envision him, dressed like a British schoolboy with knee socks and woollen shorts, studiously bent over his drawing—his concentration total.

On the adjacent wall, hang oils that indicate a greater degree of sophistication. Judging by the odd dated painting and the subject matter, I conclude that this work was created while Charles was studying in Italy.

I turn my attention to the work of his final years when I hear my hostess say, "I thought this room might capture you."

"I'm sorry, Theo. Yes, these walls could not be abandoned with a mere glance."

"I don't know why I never thought to show you these before. They actually demonstrate the evolution of an artist and I think I can say, albeit with some bias, a truly superb artist. It's strange, but I think Charles felt rather uncomfortable in here."

"As wonderful as we think his work is, he was probably never satisfied." I peer at the date on a skillfully rendered drawing of an English setter. "He would have been five or six when he drew this. That's amazing. I had no idea his talent had manifested so early."

"That was his dog, Monty. He did numerous sketches of him. When he showed me that one I knew we had to frame it. The dear boy was so proud, I can still see his little chest puffed out like a courting bullfrog." Her face reflects the memories of long ago and I hope that the upbeat mood established earlier, will not be lost.

Picking up the bowl, Theo offers me a candy. "Maud can you stay for a cup of tea?"

"I'd love to." I pull off the cellophane wrapper.

"Come back to the sun-room and I'll put on the kettle."

With the warm flavour of butterscotch coating my tongue I follow her into the kitchen and lean against the counter.

"Judging by the way Leona asked about Charles's early work, I'm sure she's never been in your living room."

"You're right. And I've so many paintings, perhaps I could let her borrow a couple." From a corner buffet Theo lifts a tray holding a china tea set. Placing it next to the electric kettle she asks, "Will you lend her your 'Hamlet'? Which I'd like to see too, if I could."

"I guess I've committed to lending it, although not happily. And of course you can see it. I'll bring it with me next time I come over, if you like. By the way, I'm very impressed with the way you handled Leona tonight."

Theo places two cups, their delicate floral pattern matching the tea set, carefully on the counter and as she does so I notice that even her fingers are more flexible.

"Thank you dear. You know, I wonder if she has any real friends."

"Why do you say that?" To me, Leona seemed to have everything. Though she may also have a drinking problem, which no one would covet.

"Maybe the world of business is all she knows. There's a falseness about her—a face she dons when she wants something and her focus does seem to be on getting things." She takes a container of milk from the fridge. "Perhaps she doesn't realize she may have something to give."

"All I know is that you got her to answer questions I'm sure she would have side-stepped if I had asked them." I pour the milk directly into our teacups.

"Well my dear, at least there are some compensations for being an old lady."

"I'm sure it had more to do with your wit than your age."

The kettle comes to a boil and as Theo fills the teapot her hand quivers under its weight. "Theo, you must be very tired. I should go and let you get to bed."

"Don't fuss. I feel better tonight than I have for a very long time and at the very least you can stay until you've finished your tea."

"How about we settle for weak tea. It's probably better for us anyway." As I pour each of us a cup, she settles into her favourite chair. "You know, Leona made a very curious comment."

"When she said you would be there for Charles now, right?" I nod and she continues.

"I think you can safely assume that she knows her Hamlet."

"I agree. It bothers me but at the same time I feel reassured."

"Reassured?"

"I don't think she's a murderer. When she got me down to the gallery to ask about my painting, she also asked about the subject matter and I lied to her."

The lines deepen in her forehead. "Really, Maud. I'm shocked."

I consider apologizing, until I see the laughter in her eyes. "I wanted to divert her from the obvious meaning behind the painting and now, based on what she said tonight, I realize she knew all along. She's tipping her hand but tipping it in the direction of innocence not guilt. Is this crazy logic or can you see what I mean?"

"Yes, I think I do. Guilt would force her to hide what she knows. Also it seems to me that Leona and Charles were good friends. In fact, he may have been her only friend. Perhaps they were lovers but more importantly, they were friends. And I must admit, at no time during the conversation did I feel the kind of jealous hatred that would lead to murder."

Though the tea tastes like a cup of warm milk it compares favourably to the glass of brandy and I enjoy a long sip before adding, "And yet, the painting she inherited from Charles was 'Theseus and Medea.' Medea was married to Theseus's father and it was jealousy that motivated her to try and have Theseus poisoned."

"If Leona was not a jealous lover, could she have been jealous of something else?"

"Perhaps of losing Charles's work to another gallery. It seems he wanted to break his contract."

"Oh dear," she sighs. "It's so much to consider."

I set down my empty cup. "And now I should be on my way. Thank you so much for a delightful meal and of course you're wonderful company."

"No my dear, it is I who should be thanking you." As we reach her front door she asks, "What was the lie you told Leona?"

"Actually, I confess to two tiny lies."

"Oh yes." She nods.

"The first was that Charles's painting of Hamlet, commemorated my high school acting debut. The second, well, that I played the part of Rosencrantz."

Her face slowly contorts into some sort of spasm and when she puts her hand up to her mouth I fear she's in pain. I begin to ask if everything's all right when the laughter erupts. Why does everyone seem to think the idea of my acting in a play is so uproariously funny? I give up on the notion of getting an answer and proceed to my car, Theo's laughter rippling through the night air.

It's after eleven when I arrive home and Kora's not waiting at the door to greet me. The forecast had been for rain so I know I locked her cat door before going out. It's not that unusual. She is a cat after all and not given to effusive displays of affection but she generally shows up within a few minutes of my arriving home. I look from the entry toward her typical resting spots—the back of the sofa and her favourite pillow, one flattened with years of use, tucked on the window ledge. I make soft kissing sounds as I prowl the living room, bending down to look under the furniture, scanning my newly created studio area, and finally I check the bathroom and kitchen. I recall losing her once when she was a kitten and she managed to wedge herself into the hollow pocket in the arm of the sofa, but she's too big to do that now. I open the door to the hall closet but there's no sign of her draped across my shoes.

Flicking on the hall light and seeing my bedroom door closed, I suddenly feel the hair on the back of my neck. In this old building, it's a heavy, ill-fitting door that often sticks and always pulls away paint from the jamb so I seldom close it. I stand still, hold my breath and listen. Silence. I walk back to the front door. No sign of forced entry. A quick survey of all the windows, reassures me that they are closed and locked. Grabbing my old baseball bat from the coat closet I step softly toward the bedroom.

Bat raised, I pause at the door. The only sound I hear is the thumping of my heart. Turning the knob as silently as possible and slowly opening the door, the light from the hall reveals an empty room but as I reach round to turn on the lamp on my dresser, I see movement on the bed. A surge of adrenaline courses through my body but it's Kora, methodically grooming her front paw while lounging comfortably on my duvet. Instinctively, I drop to my knees and check under the bed—only my portfolio and a few dust bunnies, thank God.

"Well my little fur-face, how did you possibly push this door closed?" I ask my feline companion. Although we didn't get the promised rain, a strong wind had blown earlier and with the window open, it might have pulled the door shut. I take one step backwards. But why is the window open? Surely I'd locked it closed before leaving. Maybe my sore knee and the impromptu date with Theo had thrown off my usual routine.

I now securely lock the window, draw the curtains and change into my pyjamas. Unable to shake my feelings of anxiety, I go back to the front door and recheck the lock and doorjamb before doing a thorough inspection of each room, looking in and under anything that could potentially hide a human being. Not ready for the solitude of my bedroom, I pad back to the living room, and turn on the television, hoping for comfort and company. Finding a channel playing an old movie, I curl up on the sofa, with a pillow, blanket and Kora around my feet, and we hunker down for the night. Somewhere in the twilight between sleep and wakefulness I see the image of my answering machine and a blinking red light.

Chapter 12

In the morning I find that indeed, there is a message on my answering machine. Zarina called at ten fifty p.m. and with typical aplomb, demanding I call her back ASAP.,hinting she could reveal the name of Charles's murderer. She couldn't come right out and say her meeting with Leona had confirmed her suspicions. Instead, she let me know she had spent a very profitable evening and was now ready to move on the case. Maybe she deserved an early morning phone call but getting tied up with her would make me late for work.

Before leaving my apartment I re-check all my windows and arrive at the office just before nine. I switch on the computer and while I wait, read the note my uncle has left for me. He'd be out of the office most of the day and wanted me to do some research and a couple of background checks on two clients. There's no rush so I make a call to Zarina's home number. When she doesn't answer, I try the studio, but that number sends me straight to the call answer service so it's likely she's on the phone. I leave her a message. Office work takes hold of my mind and only when I get thirsty do I realise an hour has sped by with no return call from Zarina.

Another call and once again straight to the message. Why is an art studio this busy? I do the background checks, cross them off my to-do list and call again.

Zarina is not your typical modern woman. She never makes chit chat and it's unlikely she even has any close friends so I conclude that either she or Rupert has left the phone off the hook.

I try to concentrate on the flotsam and jetsam of the office but my thoughts keep cycling round to Zarina. By lunchtime, I've had enough. My curiosity, concern and car take me to the studio.

I'm standing at the door of the studio when for the second time in less than twenty-four hours, I feel the hairs rise on the back of my neck. It was a false alarm last night, perhaps this will be a repeat performance. I turn the doorknob, find the latch is not engaged and the door falls open.

"Zarina," I call out as I enter the studio. At this point, time alters its usual trajectory. It slows while my pulse quickens. I note the drawing horses pushed at awkward angles and a couple overturned. Charles's taboret lies on its side, its contents of oil paint, medium, turpentine and brushes strewn across the floor. In the midst of this confusion is Zarina. Wearing the same colourful vest I'd seen her in the night before, she's sprawled awkwardly on her stomach, her shoulder length hair hiding her face. Both legs are splayed, with one arm tucked uncomfortably under her body, and the other stretched above her head, fingers loosely holding the portable phone.

In a bubble of timelessness, I'm suddenly gasping for air. The scene before me literally takes my breath away. I know I need to call for an ambulance but it's several seconds before I can make my muscles obey my thoughts. I fumble in my purse for my cell phone and dial 911. For a few terrible seconds after the emergency operator takes the call, I can't remember the address of the studio. Eventually, I manage some self-control and am able to relate all the important information. Ending the call, I carefully make my way through the debris to gently touch Zarina's wrist and feel for a pulse. My voice, though I barely recognise it keeps asking, "Zarina, can you hear me?" There's no response but her flesh feels warm and I convince myself she's alive. I desperately want to roll her over and provide some comfort but I know I shouldn't move her. Like an anxious flyer willing the plane to stay in the air, I will the ambulance to arrive.

Kneeling over her protectively and waiting for help, I survey the room. There had obviously been a struggle. Had she confronted burglars? What would anyone want to steal from an art studio? I looked toward the far west wall and see Charles's huge mural, the one Rupert is finishing, but his painting of Old City Hall no longer hangs above it. Turning toward the easel, I see that Rupert's painting of Grace is also missing. As that painting was unsigned, a thief might have thought it was a Venable. Before I can continue my inventory, the police make me aware of their presence and two paramedics enter the room with them.

"Are you the one who called for an ambulance?" asks a female officer.

I nod and back away, allowing the two attendants access to Zarina. Standing next to the policeman, I await the verdict. As Zarina is gently rolled over we see the deep red stain of blood soaked through her chartreuse blouse.

"It looks like a stabbing. There's a pulse. It's faint but she's alive," one of the paramedics tell us.

"Thank God," I sigh audibly.

The policeman pulls out his cell phone, dials and I hear him request crime scene investigators. I watch as the paramedics work to evaluate the necessary medical treatment and prepare Zarina for transport to the hospital. With gloved hands, the policewoman carefully dislodges the phone from Zarina's grasp.

"The light's lit on this phone. I think she was talking when she was attacked and didn't close the line."

"I've been trying to call her here since about nine this morning but I kept getting a message."

"A message?" she repeats.

"She must have call answer because when the line is engaged it flips right to the message. I left one the first time I called, but when Zarina didn't call me back, I called a few more times. Finally, I thought there must be something wrong and came over."

She looks at me suspiciously. "Why did you think there might be something wrong?"

Her accusatory tone forces me to take a step back. I note her short-cropped hair, jutting chin and military stance and my words stick in my throat as my eyes fill with tears.

"Well?" she prods at me.

"No," I blubber. I can't stop the tears from spilling over my lids. "I thought there was something wrong with the phone."

The male officer takes a step between us and says, "I'm Constable Marlow. Are you all right? Would you like to sit down?" He nods to his partner and she pulls out a pad of paper and a pen.

"I don't know if I'm all right. I feel like this is a nightmare I'm waiting to wake up from."

"I understand Ma'am. Did you know the injured woman well?"

"Fairly well. Her name is Zarina Hughes."

"Zarina? Unusual name. How do you spell that?"

I spell it for the woman officer who had not bothered to tell me her name and turn back to Officer Marlow. "I'm Maud—without an 'e,' " I add for the note taker. "My surname is Gibbons."

"Gibbons? Are you related to Sid Gibbons?"

"Yes. He's my uncle. Do you know him?"

"Only by reputation. I hear he's running a P. I. firm."

"That's right. I work for him actually."

"Are you a private investigator?"

"No." My attention is drawn to Zarina and the paramedics. "God, I hope she's going to be all right."

"Yes, me too," says Officer Marlow and I feel his sincerity. "You were saying that you work for your uncle."

"Yes, I do all the secretarial stuff."

"How did you gain access to the victim?"

"Pardon?" I'm having a problem registering his question.

"How did you get in? Was the door open or do you have a key?"

"Oh. Actually, the door must have been slightly ajar because when I turned the knob it swung open."

"Did you call for help immediately?"

"Almost immediately, after I got over the initial shock. I used my cell phone."

I know he needs to ask the questions but all I want to do is watch Zarina. As if reading my mind, he pauses until the paramedics have her ready to carry to the ambulance. Focusing once again on the uniformed man standing in front of me, I noticed the colour of his eyes. I tell him about my relationship to the studio, the late Charles Venable, Zarina's role as Charles's aide and that his former apprentice, Rupert Jaynes is now teaching in his stead. I mention the missing paintings, describing them as best as I can. He pulls out his own note book and writes down my address and phone number. When I can offer nothing else of relevance, he gives me his card—in case I think of something. Then he tells me I can go home.

I'm exhausted and desperately want to go back to my apartment but my uncle has no one covering the office so I return to work. The drive there is a blur but I arrive safely and push papers around my desk till about quarter to five. I'm developing a ripping headache and after leaving Uncle Sid a note, I take myself home.

With Kora at my heels I soak a face cloth in cold water then drop onto my bed and place the cloth gently across my forehead. The throbbing permeates the cold and though I persevere for about ten minutes, I realise only medication will dull the intense pain and down two pills from the bathroom medicine chest. Returning to my bed, I don't sleep but doze for over an hour. When I climb back to full consciousness, it occurs to me that I'd forgotten to ask to which hospital they would be taking Zarina. I pad out to the living room, get the phone book and check addresses to determine which one would be closest to the studio.

When I finally locate her, I'm told she is listed as critical and they're doing what they can. No visitors are permitted at this time but I can call back tomorrow. At least I know she's alive. I put the receiver back in its cradle and when it rings almost immediately my hand involuntarily leaps from it as if it's on fire.

"Hello?"

"Maud, it's Rupert."

"Oh, Rupert. How are you doing?"

"Maud, something terrible has happened."

"Yes, Rupert I know."

"You know? You know about Zarina?" His tone is a mixture of shock and accusation.

"I went over to the studio because I couldn't reach her on the phone."

"You found her then," he manages to say before breaking down and sobbing.

"Rupert, do you want me to come over?"

"No it's okay." His voice quavers. "I was just calling to let you know that class is cancelled. I've called everyone else. I'll be okay in a while." He hangs up. I call his name into the empty phone line and briefly consider going over to see him anyway, but then I imagine the kind of reception I'm likely to get and I change my mind and call Finella.

"Is she going to be all right?" asks Finella after I'd explained the horrifying events of the afternoon and what prompted me to go to the studio.

"I don't know. All they would tell me at the hospital was that she was in critical condition. I guess that means there's a chance. I think if they use the word 'grave' it means it's only a matter of time."

"Did you say anything to the police about the message Zarina left you last night?"

"No."

"No?" Finella echoes.

"It's not that I was deliberately hiding any-thing. I did my best just to answer their questions. I tell you Finella, all I wanted to do was get out of that studio. Not exactly your gutsy detective type."

"Now don't you worry about that," she says. "Were there any signs of forced entry at the studio? How did you get in?"

"The door was ajar. It opened when I pushed against it and I'm almost sure it was intact, no pry marks or anything like that. I don't know if it was her practice to keep the door locked."

"Do you think Zarina was attacked because she tried to prevent the theft of Charles's paintings?"

"That's what it looks like but maybe that's what it's meant to look like. Bit too coincidental, happening right after she called to say she could identify the murderer."

"I see what you mean. If someone tried to silence Zarina because of what she knows, could that someone have been Leona? You said they had dinner last night—is it likely Zarina would have confronted her?"

"Knowing Zarina as we do, it's highly likely. Hard to imagine Leona stabbing her though."

"But if she did, does she know that Zarina is still alive? I think you really have to talk to the police. Tell them about your suspicions and about the message in the painting from Charles."

"Yes, I know, but I feel like I'm letting him down somehow."

"Nonsense. Look Maud, just because the police begin an investigation doesn't mean you have to stop yours."

"You're right of course. As soon as she's allowed visitors, I'll get in to see Zarina."

"So right now no one can get in to see her?"

"No, but . . ."

"Maud," Finella interrupts me.

"I know what you're going to say," I cut in. "I'll call the police right now."

"Promise me you'll call me back and let me know what's what. I don't care how late it is."

I retrieve Officer Marlow's card from my pocket, call 11 Division but the desk sergeant tells me P.C. Marlow has left for the day. I'm just about to hang up when he calls into the receiver telling me to hold on as the officer has just walked past the front desk.

"Constable Marlow here."

"It's Maud Gibbons calling."

"Yes, Ms. Gibbons. Good timing, I was just heading out the door."

"You said if I wanted to talk to you to call and well, I have some information."

"Can you come here to the station?" he asks.

"I don't want to make a formal statement, I, well, is it possible for you to come here?"

"I'll be right over."

I hear the click and wonder for a moment if he knows where to find me, until I remember giving him my address. Hard to believe that was only a few hours ago. Time has not yet resumed its normal motion.

I make a quick survey of my apartment. He's hardly a guest but, well, one has one's pride. I fold the blanket I'd used the night before, put away my pillow, clean out the litter box and spray the apartment with air freshener. I'm dragging a brush through my hair when I hear the knock at my front door. I open it to a tall, attractive man in a sky-blue tee shirt and jeans. The blue of the shirt matches his eyes. It takes me a couple of seconds to recognise Constable Marlow and he responds to my momentary incomprehension by re-introducing himself.

"I'm sorry," I tell him. "I know it's you, it just took me a minute. Come in."

"Thank you Ms. Gibbons." His voice is steady, reassuring.

"Please, it's Maud."

"All right, Maud. I'm Paul."

I want to tell him that Paul is one of my favourite names but that might sound flirtatious. "Are you any relation to the playwright?"

"Christopher Marlowe? That would be nice, but I think he spelt his name with an 'e.' "

"And then there's Philip Marlow," I say.

"Yes . . ." He tilts his head slightly before adding, "But he was fictitious."

"Oh right." Gosh, I'm making a good impression. I hadn't even invited the guy in so we're still standing in my front hall. "Please, come in and sit. Would you like tea or coffee or something else, um, liquid."

"Something liquid sounds good." I can see the muscles of his face tightening.

"Oh God, I'm sorry," I mutter through my laughter. "I'm a little tense." He loses his reserve and laughs with me. "Why don't you follow me into the kitchen and we'll figure out something." Opening the fridge I'm relieved to find a can of club soda and a jug of orange juice.

"These two are very good mixed together. Would you like to try it?" When he agrees, I mix them half and half, and pop in a couple of ice cubes. When he steps closer to take the glass, I breathe in the warmth of his aftershave. He follows me back to the living room but before sitting down, pauses in front of one of the few pictures I deem good enough for a frame and a place on the wall.

"This is a really good painting." Glancing down at the signature, he continues, "And I see it's one of yours, I'm impressed." Well, if I couldn't impress him with my verbal alacrity, at least I could with a paintbrush.

"I painted that a few years ago, when I was a student of Charles Venable."

"The Charles Venable who had the studio we were called to today?"

I nod. "I don't suppose you know how Zarina is doing?"

"I know that she's alive." He puts the glass to his lips. "This is actually quite tasty." He holds up his drink as if to visually verify that it was possible. "And, you know, it's a bit of a miracle that she is."

"I'm glad you like it and why is it miraculous? Zarina, I mean, not the drink." I move a chair close to the coffee table and sit down, gesturing for him to do the same. He chooses the sofa across from me.

"The paramedic found that the stab wound was quite deep, but because of the way she had fallen, you know, with her left arm tucked under her body, it staunched the flow of blood."

"So, the intent was murder," I'm talking more to myself than to him. "And you're saying, that had she not fallen on her arm she would have bled to death."

"I'm sure a lawyer would argue about intent. If she interrupted a burglary, the intent may have been to wound not murder. And yes, she probably would have bled to death." He takes another sip. "Yes, very refreshing." Kora appears just as he relaxes into the soft cushions and promptly jumps onto his lap.

"I'm glad you like it." With a nod toward my cat, I say, "I'm sorry, she isn't normally that friendly. Being a calico she has more than her share of attitude. Just push her off, no wait she might bite you. Let me get her." I partially rise from my chair.

"No it's fine, I like animals." He gently strokes her head. She purrs loudly and rubs into his hand.

"Do you have a cat?"

"I did but my ex-wife got custody."

"Oh. Gee, you must miss her . . . or him."

"It's not so bad. I have visitation rights."

"Really?" I'm taken in until I see the corners of his mouth rising. "You're joking, aren't you?"

"Partly. I mean if I wanted to visit her, the cat that is, I could. But seeing her would mean seeing my ex and I don't have a lot of interest in doing that." While he talks, Kora continues to bask in his affection. I'm thinking that at any moment she'll turn on him, sinking her teeth into his hand—a peculiar predilection of hers, so it's hard to take my eyes off her.

Forcibly pulling my thoughts away from her unusual behaviour, I broach the reason I asked to see him. "I'm concerned that Zarina may not be safe in the hospital." He doesn't speak but waits patiently for me to continue. "I think the robbery was a red herring and she may have been attacked because of something she knew. I, well, I think it may have been my fault."

"Your fault? In what way and what does she know?"

"I will tell you but first I need to show you something. It's in the other room. I'll be right back." I return with my portfolio, take out Charles's painting of Hamlet and explain how I came into possession of it. Pointing out the notation Charles had written in the corner of the canvas, I relate the key elements from Act I scene v. I admit that there's no actual proof of murder and that the autopsy had cited natural causes.

"But an analysis of the tempera, I took from the fridge at the studio, revealed the presence of arsenic. I'm sure this is the tempera Charles would have been using but of course I didn't know that when Zarina confronted me about the case. She must have had her own suspicions and when I showed up at the studio for classes, she put it together and concluded that Charles had been murdered. She wanted to know what I'd found out."

He looks up from the painting. "Can we back up a minute?"

"Sure."

"What exactly is tempera?" he asks.

"It's a binder to which you add dry pigment." His expression demands further explanation. "In oil paint, the binder is oil. In tempera, the binder is egg. In oily tempera it is a combination of egg and oil."

"I take it that arsenic is not a typical addition?"

"That's right."

"And your theory is that Mr. Venable was poisoned with arsenic." As he tilts his head toward me, the table lamp warms the blue of his eyes. "Are you then suggesting that an artist would drink this tempera?"

"Oh I'm sorry, I forgot to mention the wine."

"The wine?"

"Yes, you see there was also wine in the tempera. Now, what I'm suggesting is that the arsenic was put in the wine, wine that Charles drank but that he also put into his tempera. Apparently it was something that Pietro Annigoni used to do."

"Annigoni, the Italian painter—portrait of Queen Elizabeth II?"

"Yes!" This was impressive.

"Okay, let's recap. Mr. Venable used oily tempera. He also put wine in his tempera and someone put poison in the wine. Now as you suggest, it is likely he also drank the wine."

"Right," I confirm, still tickled by his knowledge of Annigoni. "White wine was his favourite afternoon libation. It's not typical to put wine in tempera, it's certainly not in any of the tempera recipes I've ever read. I think it would probably be done to control the odour." He looks a little confused so I add, "You know, rotten eggs?" He nods. "I doubt that whoever poisoned him would have expected Charles to be adding the wine to his painting medium. I think the murderer disposed of the wine bottle but he or she didn't know it was also in the tempera."

"But you did. Very clever."

"Thank you." I have to admire this man's judgement.

"You mentioned that Zarina Hughes confronted you about the murder."

"Yes. She seems to have been conducting her own investigation and she wanted me to confirm her findings. I didn't divulge much. You see, Zarina is somewhat egocentric and rather—well, eccentric too. You can never be too sure how she will interpret things." Once again he waits patiently for me to continue.

"The message she left on my machine last night said she knew who murdered Charles. When I tried all morning and couldn't reach her on the phone, I went to the studio. And well, you know the rest. It may have been a robbery but it seems too coincidental to me."

I stare at the floor, my feelings of guilt making it difficult to look him in the face. "I intended to bring all this to the police, eventually. My hope was that the murderer would slip up, thinking he or she had committed the perfect crime. Maybe if I had come to the police in the beginning Zarina wouldn't be in the hospital now."

"From what you've told me, you did not actually involve Miss Hughes in your investigation. She came to you with her own theories, correct?"

"Yes, that's true," I concede.

"It may be that her own inquiries led to the attack, or she may have attempted to prevent a robbery. Of course, I think you should have brought your concerns to the police, but off the record, I also understand your delay. Now, I'll call in and setup some protection for Miss Hughes."

Finishing his call, he turns to me and asks if I'd be willing to come into the station and speak with his Sergeant.

"Now?" I'm instantly aware of the pain in my head.

"No, tomorrow would be fine. How 'bout I call you in the morning and we'll see what we can arrange."

I hesitate but agree.

Constable Marlow finishes his drink and gently removes my smitten kitten from his lap before standing up. "Thanks for speaking with me, I'll call around nine."

"Oh, in that case I'd better give you my number at the office." I write it on a piece of note paper and join him at the door.

"You take care now," he says, pocketing my number and bending down to pat Kora's head.

"I will and I'll talk to you tomorrow."

He opens the door, smiles at me and is gone.

"Well, Miss Mew," I look down at her furry head, "we liked him, didn't we." My watch tells me it's after nine and I understand why my stomach has been complaining. I pull two pieces of bread from the bag in the freezer and pop them into the toaster.

After pouring a glass of milk and spreading peanut butter on the toast, I decide to call it dinner, having no inclination to make anything more elaborate. I had even less inclination to call Finella but, I did promise.

I let her know that the police officer I met at the studio came over to the apartment and after our talk called in to get protection for Zarina.

"That's good news. I'm so glad you called. What else happened?"

I relate an abridged version of our conversation, ending with the verbal body language that usually leads to the close of the call. Just as I'm preparing for good-bye, Finella asks, "What about you?"

"What do you mean, what about me?"

"It occurs to me that if Zarina was attacked for her knowledge, you might be at risk too."

"I don't think so Finella. I haven't confronted anyone."

"I know but . . ."

"Don't worry, I'll be fine. Look, I'll call you first thing in the morning."

This reassures her but after her warning, I have a hard time reassuring myself.

Chapter 13

I long to open the windows, but as I value safety over comfort, I keep each one closed and locked. The small fan on my dresser will help circulate the air in my room and in consideration of my long-haired pet, I leave her little cat door unlocked to give her the option of the cool night air.

My bed is calling me but I know the events of the day will keep sleep in a tight fist. After swallowing another pain pill, I put the plug in the drain and add some scented sea salt to the running water, getting ready for a long soak in the tub. The bright light of the bathroom makes me squint and though I'm not one to use candles—it's the whole fire phobia thing—I bring a couple from the mantel and a chunky one, scented with patchouli, off the kitchen table. Grabbing a box of safety matches—now there's an oxymoron—I set the two smaller candles on the narrow counter around the sink and put the big one on the floor by the tub, pushing it away from the shower curtain before lighting it.

As I ease myself into the bath, I close my eyes and envision a luxurious spa. Starting with my toes, I consciously relax my muscles and make it all the way to my shoulders when I smell something other than patchouli wafting in the night air. In less time than it takes to say 'the cat's on fire,' I open my eyes to see the tip of Kora's tail ablaze. With cupped hands I douse the flame with bath water. As she dashes from the room, I scramble from my watery haven. Like a Keystone Cop, I slide across the wet floor, grope at the counter and tip the tall candles into the sink where the melted honey-coloured wax runs like lava on the white porcelain. I barely remain upright as I grab for a towel. Finding Kora hiding under my bed it takes much coaxing and a long reach to bring her to me and wrap her in the warm terry, giving her a few minutes of comfort before I pull back the towel to inspect her tail. Thank God it remains fur-covered.

"I'm so sorry baby cat. Mommy thought you went out your cat door." I got her one of her favourite treats, promising to give her a cuddle as soon as I clean up the bathroom, but by the time I'm ready for bed she's nowhere to be found, having escaped to the safety of her own backyard.

Too wired to sleep, I grab a pen and paper from the night table drawer and list the key points of my investigation. My uncle likes to say that 'doing beats stewing' but I also want to be prepared for my meeting with Constable Marlow's Sergeant. He wants me to call him Paul, but that doesn't feel right. Maybe when we get to know each other better . . . I complete my notes and when I turn out the light the thought of his blue eyes and the smell of his aftershave carry me into a lovely dream.

My alarm wakes me just before seven and although I feel grateful to see the dawn of a new day, I'm reluctant to leave the images of my dreams. Pulling myself from my bed, my positive attitude compels me to open a few windows before making my way to the kitchen to start the coffee. Kora has yet to show her furry face but I put some kibble in her bowl in case I forget before leaving for work. The phone rings just as I finish getting dressed.

"Hello Maud, it's Theo. I'm sorry to bother you so early but I heard something had happened to Zarina."

"You did? Was it on the news?"

"No no," she says. "My neighbour's granddaughter is in Rupert's Thursday night class. Her name is Grace. Apparently, Rupert called to cancel the class and told her Zarina had been stabbed by burglars."

"Yes, Theo I know."

She makes a clicking noise with her tongue. "Oh how silly of me. Of course, he would have called you too."

"Well actually, I'm the one who found her."

"Maud, how terrible for you!"

I explain the sequence of events and reassure her that as far as I know, Zarina is recovering in hospital. "I'm sorry to cut this short Theo but I have to get to the office. I'll call you from there, okay?"

"Of course, my dear. I shouldn't have kept you. You just call whenever you have a moment."

I ring off, and grab my purse before rushing out to the car. I don't want to miss Constable Marlow's call. The traffic is heavier than usual but I'm only a few minutes late. The note on my desk informs me that my uncle has been and gone.

I've barely tucked into the files when I hear from P. C. Marlow. We arrange a meeting during my lunch hour, which gives me plenty of time to go and return before Uncle Sid gets back. I'm less nervous about explaining everything to the Sergeant than I am about telling my uncle.

When I get to 11 Division, Constable Marlow is there to greet me. While waiting to see his sergeant, we sit in an outer office where I drink a cup of strong coffee and watch the good constable eat a doughnut. Our chit-chat centres on art and architecture, two subjects I'm pleased to learn we both have an interest in. He's curious about Charles's studio and my studies there.

"I didn't mention it at the time, but I admired the technical craftsmanship of the painting of Hamlet. Is any of his work in a local gallery?"

"They're in the Tellman Gallery in Yorkville. Actually, Leona Tellman is planning a retrospective of his work next Saturday. Do you think you would, um, like to go?"

His smile causes gentle folds around his eyes. "That would be great, I'm not working that weekend and we could have dinner afterward. If you'd like."

"Shall we meet there?"

"I'd rather pick you up and go together. That's not a problem is it?"

"No, that's not a problem. I'm sorry if I've given the impression we need to be secretive. I don't date much." Heaven knows why I feel compelled to say that.

His hand lightly brushes my arm. "That's okay. I don't date much either. Now, if you've finished your coffee, I'll check with Sergeant Joli."

He escorts me to the office and stays while I cover all the essential details.

"You were very clear and concise," Paul says when he walks with me out to my car.

"I think you have a knack for this detective work."

"Thanks, but I don't really feel like I've accomplished much."

"Sure you have. Because of you we have a list of suspects and people to question concerning the attack on Miss Hughes. We can also look at getting an exhumation order, due to your quick thinking and the arsenic in the tempera."

"I suppose. Well, I guess I should get back to the office. I still need to fess up to my uncle about all this."

Paul reaches around and opens the car door for me. "Perhaps we could get together before the art show. Next Saturday seems far away. How about dinner one night this week?"

Apparently he doesn't think I'm a complete idiot. I slide into the driver's seat.

"One day this week, then."

"Okay. I'll give you a call."

I wave good-bye as I drive from the parking lot. Wow, a date almost. But am I ready? Maybe I could begin my confession to Uncle Sid with the news that romance beckons, to calm his worries about my solitary life. As it happens I don't have long to wait to begin my tale. Uncle Sid is sitting at my desk when I walk in the office.

Eyes narrowed and brow furrowed he asks me where I've been.

"I'm sorry, I should have left you a note. I had a meeting with Sergeant Joli and P.C. Paul Marlow at 11 Division."

"The police? Is everything all right?" His concern supersedes his displeasure.

"Well, um, I . . ." I'd had this conversation many times in my head but now that I'm confronted with the actual event, words fail me. I pull the visitor's chair close to the desk and sit down. "You see," I begin again. I stand up. "You want a coffee?"

"No. I want an answer to my question."

"Sorry." I return to my chair. "The truth is I've been investigating a sort of case."

"And what is a 'sort of case'?"

"A little while ago, I inherited a painting from Charles Venable. You remember Charles?" He nods. "Well, the subject of the work was 'Hamlet, Act 1 scene v.' In that scene Hamlet learns from the ghost of his father that there was a murder. That he, the father, hadn't died a natural death, like everyone thought and that Hamlet's uncle had actually poisoned his father. That is Hamlet's father, who was also called Hamlet, by the way."

"Yes, Maud I am familiar with the play." He's drumming his fingers on my desk. "So, what you are saying is that this was Charles's way of telling you he'd been murdered."

He's quick, my uncle. I spend the next hour explaining the 'case,' ending with the attack on Zarina.

"This is very serious, Maud, very serious. Do you think the killer knows you're conducting an investigation?"

"No, I don't think so. Besides, it's not a real investigation."

"Yes, Maud, it is and it sounds to me like you've been doing a good job."

"I have? Thanks." This was a far different reaction to what I'd anticipated.

"Listen, if the killer is onto Zarina, there's a good chance you could be in danger. Where's that revolver your aunt left you?"

"Jeez, Uncle Sid. You know how I feel about guns."

"Yeah, but you got the permit and the training, and you're a good marksman. Remember, we did all that in case the time came when you needed the protection of a firearm. I think that time is now. So, you've got it at home somewhere?"

"No, actually, you've got it. I know Aunt Emma wanted me to have her pistol but I left it in your safe."

In a gesture of frustration he raises both his hands off the desk. "Listen Maud, that's illegal. We registered it with you and you're supposed to have it."

"I know but it's not a big illegal, is it?"

"It would be if it got stolen. But never mind now. I'll bring it over to your place later."

There was little point in arguing with him. While he sees a gun as a tool that can save lives, I see just the opposite. When my aunt was alive and he was still with the police force, they went to the firing range in the way other couples go bowling. Our family thought it was cute, though weird—the couple that shoots together, stays together. Anyway, it worked for them. After Aunt Emma's death, I accompanied him to target practice and it seemed to help with the grieving process. And, he takes a lot of pride in my ability.

"Also, I've met someone I rather like."

"Are we talking potential date material?" He didn't seem to mind the segue.

"Maybe. He's the constable who answered my 911 call at the studio."

"A cop?"

"His name is Paul Marlow. That's all right isn't it? After all, you were a cop."

He puts his elbows on the desk and rubs his forehead with both hands. "That's the problem. I know firsthand what some of those guys can be like."

I shift in my chair. Who do I trust if I can't trust a cop? "I'm sure you know some good ones too." He admits that he does indeed know a lot of good cops. Whether or not he wants any of them dating his niece is another story. In the end, he agrees to reserve judgement until he's met the guy. The ringing of the phone interrupts our conversation. I reach across the desk and pick up the receiver. "Gibbons Investigative Services."

"I thought you were going to call me?"

"Gosh, Finella. I'm sorry. I have no excuse. I just forgot and I don't blame you for being angry." Uncle Sid stands up and motions for me to come round and sit.

She sighs loudly before continuing. "I was more worried than angry but since you're so contrite we'll let it go. I am relieved to hear your voice though and hoping that you're still planning to visit tomorrow."

"Yes," I tell her, rolling the chair comfortably under the desk. "I intend to get an early start and as always, I'm looking forward to your company and the country air."

"That's great. Well, I won't keep you. You drive carefully and Maud, I'm looking forward to seeing you too."

"You're going to the country for the weekend?" my uncle asks. I nod. "That's good. You should be safe there." He pulls his car keys from the pocket of his suit jacket. "I gotta go but it's quiet today so how 'bout I meet you at your place at four." Not a demonstrative person, I'm surprised when he bends over my desk and kisses the top of my head. "You take care now," he says before leaving.

I'm ready to go an hour later and am in the process of locking the office when the phone rings. It's Theo. Another call I'd promised to make and didn't. At least she hadn't been worrying, just curious for more information about the events at the studio. She tells me she placed a call to the hospital and was informed that Zarina had come through the surgery but had yet to regain consciousness.

"Surgery? I hadn't even thought of that but I guess the stab wound was quite deep. I hope she's going to pull through this."

"Yes," Theo agrees. "She seems like a strong girl, I'm sure she'll make it. Do we know her family?"

"No. I've never met any of her relatives. She told me that she had been out of town when Charles was taken to hospital. Apparently her father had broken something, his hip I think and she went home to help her mother. Anyway, we know that both her parents are alive but where they live or if they're able to travel, I don't know. I'm sure they would have been notified."

"You're probably right. It's just that I hate to think of the poor girl languishing in hospital with no visitors."

"I'll see what I can find out."

On my way home, I stop at a bakery to buy cookies to take to Finella's. It seems like a cheat and though I like to bake it's just been too hot to even think of turning on the oven. It's a little before four when I climb the stairs in my building. On the last step, I'm surprised to see Kora curled up on the mat in front of my door.

Silly girl cat. Why didn't she use her own little entry off the fire escape? Maybe she scooted in past the mailman. Pursing my lips I make a kissing noise to get her attention but she ignores me. Can she be that tired? As I approach the threshold I speak her name, but she doesn't even twitch. My throat tightens as I bend down to stroke her head. "Kora, sweetie, wake up. Mommy's home." She doesn't move and my heart begins to pound wildly.

Kneeling, I reach for her and pick her up. My worst fears become real as her little body droops limply in my arms. I clutch her to my chest. "Oh, Kora what happened?" I ask through my tears. She must have hoped I'd open the door for her and I wasn't there. My tears explode into racking sobs as I rock her back and forth. "I'm sorry," I tell her. "I'm so sorry." I let the tears flow unrestrained until the worst of the shock passes, then I lay her in my lap. There's no blood, no sign of injury. She isn't a young cat but she isn't that old either. I can't tell if she died quickly or if she suffered. All I can do is sit and hold her and that's what I'm doing when my uncle arrives.

"Maud, what happened?" He kneels gently beside me.

"It's Kora, she's . . . she's dead," I manage before the tears break loose again.

"Oh, honey, I'm so sorry. Look, let's get you into the apartment." He begins to get up, stops then bends down again to pick up a piece of paper in front of the door.

"Hey, what's this?"

"I don't know. I didn't see it. Maybe Kora was laying on it."

"That's odd, it looks like a column from a newspaper with two words circled." Handing it to me he says, "Can you read them? I don't have my glasses."

Cradling Kora with one hand, I take the paper in the other. "The first word circled is 'you're' and the second is 'next.' It says 'you're next.' You're next! What the hell does that mean?"

We stare at each other blankly and then the penny drops. "Oh my God, someone killed her and . . ."

"And he plans to kill you too," Uncle Sid finishes my thought. "We may have messed up any possibility of finding prints but let's handle this paper as little as possible." He takes a cotton hankie from his pocket and carefully wraps the newspaper column in it. "Look, give me your key. Let's get inside and call the police." I nod toward my purse on the floor and he picks it up.

"The key is in that zippered pocket," I tell him. Once inside I collapse on a chair in the living room, still cradling my beloved pet, while my uncle grabs the phone.

"Maud," Uncle Sid crouches down beside me. "Do you have a box, a shoe box maybe that we can put her in? We'll need to have a vet determine the cause of death. With no obvious wounds, she may have been poisoned."

This brought on a fresh wave of tears but I direct him to a box in the bottom of my closet. He goes to the bedroom, then the kitchen and returns with the box. He'd lined it with paper towels. It's a tender gesture and I love him for it.

"Here, let me," he says as he gently removes Kora from my arms. "Maud, I'm sorry about this. I think we're dealing with one sick bastard." Placing the lid over the box he continues, "I'll put the box by the door and get you something to drink, okay? P.C. Marlow should be here shortly."

"Paul's coming here?"

"When I called, I requested that he come over since he's familiar with the case and you know him. Makes it a bit easier on you. Are you okay, sweetie?" he asks softly.

I nod. "Okay then, I'll put on the kettle. I don't suppose you've got any booze in the house?"

"I think I have a bottle of white wine—no, maybe not, I don't know. Anyway, tea will be fine."

Reaching into his pocket he says, "Oh, here, I brought the gun and some bullets. We need a safe place for this."

I'm not thrilled about having a gun in my apartment but it gives me something else to think about. "I've got a jewellery box that locks, shall we keep it in there?"

"I guess it will have to do. We'll hide it at the bottom of your laundry hamper because I think, at least for tonight, you should come stay with me."

"Okay." I think I surprise him by agreeing so quickly but it also gives an indication of how terrified I feel. I get up and bring him the jewellery box. I've just closed the lid of the hamper when Paul arrives.

"Paul, I'd like you to meet my uncle. Uncle Sid this is Constable Paul Marlow."

They shake hands and move toward the living room while I go to the kitchen to pour the tea. Returning with the tea tray I'm relieved to see them sitting amiably opposite from one another, my uncle in the comfy old arm chair and Paul in the corner of the sofa, his left arm stretched across its back.

"Maud, honey, I know it won't be easy but Paul needs to hear what happened."

I sit in the straight-backed chair to form a conversational triangle and tell him about locking all my windows the previous night but leaving Kora's cat door open because of the heat, a decision I now deeply regret. "I should have kept her in." I try to control my emotions but fail as I stifle a sob. Both men rise toward me and there's an awkward moment until Paul takes a step back to his place on the sofa while my uncle wraps a loving arm around my shoulder, waiting patiently for me to calm myself.

"It's understandable that you would blame yourself but it's not rational. No one could have foreseen something like this," says Paul.

"I know but I could have prevented it. Anyway, as Uncle Sid probably told you, she was lying on the mat at my front door when I got home from work."

"And this," Uncle Sid takes a step toward the table motioning for Paul to join him for a look at the newspaper column. He unwraps it, explaining that although we had handled it initially, he's been careful with it now that we understand what it is.

"Okay," says Paul, "we'll check it, but as you know, we're not likely to get any prints." Turning toward me and then tilting his head in the direction of the front door he adds, "Your uncle tells me you have Kora, um, ready. I'll take her now and hopefully a veterinarian can determine the cause of death." I appreciate the way he refers to her by name. "But Maud I don't think you're safe here so . . ."

"I know," I interrupt him. "I'm going to stay with Uncle Sid tonight."

"Good. Okay well, I'll get going then." He places the paper, securely wrapped, on top of the box, which he gently picks up from the floor. His hand on the doorknob, he turns toward me, "Maud, I'm truly sorry about the loss of your companion. If it's any consolation, we'll do everything we can." He opens the door and is gone. Looking back toward my uncle I see the tea tray on the coffee table. "I never even offered him a cup of tea."

"That's okay, honey. I think he'll forgive you. But you should have one. It's probably good and strong now." He pours a cup for each of us before sitting down.

"What about your plans to visit your friend? Do you want to wait and see how you're feeling tomorrow? Or do you want to give me her number and I'll call her now?"

"I don't know. Maybe I'll call her later. It would probably be a good thing to get out of the city. What do you think?"

"I think you should drink your tea, then pack up what you need. We'll get something to eat on our way and you can see how you feel tomorrow."

"That sounds good to me," I say.

"And if you don't want to go away tomorrow, we could drop by the Humane Society."

"The Humane Society?"

"I've heard that the best remedy for the grief of a lost pet is to get another one. They've probably got a cat that would be happy to come and live with you. What do you think?"

I stare at him for a few minutes. "Well, I guess. . ."

"Naw," he waves his hand in the air. "Tomorrow's too soon. But you think about it, okay?"

"Okay," I promise. "I'll get my stuff together." I set my empty cup on the table.

"And I'll wash up the tea stuff."

Within a few minutes I've packed what I think I need and made sure the apartment is secure with all windows locked. Then I'm ready to go. Uncle Sid has finished in the kitchen and is waiting for me by the door. "Do you want to eat out or should we just pick up something to take home?"

"I'm not really that hungry," I tell him. "Maybe just a salad."

"They have takeout salads?" He puts his hand on the doorknob.

"For sure. Almost all the fast food places have them. Where have you been?"

"Sweets, I've been brown baggin' it for years." He takes his hand off the doorknob.

I stand in the living room, scrutinising. "You're in for a treat then. They make more than hamburgers now."

"Okay," he says putting his hand back on the doorknob. "You ready to go?"

"Yes, but I'll just check the kitchen."

"Everything's off!"

"I know but I have to check it one more time."
I do my tour and in the kitchen see Kora's food and
water bowls, washed and in the dish rack. "Okay."
My voice quavers. "I'm ready to go."

Chapter 14

I walk into my uncle's kitchen and without thinking find myself looking out the window expecting to see Aunt Emma in the garden, and when I stow my overnight bag in the room that was once mine, I can almost hear her voice. Death does not erase the well-trod pathways in the brain.

Before he retired, my father was an army man and we did a lot of moving around when I was a kid. Every few years, it was another neighbourhood, another house, another school and a new set of faces. We were living in Toronto the year I started grade 11. Two years later my dad was posted to Vancouver, British Columbia. After a family meeting, it was decided that I would live with my childless aunt and uncle until I finished my final year of high school. When it came time to choose a university, I decided to stay in Toronto, not willing to give up my newly-found stability. This caused a rift with my parents, one that's lost its edge over time but hasn't completely healed.

The table is set and Uncle Sid pulls out a chair for me when I re-enter the kitchen. "It's nice to have you home, Maud."

I give a nod toward the window. "I always liked the pattern of yellow daisies on those curtains and the quilt Aunt Emma made is still on my bed—or the guest bed."

"It's your bed whenever you want to be in it. Been quite awhile since you were here. I'm sorry about that and I'm sorry too, about the circumstances that finally brought you home."

"I know. Poor Kora. I should have kept her in last night."

"Now Maud, you know . . ."

"Yes I know," I interrupt him. I try to ignore the lump forming in my throat. "What kind of person would kill a defenceless cat?"

"A very dangerous person and one we are going to put behind bars before he or she can hurt anyone else. If you feel up to it, I'd like to hear more about your suspects. But first eat your dinner."

Half a salad is all I can manage. Pushing it aside I begin with my letter and my visit to the lawyers. I described, as detailed as possible, the subject matter of each painting bequeathed as Charles had directed.

"On the surface," he says, "it would appear that Charles suspected each one equally. I would imagine, though, that he mistrusted one or two over the others. We need more info. Did you bring your notes with you?"

"No, I left them at the apartment. How did you know I took notes, anyway?"

"Because that's what a good detective does." He smiles. "Well, we'll pick 'em up later. You think we can eliminate that agent, what's his name, from the list?"

"Teddy Baer."

"Oh yeah. How could I forget? I think that's cause for a warped personality right there."

"His real name is Evelyn, actually."

"And that's gonna make a difference?"

"He's a nice guy," I insist. "A really nice guy."

"And that's why you eliminated him? Maud, I remind you that some of the most abominable men in history have given the appearance of being 'nice guys.' "

I stare at my half-eaten salad. "I know, but, well, it's more like intuition. I could be wrong, I guess."

"Maybe not." He reaches across the table and touches my hand. "Sometimes we have to go with our hunches. It looks like your friend Zarina is in the clear. At least we know for sure that she could not have hurt Kora."

I'm beginning to feel pressure around my temples and rub them with my fingertips.

"Sorry, honey. I can see you're getting tired. Let's find a distraction, or would you rather rest?"

"It's too early to go to bed. How about a game of cribbage?"

He leapt from the table. "What a great idea! I'll get the cards and the board."

I have the table cleared when he returns. I do my best to give him a challenge but my concentration is off. If he noticed he didn't say and we play until my eyes are heavy. It's after ten when I join him in the kitchen the next morning.

"Did you sleep okay, Sweetie?"

"I was exhausted but it was hours before I drifted off. Poor Kora. You know, I never really considered myself to be a cat person. I hope I gave her a good life. Maybe I left her alone too much and I wish I hadn't burned her tail with that stupid candle. God, I'm rambling—sorry."

"Her tail caught on fire?" he asks and I tell him the whole sad story. At least I thought it was sad but I was sure the hand he held over his mouth hid a smile.

"I'm sorry Sweets, I know you're unhappy but the image is kinda funny—wouldn't have been if she'd been badly burned, of course. Look you'll feel better after you have some coffee."

He hands me a mug. "What do you think about going to visit your friend?"

"I don't know." I take a sip and feel instant regret. I'd forgotten just how terrible my uncle's coffee could be.

Looking at my face he chirps, "Good and strong isn't it?"

"It's strong all right."

"What about the good part?"

His look reveals sincere innocence and though I risked hurting his feelings, I can't stop myself. "Uncle Sid, you make the worst coffee I've ever tasted. I think we could probably run your lawn mower with this."

"What? You don't like it? How come you never complained before?"

"I know. I should have been honest. Look," I tell him, "let's dump this and I'll show you how to make a good cup of coffee."

"Maud, I'm cut to the quick."

"No, you're not." I pour the coffee down the drain. "Do you have a scoop for the grounds or do you use a tablespoon?"

"Neither. I just pour it into the basket till it looks right."

"That explains a lot," I proceed to demonstrate the fine art of coffee making. When it finishes brewing, I pour him a cup. "Well?"

"Yeah, it's okay," he admits. "So, what do you think about going to Finella's?"

"I don't think I'm up to it. I'll call her and make it for another time. I wish I could avoid getting into the whole explanation about Kora."

"How 'bout I call her?"

"Would you? That would be great. I really appreciate it." I give him her number and go to my room to get dressed. When I return, he's looking in the phone book.

"What are you doing? Did you call Finella?"

"Oh, yeah. She wanted to talk to you of course but she understood. She said to call her or visit whenever you like. I was just looking in the phone book for the address of the Humane Society. What d'you think? Shall we pop over and have a look-see?"

I'm not sure if it will make me feel better or worse but it will provide a diversion.

"You don't need to get one today, in fact it's probably too soon" he says, "but at some point it would be a good thing, in memory of Kora, to provide one of her brothers or sisters with a home, don't you think?"

"Okay and after that we can stop by my apartment and pick up my notes on the case."

During the drive I try unsuccessfully not to think about Kora. Finally, I give in to the need to mourn and remember.

In my final year at the art college one of my classmates had a cat that surprised her with a litter of kittens two months before she was planning to move from Toronto. She was desperate to find homes for them and though I didn't want a cat, I fell victim to her pleas. Being the first to do so meant I had the pick of the litter and Kora, the cal-ico, had been chosen for her beauty. Had I known that tricolour cats tended to have even more atti-tude than the average feline, I would likely have made a different selection. But I came to love her and I think she loved me, in her own way. I knew when I returned to my apartment it was going to be painfully lonely without her.

Kora, I thought, I'll get the sick bastard who mur-dered you. My hands involuntarily form fists in my lap and my teeth clench firmly in my mouth. Uncle Sid must have noticed the whites of my knuckles or felt the anger emanating from my body.

"Maud, honey, are you all right?" he asks, briefly placing his hand over mine.

"I was enjoying kitten memories, when I was suddenly filled with anger or maybe it was hate. Whatever it is, I want to get the lowlife scum-bag who would kill a poor defenceless animal." I pound the dash then quickly apologise for my outburst.

"You don't have to say you're sorry. Anger is good. Anger is energy. We just have to be sure to direct that anger in a constructive way."

"I don't know if I am up to getting a new cat. It might be a good idea to keep this anger. It's prob-ably a better motivator than grief."

"I think that's true but, we're here now. Do you want to have a look? You know it doesn't have to be another cat. Maybe they have gerbils, hamsters, maybe a bird. Or we could just go directly to your place?" He pulls the key from the ignition.

I get out of the car and Uncle Sid joins me as I walk toward the entry door.

"Somehow I don't think they get many small rodents or birds needing a new home. I knew somebody who got a ferret here, but I don't think I want a ferret."

At the front desk I'm greeted with enormous enthusiasm by the ugliest dog I've ever seen. His face is wrinkled and droopy, his limbs gangly and his co-ordination suspect. The woman who holds his leash turns toward me, her cheeks damp with tears.

"He certainly likes you. I was just telling the attendant here," she tilts her head toward the young man behind the counter, "that he's nine months old. I love him dearly but my husband says we can't take him to Europe. I don't know what to do."

I lean over to pat him and he pushes his body against me. We make eye contact and a bond forms instantly. I had lost my companion and he was about to lose his home. His owner continues, "He's a bloodhound and his name is Sherlock. My husband has just been transferred to England." She dabs her eyes with a tissue. "He really does seem to like you."

"I think he's the ugliest, most beautiful dog I've ever seen." I drop on one knee and grab the heavy folds around his neck.

"Are you here to adopt a dog?" she asks.

"Well actually . . ." Sherlock began covering my face with slobbery kisses. "Actually," I begin again. Then I look deeply into his soulful brown eyes. "Yes."

"But Maud," my uncle interjects.

"I know Uncle Sid, but isn't he gorgeous?" I turn my attention to the woman who is looking at me intently.

"My name is Maud Gibbons." I stand up and extend my hand.

Receiving it, she responds, "And I'm Sarah Jenkins. It's a pleasure to meet you."

"This is my uncle, Sid Gibbons, he's a private detective and I work for him at the Gibbons Investigative Services."

"Actually, we're both detectives," he tells her.

"Cool," says the young man from behind the desk. "What better dog for a couple of detectives than a bloodhound named Sherlock."

"He's right," says Sarah. "I think you're an answer to my prayers."

"You want me to adopt him? Wow! I'd give him a good home and you can visit if you like and I'll even take him with me to the office so he's not alone all day." I ignore the sound of my uncle clearing his throat.

"It's hard to give him up. I've been fretting about it for weeks, but if you want him, well it feels better at least knowing his new owner," she said. "What do we have to do?" she inquires of the Humane Society employee.

"As you haven't signed him over to us, we're really not involved. The arrangements can be made between the two of you."

"I may not be able to but I'd like to think I could visit Sherlock before we move."

"Yes, of course," I tell her, digging in my purse for a business card.

She takes the card. "I brought his bed and a few of his toys. They're in the car. I didn't know what the Society would let me leave with him."

I'm only half listening as I kneel next to my dog—my dog, I can hardly believe it. I hug him and bury my face in his furry neck. "He smells good too," I say, looking up at my uncle.

"Yeah? Wait till he gets wet." He turns to Sarah. "Is he housebroken?" I can see he's going to ask all the important stuff.

"Oh, yes and he's had all his shots. He'll need boosters of course. Do you have a good vet?"

"Maud, do we have a good vet?"

"Yes Uncle Sid."

When we get to the parking lot, Sarah hands me Sherlock's leash. "I'm parked over there," she points to a red SUV.

"Maud you wait here and I'll pull the car up beside Mrs. Jenkins' car so we can transfer the dog's belongings."

I lead Sherlock to a grassy area, before walking him over to the cars. "He did his pee-pee," I reassure my uncle.

"Swell, that's a relief for the two of us."

We put all his doggy accoutrements into the trunk and settle Sherlock in the backseat. We're saying our good-byes when I realise I've neglected to ask Sarah how much money she wants.

"Oh, I don't want any money. I'm just happy to know he'll have a good home. He was a gift from my sister-in-law, she breeds Bloods, and you know, it would be a good idea for you to have her name and number in case you have any questions. She lives in Saskatoon." Sarah pulls a piece of paper from her purse and writes out the information. She turns toward Sherlock, his head hanging out the open window. "Now, you be a good boy. Mommy will come and see . . ." She turns away, unable to finish her sentence and I put my hand on her shoulder. "I'll be fine in a minute." She forces a weak and crooked smile. "It's probably best to make this quick, but I really am happy to have found you."

I thank her again and get into the car with my new 'baby.' Before we drive off Uncle Sid leans out the window. "Excuse me Mrs. Jenkins, has this fellow finished growing?"

"Not quite. As an adult he'll be about three feet tall and about a hundred and twenty pounds." He turns back to me, "You heard that?"

"It'll be fine. I'll take good care of him." I turn and look at the back seat where Sherlock is happily drooling all over my uncle's leather upholstery.

"What's important for me right now, is that I think he will take good care of you. However, he is still a pup and I don't know if you should be bringing him to the office."

"How about on a trial basis? If it doesn't work out then I'll leave him at home. I'm sure I can train him, maybe even enrol him in obedience school." I swing around and pat his beautiful head, telling him all about his new home. I hope I have a tissue to wipe those seats.

"Maud, we're here."

"Where?" I ask swivelling around.

"Your apartment. Remember we were going to pick up those notes."

"That was fast. Come on Sherlock, we're home." I hop from the car and flip back the seat to help him out. Grabbing his leash, I grimace when his claws add a few scratches to the dampened leather.

"Hey, what's all over the back seat?"

"Oh. That's just a little saliva. I'll bring some paper towels."

"Nix the towels. Bring down a blanket or whatever we can use to cover this leather."

"We won't need it. I'll follow you back in my car. I'll need it tomorrow anyway."

After Sherlock waters the bushes we climb the stairs to my apartment. I'm stopped at the threshold by the image of Kora, lifeless on the mat in front of the door. Fortunately, it's replaced with Sherlock's goofy face staring up at me in anticipation. Once inside, he makes a thorough search of the apartment, running into each room, and finally sliding on the tile in the kitchen. I figure the poor fella could use a drink of water and automatically reach for Kora's dish from the drain board. I look at the dish. I look at the dog.

"I think you might need something a bit bigger than this. We'll keep these aside, in memory of Kora." I use one of my stainless steel mixing bowls.

"Maud, are you talking to me?" Uncle Sid calls from the living room.

"No. I'm talking to the dog. I'm just getting him some water. You know, I'll have to stop at the store and get him some food. I forgot to ask Sarah what he likes to eat."

"He looks like he'd eat anything."

I check my messages and find one from Rupert, saying he will be teaching on Tuesday evening and one from Leona, about Charles's retrospective and my painting. This reminds me to show the work to my uncle. He's duly impressed and with a keen eye, notes the resemblance between Hamlet and myself. There's no need to hide it now, but I feel more comfortable stowing it in the portfolio under my bed. I grab my notes plus a couple of other things I'd forgotten and we're ready to go.

Sherlock has greedily lapped up the water, spilling half of it on the floor. Cats are so dainty. I clean the floor with some paper towels and hand some extras to my uncle for his back seat.

"So, what are we doing for dinner?" I ask.

"Dinner? We haven't had lunch yet."

"Oh, you're right. Well, for dinner I have one of these new frozen meals, a pasta thing. It's pretty good. I could bring it."

"Okay. I'll stop at the bakery and get a loaf of french bread to go with it."

"And I'll go to the pet store and get food for Sherlock."

"Don't hang around there too long," he cautions. "I'll make some sandwiches as soon as I get back."

"Don't wait for me. You go ahead and eat."

"No the sandwiches will keep until you get there."

Having secured my apartment, we go out to the cars. I decide it's prudent to let Sherlock have a short walk before we pile into my little car and drive to the pet store. Sherlock is preoccupied during the short drive along Bloor Street. Rustling around in the back seat, I assume he's familiarising himself with all the new scents, but when we pull into the parking lot, I discover the source of his amusement. He's consumed most of the now day-old goodies I'd bought to take to Finella's. Leading him from the car, he leaves behind a trail of partially eaten peanut butter cookies.

"Good thing I didn't buy chocolate, little buddy. We could be taking a trip to the vet's on our first day together." I hold onto his leash and do my best to clean up the crumbs. "Now if we're late for lunch, your uncle won't be happy." He wags his tail.

In the pet store I look around for some assistance. Not only do I want recommendations on food and some big bowls to put it in, I also need an education. We had a dog when I was a kid but I hadn't been involved in much of her training. Along with what is apparently the best in dog nutrition, I also buy two highly recommended books. Having already learned one important lesson, I put my purchases in the trunk of the car and Sherlock in the back seat. I'd been cat trained; now I would be dog trained.

By the time we reach my uncle's, Sherlock had done a thorough job of cleaning up all the crumbs. I heft the bag of food and my other purchases from the trunk and with some difficulty carry it in one arm while holding the leash with my other hand. Sherlock lifts his leg against the hedge by the front door, leaving a puddle on the first step.

The table is set, the sandwiches made and my uncle has even bought some fresh flowers to grace the table. He's put Sherlock's bed in the corner, with the cardboard box containing his toys and some large bowls for food and water. Seeing his bed, our tired boy hops into it, his big wrinkly head hanging over the edge.

"I should have known Sarah would have given us his bowls." I held up the bag. "Now he has another set." I compliment my uncle on the lunch preparations. "You bought flowers and put out pickles and everything."

"Yeah, well, this is a special day. I thought we could celebrate Sherlock's arrival to our family."

"That's so thoughtful. Thank you. Thank you so much for everything."

"It's nothin'. Just sit down and let's eat."

Over lunch I show him my new books and he reminisced about the dogs of his childhood. My aunt's allergies had prevented him from having a dog when they got married and I think after his initial concerns, he's now almost as thrilled about Sherlock as I am, though I don't expect him to admit it.

After savouring the last sip of his coffee he says, "I've got to go to the office for a couple of hours."

I set my cup on the table. "Do you want me to come with you?"

"No need. You stay with 'Mr. Holmes,' here. The two of you can learn something from those books you just bought. I won't be long."

Sherlock has been snoozing in his bed but wakes up when he hears Uncle Sid leave. I'm not sure if my new pooch should be eating twice or once a day but I put a little food in his bowl to see if he's interested. He attacks it like a vacuum cleaner then he takes off down the hall with me running after him. "Whoa, horsey. This is your uncle's room, and it's off limits." I smack my thigh a couple of times and he turns to follow me. "Good boy! Now, this is my room, soon to be our room, once I bring your bed in here." He jumps up on my bed and I grab his collar, pulling lightly to encourage him down. "Come on boy, it's not bedtime yet."

He follows me from the room and I grab my new books as we pass the kitchen. Once in the den, Sherlock curls up on the couch with me, after a futile attempt to curl up on my lap. I had worried that he might pine for his previous home but instead I marvel at how well he's adapting.

Maybe it's a breed thing. I had a friend in college whose family had to give up their golden retriever when they lost their farm. They put an ad in the local paper and within a couple of days got a response from a farmer in the next county.

When he came to pick up their beloved companion, they stood teary-eyed on the drive while five year old "Rover" leapt with no hesitation onto the passenger's seat and hung his face out the window with an expression that said "Bye, thanks for the memories."

I scan through both books and select a few chapters to read from each one. Forcing myself to focus and feeling the warm body wrapped around my feet helps repel painful thoughts of Kora. I find no reference to the faithfulness of bloodhounds but after a couple of hours study, do feel better equipped to care for a dog.

By four o'clock I'm ready to put some of my new-found knowledge to the test. I pocket a couple of dog treats then hook the leash to Sherlock's collar. I do my best to shake off any negative energy, push my shoulders back and at least act like I know what I'm doing. When he tugs, I pull him next to me then let the leash go slack until he tugs again. In the backyard, we practise sit and stay until all the treats are gone. It's going to take time and patience but I just know he's the smartest dog on the planet.

Uncle Sid arrives home as I finish dinner preparations. He had stopped at the video store and rented *Turner and Hooch*, a good dog movie. Hooch attracts Sherlock's attention every time he barks, so we agree the film was enjoyed by all. It strikes too close to home when Hooch is killed, but then there's the puppy and a happy ending.

I bring Sherlock's bed into my room and he circles the cushion until I tuck myself in. Then he's up next to me and I can't say no. It is his first night away from his family and despite sharing my bed with a ninety-pound canine, I sleep like a contented child. In the morning, the sun, the dog and I rise as one. He covers my face with good-morning kisses and his excitement at the beginning of a new day is contagious. We spring into the kitchen, four legs having slightly more spring than two. I release him into the backyard and make some coffee. Uncle Sid wakes up to its aroma and we carry our steaming cups out to the deck.

"If you feel up to it, Maud, I did a little research at the office yesterday, and would like to discuss some curious aspects of your case."

"You did? That's great. I definitely feel up to it."

Chapter 15

Breakfast eaten, its remains tidied, my uncle and I sit down to discuss his findings.

"I was hoping to add to your research and insights into the case, so I took your notes with me to the office yesterday." He puts a manila folder on the table.

"You did? Why didn't you say something last night when you got home?"

"I wanted you to have a break, just enjoying the evening."

"Thanks. It was fun. So what did you find out?"

"I swam the Internet but without an address I'm not too good at that stuff, so I went to the library. The librarian was really helpful and hey, why are you smiling?"

I suppress a giggle. "Sorry, but one surfs the Internet. One does not swim the Internet."

"Well the way I do it, it's more like swimming and against the tide. Anyway, in my notes here," he flips through the pages, "I found a couple of things that have prompted some questions. In connection to them, I'd like to hear your gut reaction to each suspect. Give me a kind of Rorschach personality sketch."

"Okay. I'll give it a go."

"First up, Alissa. What comes immediately to mind?"

I form a mental image of Alissa. "She's one of those needy females. The type that brings out the Sir Galahad in men. I admit she's pretty but too blonde, too thin, too made up and I don't think she's quite as helpless as she appears."

"You mean under that frail exterior beats a heart of steel?"

I nod. "I think that's a fair assessment."

"Her painting was of Hercules and his wife," he pauses to check the notes, "Deianira."

"Right and according to the myth, Deianira feared losing her husband's affection. In an attempt to rekindle his passion, she applied what she thought was a love potion on his robe. Unfortunately, she was beguiled by an evil centaur and the potion was poison."

"You said that Alissa was planning to divorce Charles, but was that a last resort? Would she have tried anything to get him back?"

"I don't think she would grovel and beg."

"But she might like him to," he adds.

"Yes," I agree. "It may have been that she was hoping to use the arsenic to debilitate rather than kill. Thus putting her husband in a position where he needed her."

"And, getting some revenge for her suffering at the same time."

"You're right. I hadn't thought of that. She probably didn't know about the fragile state of his liver."

"Okay, now Charles's apprentice, Rufus."

"Maybe my writing's not too clear. His name is Rupert."

"Rupert, all right. So, is this Rupert," he puts extra emphasis on the "t," "gay?"

That takes me aback. "Gay? No." I see him fawning over Grace. "Why do you ask?"

"The painting, 'Socrates and Meletus.' Socrates had a fondness for boys and given the time and place, this Meletus character probably did too. It was just a thought. Describe Rupert for me."

"He's young, late twenties maybe, a little shorter than average and I think for some men that's a problem. He's also quiet, unless you get him onto his favourite topic: Art. There's something else though, that's hard to describe. He's socially inept but maybe it's shyness. He was devoted to Charles and had worked with him for years. I think Zarina's hard on him but he's turning out to be a pretty good teacher."

"Any chance he thought Charles was corrupting the youth, as the painting suggests?"

My thoughts turn back to Grace. "In talking with Grace—she's one of the students at the art school—she told me that while Charles was helping with her modelling career, he allowed others to think they were having an affair. Rupert may have felt it wrong for Charles to have a relationship with a woman thirty years his junior, but I can't see that as a motive for murder."

"Maybe not, but he did have opportunity."

"Yes and so did Zarina, and everyone else who visited the studio, for that matter." I counter.

"Too true. So, tell me about Zarina. What did you think of her painting of Guinevere and Sir Gawain?"

"My first thought was that it was appropriate, since Zarina seems to live in another time. She's probably in her early thirties, but she acts, oh, I don't know, older and, well, odd. It should be obvious that she's difficult to know and quite unpredictable. Prior to our discussion about Charles, I'd never seen her display much in the way of human emotion, but over lunch, she sobbed hysterically."

"Her painting would seem to imply that the poisoning was without her knowledge."

"Yes and it would have been, if someone else had put the poison in the wine. Zarina, tending to Charles, would have been the one to serve it to him."

"Just as Guinevere inadvertently served the poison apple. That fits rather nicely then, doesn't it?" Uncle Sid is pleased we have something conclusive. "Also her attack and the fact that she was in hospital and couldn't have harmed Kora, makes her an unlikely suspect. Now, the charming Mr. Baer. Could he have been siphoning funds?"

"Stealing from Charles?" I ask.

"Nero was a very corrupt emperor. From your notes, I see that this agent owns a house in a very expensive part of Toronto, not to mention that car of his, make that two cars, that you're so fond of. How much do you figure artists' agents earn?"

I had to admit Teddy's life style was rather grand. "Maybe he inherited money, Alissa did. Or maybe he married into it." I'm reluctant to consider Teddy a thief and a murderer.

"I'll see what I can find out about his financial status. Finally, the one Zarina suspected, Leona Tellman."

"Sorry, Unc. Can't help you too much there. I don't know her and she's secretive. The strong independent type. Theo thinks she's all business. From dinner the other night, I learned that she and Charles were good friends, that they went to Italy together on business and that she has a particular fondness for Bloody Marys."

"You know, some people try to bury a guilty conscience in booze. Speaking of liquid refreshment, I think I'll get another coffee. You want one?"

"No, I am fine. Another thing, Leona is having a retrospective of Charles's work this Saturday."

He rises from his chair, empty cup in hand. "Is she likely to hang the paintings Charles gave each of our suspects?"

"I think so, she certainly wants mine and she asked Zarina for hers. I think that's what started Zarina's suspicions. She believed Leona had plans to destroy the paintings, in the belief that they were the only link to the murderer."

The phone rings and my uncle leaves to answer it. I see that Sherlock is no longer sleeping in his bed near my chair and find him in my uncle's room chewing happily on a slipper. I'm wrestling it away when Uncle Sid appears in the doorway. "It's Paul, for you. Hey! What's that dog chewing on?"

"He just got the one, the other slipper's untouched."

"Well that's okay then," he says, sarcastically.

"I'm sorry Uncle Sid. I'll get you a new pair," I take the phone from his outstretched hand. "Hi Paul. How are you?"

"I'm fine, is everything all right there?"

"Oh yes, we're fine." I offer my uncle an apologetic smile.

"I'm calling for a couple of reasons. First, I have the report on Kora. You probably knew this already but it was arsenic, likely put into tuna fish."

"She loved tuna."

"I also spoke with your neighbour from the first floor apartment."

"Mrs. Sperdakos?" She's an elderly widow who seldom leaves her apartment.

"Yes. I wanted to know if she had seen or heard anything suspicious. It seems she's almost deaf and goes to bed early, so no luck there. We weren't able to locate your upstairs neighbour. Is he away?"

"That's Bill Peters, the landlord's nephew. He's a teacher and travels every summer."

"We also looked over the property but it's been dry and the ground is hard, so no visible footprints. Sorry, Maud. I wish I had something for you."

"That's okay, Paul. It's early days. Any word on how Zarina is doing?"

"Still in a coma, I'm afraid. Looks like she received quite a blow to the head, as well as the stabbing."

"Coma? That sounds ominous."

"I know, Maud, but people survive comas."

"Of course they do," I try to be positive, despite my misgivings.

"One other thing."

"Yes?"

"Would you like to have dinner with me on Wednesday? We can make it an early evening, since I'm sure you're working Thursday. I don't want to wait until Saturday to see you."

My face gets warm but I try to ignore it. He's a policeman, if I can't trust a cop, who can I trust? "Okay. What time?"

"I'll pick you up at around six, if that's okay. Will you be at home or at your uncle's?"

"Six is fine and I'll meet you at my place."

When I hang up the phone I notice my uncle massaging the leather of his slipper.

"Got a date?" he asks.

"Wednesday night for dinner. I'm sorry about the slipper. I should have been watching him."

"That's okay, I was due for a new pair. But these were so comfortable." He puts both slippers into his closet and closes the door. "Well, shall we get back to work?"

"Sure, come on Sherlock, you stay where we can see you. Maybe we could sit outside, don't you think?"

He gathers up the papers from the kitchen table. "You bring the dog, I'll bring the notes."

Once settled on the patio, I tell him that Kora had indeed been poisoned with arsenic.

"You know," he says, placing the papers on the patio table, "that stuff is not easy to come by. I wonder where our murderer is getting it. Can you think of any of the suspects that would have access to it?"

"Not really. But what are we talking about here, someone related to a chemist?"

He settles back in the chair, placing his mug of coffee on top of the notes to prevent the light morning breeze from blowing them off the table. "Could be someone in manufacturing. I think it's used to treat wood and of course, in things like rat poison."

"I don't know of anyone associated with those things but then, I don't think it's ever come up. I'll have to give it some thought." I push back my chair. "I think I will have another cup of coffee. Do you want yours topped up?"

"Sure, honey, thanks." I lift his mug and he picks up the papers, holding them on his lap. When I return he asks, "What do you think of this painting of Theseus and Medea?

"Can't tell you too much on that one. The night I was researching, my computer kept crashing and I haven't gotten back to it."

"Our librarian was helpful with this one. Apparently," he reads, "Medea was a sorceress and wife of Aegeus, who was the father of Theseus. Medea feared losing power over Aegeus, if he were to recognise Theseus as his son. She made the potion but she tried to get Aegeus to administer it.

Things didn't go as she'd hoped and she was forced to flee."

"Since Charles wanted out of his contract with Leona, Theo and I thought it possible that she was jealous of another gallery getting his paintings. The story of Theseus and Medea would suggest that Leona put the poison in the wine ready for someone else to serve it. That someone being Zarina of course."

"So she wants him dead but she doesn't actually want to do it herself."

"That seems to be a pattern. One person puts the poison in the wine and another unwittingly does the serving."

"I have another question for you to consider," says Uncle Sid.

"Yes?"

"Among our suspects, who knew you had a calico cat?"

"Well, let's see. Alissa, because shortly after I got Kora, she and Charles dropped by my apartment. I don't think that it would be something she would bother to remember though. And none of the other suspects has ever been in my apartment."

"Is there anyone you may have mentioned Kora to? You know, had some occasion to talk about cats."

"I recently started a painting of her and I know I've mentioned that to a few people. Teddy maybe, yes, he asked me what I was working on. But Teddy wouldn't hurt her." My uncle raises his eyebrows. "Oh, and Rupert when I met him at the paint store and maybe Leona because we talked about painting. I don't know if I mentioned it to Grace. Gosh, if I hadn't been bragging about it, we might have been able to narrow this down."

"Don't worry about it now. Do you think our Mr. Holmes would behave himself if we went to the range and fired off a few?"

"One of those books I read, said that you should leave the dog in an enclosed space—a crate would be good but we don't have one."

"What about the back porch? It's closed in and there's a cool breeze if we keep the window open. We can put his bed in there. He'll be okay."

"I guess. Could he hear the radio, if we left it on in the kitchen?"

Uncle Sid walks to the kitchen counter, bending over the old radio. "Sure what station do you think he would like? Contemporary, classical or one of the all-news stations?"

"I think classical."

He turns and stares at me. "Jeez Maud, I was kidding." But he turns it on, rotating the dial until he finds suitable music. "There we go, maybe this music will soothe the savage beast. Come on let's get outta here."

My uncle and I spend a pleasant afternoon shooting targets. As much as I'm ethically opposed to guns, I admit to enjoying target practice. I think it's a combination of the challenge and my ability to meet it. My uncle has such a great time, I resolve to accompany him on a regular basis.

We return home and find the back porch intact and a pup so ecstatic to see us, he seems in danger of wiggling himself right out of his skin. I knew, from the material I'd been reading, that a good dog is a tired dog, so I leash him up and we go for a long walk around the neighbourhood while Uncle Sid prepares our dinner. I could certainly get used to having my meals ready for me but I was missing my own space. I decide to stay one more night. With a gun and a dog, I figure I have enough protection. I broach the subject over a dessert of chocolate cookies.

"I don't know that it's any safer now than it was on Friday," cautions my uncle. "After all Maud, we haven't caught the creep."

"I know, but I feel safer and stronger now. I know he's young but I think Sherlock will be some protection, at least he can look scary and I do have my gun. I'll talk to Mrs. Sperdakos and we'll keep the ground floor entry door locked. If it were you, wouldn't you want to get back to your home?" He had to admit that he would, and to his credit he avoids any chauvinistic references.

We spend a quiet evening. I read my dog books while my uncle reads the newspapers. Maybe he's brooding over my decision to return home but unable to come up with a reasonable counter-argument.

Monday morning I'm getting ready for work and it occurs to me that my uncle is enjoying my company, and perhaps his reaction is not simply due to concerns for my safety.

Sitting at the table for a light breakfast, I pass him his favourite strawberry jam.

"I've been thinking. I know I said I wanted to get back to my apartment tonight but I've changed my mind. Can I stay till Wednesday? I have to go to the studio for an art class on Tuesday evening, and I had hoped Sherlock could stay with you while I'm out? Would that be okay?"

"Sure. If that's what you want." He sounds so nonchalant but his grin betrays his pleasure and relief.

"With regards to the case," he begins, "I'd like to get a look at those paintings Charles gave the suspects. How 'bout you call Miss Tellman and see what's happening with the show. Find out if she's got the paintings and when she's going to hang them. Her response to our interest in them might also shed light on her role in all this."

"Okay. I'll call her this morning. If you're ready to leave now, go ahead. I'll take the pooch around the block and meet you at the office." This being Sherlock's first day on the job, I want him well behaved and since that's best achieved by some exercise, we go for a run. Returning to the house, Sherlock is refreshed, but I can feel the burn in my calf muscles. After hauling his bed from the kitchen and stuffing it awkwardly into the back seat of my car, I resolve to get him a big cushion to leave at work. He seems thrilled to be on this adventure and once in the office, sniffs every reachable bit of floor and wall space before settling into his bed for a nap.

"Well, he sleeps a lot, that's good," says Uncle Sid. "I'll be out for a couple of hours. Make that call to the Tellman woman, will you? I'd like a sneak peek at those paintings."

"I'll call her at ten. I think that's when the gallery opens."

I push myself into the paper work and am lost in the computer when the office door opens. Sherlock lets out a bark to wake the dead.

"Whoa." Al plasters himself to the door.

My fearless hound moves toward him in a flash, sits down and proceeds to make what sounds like snorting growls.

"Sherlock it's okay," I call out but he ignores me. I jump from my desk and grab his collar. "Sherlock," I repeat. "It's okay boy, he's a friend." Instantly, his body relaxes and he greets Al with much wagging and slobbering.

Unconvinced, Al remains pressed against the door. "That's quite the watch dog you have there."

"Sorry Al. I had no idea he would do that."

"Is he yours?" His expression yearns for me to deny it.

"Yes, Uncle Sid and I got him on the weekend. We stopped by the Humane Society and met his previous owner just before she turned him over to them. We were really lucky."

"Yeah, lucky." Al echoes my words but not my sentiment.

"He's still a pup. Nine months old, actually."

"Sure looks grown up to me. Whoever owned him before must have been training him to guard. As far as I know, bloodhounds are not naturally aggressive."

"I just read that in one of my new books. Maybe I should call his former Mom and ask her."

"It is something you should know," he says.

Al slides into his office while I search in my purse for Sarah Jenkins' number. After eight rings I'm ready to hang up but before I do she answers. She tells me that in the midst of packing, she had temporarily misplaced the phone. I reassure her that Sherlock is fine, and explain his aggressive reaction to Al.

"Sorry Maud, I should have told you. Hounds tend to be friendly but my husband was determined, since he travels so much, to train Sherlock in protective skills. We taught him to sit in front of a stranger, so his wagging tail wouldn't betray him.

That way he will at least look menacing," she told me. "Also, like most dogs he has an instinct to guard his owner. Don't worry though, he's never actually bitten anyone and the sounds he makes are not really growls, just hound talk."

"What should I say to him to let him know when the person is a friend," I ask.

"That's it, you just say the word "friend." In no time at all, he'll get all warm and cuddly. I am sorry. I was so pleased he was going to a good home I never thought to tell you. So is everything else okay?"

We chat about how he's settling in. I need to know I'm not over feeding him and after reassuring her that he seems happy I leave her to her packing.

"So you're going to be my protector." I give his furry head a pat.

Al's office door opens slightly and his disembodied head seems to float six feet above the floor.

"Is it okay to come out?" he whispers.

"Yes. I have been given the password," I tell him. "I just have to let him know you're a friend."

"So."

"So—what?" I ask.

"Tell him I'm a friend so I can come out of my office."

"Oh, I'm sure he already knows, but if it makes you feel better. Hey, Sherlock," I call and he bounces out of his bed. "Here's our friend Al!" On hind legs and with both front feet he reacts by pushing open the door and covering Al with slobbery kisses.

"Jeez, maybe we should tell him I'm just an acquaintance," Al grunts, as he pulls Sherlock's two front feet off his chest. "Gotta go now, tell your uncle I'll see him tomorrow."

I give him a nod and a wave and return to my computer. My companion does another sniff search of the room. By ten thirty I remember that I'm supposed to call Leona at the gallery.

"Maud, how are you?" she asks.

"Good thanks. I'm calling because I'd like to meet you for lunch. Which day would you prefer, Tuesday or Wednesday?" I hope to improve my chances of a positive response by giving her a choice.

Although she hesitates for a second, she does agree to meet with me on Wednesday at noon.

"You'll be bringing me Charles's painting at that time, of course."

"Of course. And do you have the other paintings from Charles's will?"

"Only Zarina's, the others should be in the gallery by Thursday. She loaned hers before the, um, accident. Do you know how she's doing?"

"It was an attack, not an accident, Leona and as of yesterday she was still in a coma."

"Oh poor thing. Well, I must fly. See you Wednesday, Maud."

She hangs up without saying good-bye. I hate that. And she wasn't too sympathetic about Zarina either. Damn, I wish I'd asked her exactly when she got Zarina's painting.

Chapter 16

Dividing my time between paperwork, the computer, the phone and the dog, I get through the day. There's one slight hitch when, during our lunch time walk, Sherlock finds an irresistible scent and drags me along a side street. Both his strength and determination surprise me but I finally get his attention. Either the scent had obliterated everything he learned at obedience school or the honeymoon was over.

My uncle arrives back to the office minutes before five. Fortunately, Sherlock recognises his friend and gives him a boisterous bloodhound greeting.

"How's our boy? You been a good doggie?" He places a large plastic bag on my desk then bends down to hug our gangly canine.

With pleasure I watch their mutual exchange of affection.

"Open the bag Maud." Uncle Sid scratches Sherlock's hairy chin. "There's something for you and something for our droolie buddy here." He grabs a tissue from my desk.

Rolled up in the bag is a big dog cushion. I put it on the floor and Mr. Holmes begins an immediate investigation. "This is great, Unc. Now we can take his bed back home." At the bottom of the bag is a package of stickers, the kind you place on your doors and windows warning of an alarm system. "But Uncle Sid, I don't have . . ."

He places his index finger in front of his lips. "I know, but that will be our secret. There's one more in that bag."

I reach in and pull out a rectangular sticker that reads, BEWARE OF DOG. "Okay, I do have a dog. Actually, I had occasion to call Sarah Jenkins this morning and she told me that they trained Sherlock as a guard dog. Seems her husband travels a lot."

"Oh yeah? That's good but what was the occasion that prompted the call?" asks my uncle the detective.

"We had this little incident when Al arrived at the office this morning." He crosses his arms in front of his chest and waits. "Sherlock didn't actually attack him," I add.

"Well jeez, that's a relief. So what did happen?"

"He blocked him, you know kept him up against the door. He just kind of sat there, watching Al and growling. Well, not growling, more like a serious snuffling. No, maybe not snuffling."

"Okay Maud, I got the picture."

"The thing was," I continue, "he wouldn't back off. I called him and he ignored me. Finally, I said that Al was a friend and everything was fine. So, that's why I called Sarah. Turns out the password is friend."

"That's something we need to know." He cups the base of each of Sherlock's ears in his hands, "You're going to take good care of my Maudie, aren't you buddy?" After a moment of mutual admiration, dog and man staring into each other's eyes, my uncle clears his throat and walks over to my desk. "So did you get a hold of that Tellman woman?"

"Yes, I'm going to meet with her on Wednesday for lunch. She wants me to bring in my painting of Hamlet."

"And the other paintings?"

"She said she only has Zarina's but expects to get them all by Thursday."

"How did she get Zarina's?"

"That's one of the things I hope to find out when I meet with her. We also got a call from Jeff Williams. Seems there's a probable arson they want your help on."

His eyes light up. I have a serious phobia of fire and my uncle delights in investigating them.

"Have you got the number? I'll give them a call right now." He doesn't bother to use the phone in his office but grabs mine. After a series of affirmatives, negatives and maybes, he scribbles down an address and hangs up.

"So what do you think, honey? Shall we call it a day?"

"Sure, I'm ready. What do you want to do for dinner?"

"The daily question. Too bad I don't have a cook, eh?"

"How hungry are you? I saw a couple of cans of soup in the cupboard and I could make us some sandwiches."

"Yeah, that'd be great."

"And after dinner we could have a game of cribbage."

"You're on!"

I'm in a better frame of mind for our second cribbage challenge and I win the first two games. My worthy opponent narrowly beats me in the last challenge, allowing him to end the evening with a modicum of his dignity intact.

With Al out of town and Uncle Sid at the site of the probable arson, Sherlock and I spend Tuesday on our own at the office. It's a quiet day, and I finish everything that needed doing by four o'clock. I decide to surprise my generous host with his favourite dinner. After writing him a note requesting that he call me before leaving the office, I take Sherlock out to my car. Having him along for the ride complicates things a bit but I do my best to get through the grocery line quickly while he waits in the car. Stopping at my apartment for my art supplies I decide to take him in and introduce him to my downstairs neighbour, and to let her know I would be returning home on Wednesday.

I prepare Sherlock, pushing his hind quarters into a sitting position and repeating the word friend a couple of times. Then after a minute of bruising my knuckles on her door, I vow to buy the woman a proper knocker. Finally a crack of light appears, and the door opens only as far as its chain will allow.

"Mrs. Sperdakos," I yell. "It's Maud."

"Oh hello Maud." She unhooks the chain and opens her door. A tiny woman, she's closer to Sherlock's eye level than to mine. "And who is this big boy?"

"This is Sherlock." I want him to make a good impression on my neighbour and am thankful when he shows an awareness of her frailty, greeting her with a polite wag of his tail.

"I was so sorry to hear about your little pussy cat. The police tell me, you know. So sad, so terrible. But now you have big dog to protect you. That is good."

"Yes," I agree. "I wanted to let you know that I'm still at my uncle's but I'll be back here tomorrow."

"What you want to borrow?" she hollers, her hand cupping her ear.

I repeat myself a few decibels louder and add that we should keep the front door locked.

"Oh, yes, fine, we keep it locked up tight. I glad you be back here."

I thank her, and Sherlock and I proceed up to my apartment. Listening to my telephone messages, there's one from Finella, checking to see if I had returned home, and one from Theo—a surprise since I know how she feels about answering machines. I have just enough time to return her call. When she answers I apologise for not calling sooner, explaining that I'm staying with my uncle and why.

"Oh, Maud, how dreadful for you. You certainly have had a time. I'm so sorry."

"Thanks Theo but I'm all right now. How have you been?"

"I'm just fine. I called to let you know that Leona has been pestering me about Charles's paintings and although I find her rather annoying, I've decided to let the gallery borrow a few. What about you, have you given her your 'Hamlet'?"

"Not yet. I'm taking it tomorrow. I could take yours too, if you like, or have you made other arrangements?"

"Leona said she would pick them up but it would be lovely to see you. Would you have time for tea?"

"Sure, I could drop in after lunch." She agrees and I add that I look forward to seeing her.

Having left my painting of the goose egg and feathers at the studio, it's just a matter of collecting my paint and brushes. On my easel sits my unfinished painting of Kora. Poor baby—I know it will take time, a lot of time, before I'm able to work on it again. I also know it's too painful to leave it on my easel and decide to store it under my bed. Just before leaving the apartment I remember the book on Annigoni I had borrowed from Rupert and slip it into a bag.

I arrive back at my uncle's in plenty of time to ready the steaks I'd bought for the barbecue, pop in some potatoes for baking and prepare a garden salad. The phone rings as I finish making an oil and vinegar dressing. .

"Hi Maud, it's your uncle. I got your note."

"Are you on your way? I've started dinner."

"I've got a few things to do, but they'll only take a couple of minutes. I should be there in half an hour."

I sometimes think there is 'real time' and then there is 'guy time.' The men I've known have been pretty consistent in underestimating the time it takes to do anything from changing a washer to renovating a kitchen. Uncle Sid's ETA of thirty minutes turns into sixty. I put the steaks on the barbeque when I hear his car pull into the drive and though our potatoes are overcooked, the rest of the meal is perfect. By eating quickly I manage to get away before six-thirty, leaving Sherlock in the capable company of his adopted uncle.

The traffic is light and I arrive at the studio at ten minutes to seven. The door is open when I enter but Rupert doesn't respond to my call. I'm experiencing déjà vu but the room is in order. The drawing horses are set up appropriately in front of the still life, so he can't be too far away. At least his body is not sprawled on the studio floor.

Rupert had, once again, placed student names on all the drawing horses and easels, so it was easy to find my spot. Leaning my art box against the base of the drawing horse, I pull the Annigoni book from the bag and carry it to the bookcase next to the painting rack. Squeezing it in between the existing publications, I spot a small paperback about famous murder trials. It's so out of place amongst the art books, I remove it for a closer look. Scanning the index, I see the name Madeleine Smith. Is this how Charles knew about her? I flip to the front cover and see one of those *ex libris* inserts indicating that it's the property of Leona Tellman. I'm returning it to the shelf when I hear footsteps behind me.

"Hi Maud, you're here early."

"Oh, Rupert. I was just returning your Annigoni book and left it in the bookcase as you asked. Thanks for letting me borrow it."

"Not a prob. Happy to let you borrow it and happy to have it back, thanks. So, are you ready to paint?"

I wonder if his cheerfulness is sincere. "How have you been doing since Zarina's been in hospital?" I ask.

"Just fine, Maud, fine." He glances down at his feet. "I miss her, of course and hope she can come back real soon."

"Hi, y'all!" It's the chirpy little voice of Alissa. She's practically skipping into the studio. "Ruppie, did you get the cream for the coffee?"

Ruppie? Did I hear that correctly?

"Yes, I have it here." He holds up a small brown bag. "I'll put it in the fridge now."

More students begin arriving and Alissa greets each one. I'm placing my picture on the easel when Grace arrives.

"Hi Maud, what's going on?" she whispers.

"I assume you're referring to the presence of Alissa?" She nods. "It looks to me like she has filled Zarina's position."

"I wonder if Rupert asked her or if she offered?"

"I don't know but I'll see if I can find out."

Rupert strolls to the front of the class. "Welcome everyone. I'm sure many of you are wondering about Zarina. I spoke to the hospital personnel and was told that although her condition is stable she has yet to regain consciousness. I know you join me in hoping for a speedy recovery." There's much affirmative murmuring.

"Now," he begins, "you seem to have found your places and are ready to begin where you left off. When most of you have reached the point of transferring your drawing to canvas, I will interrupt the class and give a demonstration. For now, I will go around the room and insure that the drawings are correct. Please carry on." He leaves the front of the room and begins his inspection. I had hoped he would say something about Alissa's presence. If he didn't volunteer the information, I would ask him. I'm mixing my paint when he finally sidles up to my easel.

"Maud, I wonder if I might use your canvas again as a demonstration. Yours is coming along quite nicely and you're ahead of everyone else."

I agree and he lifts my work off the easel. "Excuse me everyone. I want to show you Maud's painting. She put the veil on last week and is now at the point where she will begin to lay in the values. This is to be a monochrome, if you remember, so Maud will be using greys. For now, I want you to note that she has transferred her image using tracing paper and charcoal. The lines were redrawn with India ink and then a veil of grey at a number five value was applied. You will recall that our value scale goes from white at number one, to black at number nine. The number five then, is the mid-tone and that is what you are striving for in this veil. Be sure to thin the veil with enough turps and medium so that your inked image is visible." He hands my canvas back to me. "Thank you Maud. I assume you know how to proceed."

I tell him I do and continue mixing my paint.

"When are you going to ask him?" whispers Grace. "I admit that I don't like that woman. If she's replacing Zarina for every class, I don't think I want to be here."

"Oh Grace, don't let her keep you away. Maybe I can find out something during the break."

She steps closer to me, her voice barely audible. "I heard that you found Zarina. That must have been pretty awful."

"It was, but who told you?"

"My grandparents are neighbours of Miss Theo Venable."

"Theo did mention that."

After about half an hour, Rupert returns to the front of the room.

"I think most of you are ready for this demonstration. If you would gather round the table on the far wall, I'll go through the transferring process and the inking. If you don't feel you need this information, stay at your easels and carry on with what you're doing."

The new students follow him to the other side of the room. The rest of us stay put and plod on. I see Alissa go into the kitchen and on the pretence of needing a glass of water I join her.

I adjust my smile for maximum warmth. "Hi Alissa, nice to see you here."

"Nice to see you too, Maud." Her smile was on then off her face like a bride's nightgown.

Pouring water into a glass, I keep my voice light and breezy. "Good of you to come in and help Rupert. Did he have a hard time asking you?"

Her eyebrows narrow. "He didn't ask me. He was in pretty rough shape when he called to tell me about the robbery and he was so concerned about handling things on his own, well, I just had to offer to help."

"How nice of you." I gently pat her arm. "I'm sure he appreciates it. And what about your pastel class? Are you going ahead with that?"

"I think I'll wait until Zarina gets back. Things are too disrupted right now."

"Yes, understandable. So, are you going to help out with every class?"

"I sincerely doubt that. Now if you will excuse me Maud, I was just going to make the coffee. They'll be taking a break soon."

When I return to my easel, Grace gives me a questioning look. I promise to fill her in during the break and continue to mix my greys in their appropriate values—a job that only looks easy. I apply them, as they appear on the still life, beginning with the lightest greys, since it's always best to go from light to dark. When I reach the point of establishing the transition values, Rupert announces our break.

Grace turns from her work to look at mine.

"Maud, that's really good. You have a great eye for the values."

"Thanks. I've had lots of practice. Remember you need to squint, and then it's like viewing objects under low light, everything starts to look like varying shades of grey."

She squeezed her eyes almost shut. "I know that but I always forget to do it."

Lowering her voice she continues, "So what did you find out from Alissa?"

"Well, she said . . ."

"How's it going here?" Our dedicated instructor is hovering again. "Are you almost ready to transfer your drawing Grace?"

"Oh, Rupert. I don't think it's accurate enough yet."

Examining her work he hesitates before saying, "Yes. I see you're having trouble with the ellipses. Don't worry. They are very difficult to draw but I can help you after the break." He grazes her shoulder with his hand before strolling off in the direction of the kitchen.

"Pompous ass," Grace murmurs. She slides from the drawing horse and arches her back to stretch out her muscles.

"I know but he's right. You might as well have him work for your money and let him help you."

"Yes, but I just don't want to feel owing to him."

"What 'owing'? As I said, you're paying him to teach you. Come on girl," standing next to her, I tap her drawing board, "you got to have the right attitude."

"Okay, okay." She laughed. Lowering her voice again, she asks about Alissa but before I can reply the merry widow is asking to speak to me.

"Maud, I need to know something." Alissa motions for me to move closer to her.

"Have you talked to Leona? I was wondering what you had decided to do with your painting, you know, 'Hamlet.'"

"I decided I would let her borrow it. What about you?"

With an exaggerated sigh she says, "I guess I'll have to. It wouldn't look good for me to refuse. He was my husband after all."

"You know I forgot to ask. Do you know how long she intends to keep our paintings?"

"According to the invitation, the show runs for a month. Maud, didn't you get an invitation?"

I hadn't checked my mail in days but didn't want to tell her I'd been staying at my uncle's.

"I have mail I haven't opened yet. It's probably there."

Her expression suggests she thinks it odd to leave one's mail unopened but she refrains from saying so.

"Did she offer to help Rupert or did he ask?" queries Grace when I rejoin her.

"She told me she offered." I watch Alissa go into the office.

"So will she be here for every class?"

Rupert interrupts before I can answer.

"Okay, everyone, shall we return to our drawings? If possible I would like everyone to have their veil applied before leaving tonight."

"It's impossible to talk here," I say to Grace. "Let's go for a drink after class."

She gives me the thumbs up sign in agreement. Rupert returns with his offer to help Grace draw the ellipses, and she allows him to take her place on the drawing horse.

I begin the delicate job of rendering the transitions. A transition is the area where one value graduates into another. Done well, it helps produce the effect of three dimensions on a two dimensional surface. At the same time, I work to soften the edges of the individual elements. I can hear Charles's voice in my head. "There are no hard edges in nature."

With Rupert's assistance Grace finishes her drawing and he leaves her to transfer it and do the inking. I've mixed more paint than I need, so I give her my number five for the veil. At the end of the class time, I clean my brushes and return my painting to the drying rack.

Rupert comes by as I pack up my supplies. "You did some good work tonight, Maud."

"Thank you Rupert. I'll see you Thursday?"

"I'll be here."

Grace is waiting for me at the door and we leave together.

"Same little café as last time?" she asks.

"Sure. Shall we walk again? It's not far and it is a nice evening."

Not wanting to carry my art box and bag, I tell Grace I'm parked a block north of the studio and ask if she wants to walk with me or wait.

"I'll walk with you. Does it seem darker to you than usual?" she asks when we reach the car. I follow her gaze to the streetlights. "Is there an electrical problem or do those things have bulbs that burn out?" she wonders aloud. "It's kind of spooky?"

I quickly store my things in the trunk and like anxious moths, we fly back toward the light.

"By the way," Grace begins, when we're safely on the main street, "I think your painting is coming along beautifully. You definitely have talent. Have you thought of making it a career?"

I thank her for her encouraging words. Although I'd certainly thought about painting full-time, I realise I don't have the personality to deal with a sporadic income.

"I know what you mean. Our artists don't get a lot of support do they?"

At the café, we find a quiet corner and place our order.

"So, what exactly did Alissa say?" Grace asks, while we waited for herbal tea.

"She said she volunteered to help Rupert after he expressed concern about dealing with the class on his own. Apparently he didn't come straight out and ask her, but I think he set her up to make the offer. She also said she didn't think she would be at every class."

"That's good. But on the other hand, I prefer Rupert to direct his attentions at her instead of me."

"They did look cosy. Were you there when she called him 'Ruppie'?"

Grace raises her hand to her mouth. "Ruppie? Good grief. Well as I said, better her than me. On a sadder note, it must have been terrible for you, finding Zarina at the studio. Were you supposed to meet her or something?"

"Actually, I was trying to get her on the phone and when I couldn't I went to the studio."

"I heard there was a robbery, that the thieves took the painting Rupert had almost finished of me and the one Charles painted of City Hall. It gives me the creeps to think of my portrait in the hands of some thugs. I wonder if he'll ever get them back?"

I sip my tea. "It's hard to say."

We sit quietly for a few minutes, each of us with a cup in hand and lost in thought. Grace breaks the silence. "I remember when Charles did that painting. He took the photos for it on one of the days he accompanied me to a fashion shoot. The weather wasn't ideal but he was determined to get the pictures. I think he wanted to get the painting finished before he left on a trip."

I put down my cup.

"Left on a trip, was that when he went to Italy?"

"No, he was already back from Italy by then. I don't know exactly. It's just that when I suggested he come back on a better day he said no, he wanted to get it done before he left."

"I wonder where he was going?"

"I guess we'll never know. He died shortly after he finished it. I think that's why it was still at the studio. Rupert was waiting for it to dry completely so he could varnish it," she says. "I hope you don't mind Maud, but I have to get going. I don't like travelling on the city transit system at the best of times but it's even worse at night." I offer to drive her home but she declines, asking only that I wait with her at the bus stop. Seeing her safely onto the bus I walk the dark road back toward my car.

The leaves at the top of the trees sound like a hundred people rubbing their palms and the dust from the city streets blows into my nostrils. There's a storm in the making. As I turn onto the street where I'd parked my car, I can't see it. I'm concentrating so hard on getting a visual of my car I only gradually become aware of the footsteps behind me. Without slowing I swivel my head and see what looks like a shrouded figure ducking into the alley.

I break into a fevered run, praying my car is not one of the 10,000 stolen every year. Thank God I'm not hauling my art supplies. God receives my further gratitude when I find my car and my keys in record time. Once inside, I start the ignition and drive away like the proverbial bat. I don't exhale until I'm safely in my uncle's driveway. They say the Lord helps those who help themselves, so until the killer is behind bars, I'm totin' my gun.

Chapter 17

When I feel sufficiently calm, and consciously aware of my actions, I exit the car and go into my uncle's house. He can be acutely perceptive and I don't want him to worry about what may have been my overactive imagination. There's much wiggling and tail wagging by Sherlock and relief on Uncle Sid's face.

"I thought I heard the car pull in awhile ago. Certainly, your pal here thought you'd arrived. He's been sitting by the door for the last five minutes."

"Oh, my paint box slid off the back seat and I had to check to make sure nothing had spilled." Sometimes the ease with which I deceive amazes me.

"So, come on in, tell me about your class."

Sitting across from him, I relate the story of Madeleine Smith, a woman accused of poisoning her lover. I explain that Charles had left a clue, although I couldn't be sure if it was deliberate, by writing her name on a piece of paper and leaving it in a book of poisons in Theo's bookcase. I conclude by telling him I'd found a book at the studio on true crime, and it contained a chapter about her trial.

"If Charles thought he was being poisoned, he may have identified with the plight of the wily Miss Smith's fiancé."

"I agree. Of further interest, the book did not belong to Charles. On the inside cover, I found a book plate signed with the name of Leona Tellman."

"Ah, a further bit of incriminating evidence toward the gallery owner." He lifts his feet to the hassock and leans back in his chair.

"What time are you meeting with her tomorrow?"

"Noon, I hope that's not a problem."

"No it's okay. I knew you were going out so I planned to spend the day at the office anyway. You're not taking Sherlock with you, right?"

He's been sitting on his haunches and resting his chin on my lap but with the mention of his name, my canine ambles next to Uncle Sid's chair, resting his body firmly against it. My uncle drops his hand over the side and massages the bony head.

"I could leave him at my apartment," I offer.

"No, no, he can stay with me."

"Are you sure? That would be great. Oh, and the other unusual incident tonight, was the appearance of Alissa."

"She's not normally at the studio?"

"No, other than that one time she came by to make sure Zarina and Rupert knew who their landlady was. When I asked tonight, how she came to be there, she said she had volunteered to help Rupert, who, by the way, she called 'Ruppie.'"

"Say, that sounds chummy. Is there something going on between those two?"

"I don't know. It's hard for me to imagine the two of them together. Finally, one last bit of info. I had tea with Grace after class and she told me that the painting of City Hall, the one that disappeared from the studio, was something Charles was anxious to finish before he left."

"Before he left for where?"

I answer by shrugging my shoulders. "I thought I could ask Theo if she knew of any travel plans."

"That's what I love about detective work, there's always a new clue for every new question. But, on the down side—a new question for each new clue. Well, honey," he pushes the hassock aside and rises from his chair "I'm gonna hit the hay. See you in the morning." He leans over and kisses the top of my head.

"I'll let Sherlock out and then I'll get some sleep too. Good night."

"Oh, Maud?" He starts down the hall to his room but steps back into the doorway.

"Yes,?"

"You still planning to return to your apartment tomorrow?"

"Yes."

"You'll take extra care?"

"I'll be locked up tight with a pistol under my pillow and a guard dog by my side."

"Okie dokie," he acquiesces.

I awake early, shower and pack up my belongings and the pooch's. In recognition of my lunch with Leona, I dress in a matching linen skirt and blouse. I try to get my natural curls to curl unnaturally, give up after five minutes and go for the tousled look. I even apply some mascara, although it will likely be smudged before ten. After brewing the coffee, I put Sherlock in the backyard and put my stuff in the car. My uncle is sipping his coffee when I re-enter the kitchen.

"Morning Maud. You're looking very spiffy."

"Thanks Unc. This is for Leona," I say in reference to my outfit. "I thought I'd have some toast. You want some?"

We have a light breakfast before leaving for the office. Just after eleven, I take the hound out for his constitutional. On our return, I pop into Uncle Sid's office to let him know I'm on my way to Leona's.

He's on the telephone but signals to me to hold on a minute.

"She's right here," he says into the receiver. "It's Paul."

"Hi Paul, how are you?"

"Fine Maud. I'm just calling to tell you that Zarina has regained consciousness."

"Wow! That's great news. Can I visit her today?"

"Sure. I thought maybe you could meet me there. When's a good time for you?"

"I'm meeting Leona Tellman at the gallery at noon. How about two?" I ask, looking at my uncle for confirmation. He gives me the nod.

"All right then," says Paul. "How about we meet in the cafeteria and go to her room together?"

Seems like a good idea to me and I tell him so. "I better dash. I forgot that I have to pick up my painting." I give Sherlock a scratch under his chin. "You behave yourself. I'll see you both soon."

My uncle calls out as I hurry from the office. "Drive carefully. Remember you want to arrive alive!"

The detour to pick up my painting and drop off my belongings makes me ten minutes late but when I get to the gallery Leona is busy with a customer. I amuse myself by looking at the paint-ings. Against one wall lean some of Charles's early works and the piece that must have been Zarina's 'Guinevere and Sir Gawain.'

Guinevere resemblances Zarina but Charles had painted her as a blonde. Of course, for all I know she may have been a blonde at the time he painted it. In contrast to my 'Hamlet,' Charles made elaborate use of colour, perfect for an epic legend. I'm certain the story Finella told me had Guinevere giving the visiting knight an apple but Charles had painted a glass of wine in her outstretched hand.

"Hello Maud. Sorry to keep you waiting." It was Leona's voice over my right shoulder.

"Not a problem. Besides, I was a little late. This painting Charles did for Zarina is beautiful. When did she bring it to you?"

"Actually, I picked it up the day before the um, attack." She looks down at my portfolio. "You brought your painting, excellent."

"Yes." I unzip the case and remove it.

"Ah, I see it's a grisaille. That's very unusual for Charles. Beautifully haunting though, isn't it?" She takes it from me then leans it against the wall. My feelings of protectiveness are heightened and I move closer to it.

"Maud, don't worry it will be quite safe. I plan to hang it in this spot here," she points to the wall on my left.

"That way you can see it from the window, and even make periodic checks if you want to.

Now if you're ready, I thought we could have lunch across the street. I'll just let my assistant know I'm leaving."

Aside from proximity, I immediately understand Leona's choice. The restaurant has an elegance revealed in sparkling white table cloths and gleaming crystal. Our impeccably dressed waiter appears with menus and takes our wine order. While perusing the menu, I also observe the woman sitting opposite me. Her makeup is flawlessly applied and her auburn hair expertly coifed. She's fashionably thin but I sense her heart is uncomfortably heavy.

Our waiter returns with the wine and we're ready with our selections. I allow her a couple of sips, before a direct confrontation.

"Did you poison Charles?"

Her eyes hold mine. "No, Maud. I did not."

"You know I had to ask."

"Yes." Leona presses her shoulders into the back of her chair. "I figured Charles had appointed you as his finder."

"From the subject matter of my painting?"

"That and other things."

With both elbows on the table, I lean toward her.

"Who do you think murdered him?"

"I thought," she begins slowly. "I thought, he committed suicide."

"Suicide?"

"Or Zarina," she adds quickly.

"Really? Zarina thought it was you."

"I know. She made that abundantly clear the evening I met her for dinner. The same evening you dined with Theo."

I don't reveal that I'm aware of their meeting and when the waiter arrives with our salads, I let the interruption provide a pause in our conversation. Setting down my fork, I ask, "Were you and Charles lovers?"

"There was a time in our relationship when I would have welcomed his attentions but Charles was a tortured soul and he needed a friend more than a lover. I loved him but we were never intimate."

Watching her sip her wine, I rest my forearms on the table, my face inching a little closer to her own.

"Leona, you were so, so, off-putting during our earlier contact. Why are you so candid now?"

"Because it's not going to go away. Because it's what Charles wants and because I've come to see that it matters."

"What matters?"

"Finding Charles's murderer."

My jaw drops as I fall back into my chair.

"Matters? Of course it matters. Why would you even consider any other possibility?"

"Because Charles was dying." I watch as a solitary tear falls like a raindrop from the corner of her eye. "He would have died anyway."

"Dying!" I make an effort to turn down the volume and continue in hushed tones.

"Dying from what?"

"AIDS."

"But Leona how did he get . . .? I mean how did he know?"

"Charles had a very good friend, a doctor in Italy. The tests were done there."

"But there are treatments, couldn't he . . .?

She compulsively straightens her cutlery. "I think it was too late for that."

"But how?" I can't seem to form a complete sentence.

"You want to know how he contracted it in the first place?"

"Yes."

"There was a part of his life Charles preferred to keep very private. He was married, after all and I think he truly loved Alissa, but well, it wasn't enough. As I said, he was a tortured soul."

My mind goes into overdrive and I understand why Charles appeared to do so little when he thought he was being poisoned, why he shunned Alissa's affections, the reason for his heavy drinking and why he was in such a hurry to finish his painting of Old City Hall.

"Do you see why I was so evasive?" Leona asks. "I hoped you would do a little detective dabbling, then give it up. But you found enough evidence to have his body exhumed and I'm sure this time they will do a more thorough job."

"How did you know about the exhumation?"

"Theo told me when I spoke to her yesterday. And no, I did not tell her about her nephew's illness."

"Did you tell Zarina about it?" I ask.

"Yes, it was the only way to convince her of my innocence."

"Last night, at the studio, I found your book on famous murder trials with the case of Madeleine Smith."

"Is she the one who was accused of poisoning her lover with arsenic?"

"That would be the one," I said.

"I see where you're going with this, but Charles was not my lover and he had the book because we shared an interest in criminology. I'm sure if you thought about it, and if the situation warranted, you probably have some incriminating books in your library."

I have to concede that I do. "I wonder if Charles saw the similarities in the symptoms between himself and the unfortunate fiancé?"

"That could explain his interest," she says. "But he borrowed that book some time ago, before our trip to Italy and at that time, it would have been just an interesting read."

The waiter returned with our coffee and I check my watch. One-thirty, I needed to hustle.

"Leona, thank you for being candid with me."

"You know I wouldn't have told you any of this, if it hadn't been provoked."

"Yes, but it was and you did. I think it's what Charles would have wanted. We can't allow his killer to go unpunished. Regarding the paintings he bequeathed, do you expect to get the rest of them by tomorrow?"

"Well actually, I gave Friday as the absolute deadline. They may not arrive until then."

I finish up my coffee and signal the waiter for the bill.

"Let me get this," Leona says.

"No, no. I invited you for lunch, remember."

"That may be but I chose the restaurant."

"Moot point," I counter.

"Then, you pay for your lunch, I'll pay for mine."

When I see the bill I consciously suppress a sigh of relief. The hospital is a short drive away and I find the cafeteria just after two. Paul is at a table by the door.

"Hello Maud, nice to see you." I feel the warmth of his smile.

"Hi Paul. Nice to see you too."

"Would you like a coffee or shall we go directly up to Zarina's room."

"I'm ready to go if you are."

Thanks to my navigator, we arrive at her room without a misstep. Hospitals are a maze to me and as I have difficulty distinguishing left from right, I invariably get lost. When we enter her room, Zarina is sitting in a chair instructing her nurse on the proper way to make a bed.

"Zarina, it's great to see you awake and aware." I rush to give her a hug, but pull myself back, worried about how it might be received.

"Ah Maudlin," she drawls. Her once plump cheeks now have a hollowness revealing her ordeal. "Lovely to see you too." She stretches out one hand and I take it, not sure if I should hold it gently or give it a shake. I decide on the former. "I gather I've been incommunicado for some time."

"Yes you have, but you're back now. I'd like to introduce Constable Paul Marlow. He and his partner answered the 911 call the day I found you in the studio."

"Enchanted," she coos.

Paul bows slightly. "Glad to see you are on the mend, Miss Hughes."

"On the mend perhaps but not quite out of the woods." She grimaces as she attempts to shift her weight in the chair. To her nurse she snipes, "My bed is calling me. Are you quite finished?"

"Yes, your ladyship. Inch to the end of that chair and I'll help you up."

Zarina waves an impatient hand at her. Raising her eyes toward Paul, she asks, "Would the officer be so kind as to assist me?"

He steps up to offer his arm, changes his mind and scoops her up, placing her gently on the bed.

"Thank you, kind sir."

The nurse abruptly pulls up the sheets and yanks the bed's side rail in place.

"Before you get too comfy, I want you to take this medication."

Taking the pills as directed, Zarina asks, "Has anyone ever told you, you have a wonderful bedside manner?"

"No," replied the nurse, a hint of pleasure evident in her voice.

"I'm not surprised," murmurs Zarina. Her attendant grabs the glass of water and stomps from the room. Zarina gives us a weak yet impish grin.

"She fell right into that one didn't she. Really Maudy, there's so little to entertain one in this place."

"I know, Zarina. And as you begin to feel physically better each day, you're going to have to deal with the boredom."

She rotates her attention between Paul and me.

"I suppose you two are holding your respective breaths anticipating an enlightened disclosure of the distressing events that landed me in these calamitous circumstances."

"We had hoped you would remember something about the attack," I said.

"Matty, Matty, I fear I am going to disappoint you. Although my attempts have been heroic, they have been in vain. I regret to tell you I have drawn the proverbial blank." She makes a theatrical wave with her hand.

"Don't worry about it Zarina. What's the last thing you do remember?"

"I have mental images of my dinner with the Lovely Leonid, who by the way managed to persuade me of her innocence."

"I just had lunch with her and after our discussion I agree with you. I saw the painting Charles gave you. It is beautiful!"

"Unearthly, isn't it. It was Miss T's arrival at my doorstep and her demand for my painting that aroused my initial suspicions. I do hope I can attend the retrospective on Saturday. You are going of course."

"Yes. I am planning to."

"I would suggest you take this charming police officer with you. I believe you two are very well matched."

I feel my face flush and feign an interest in the wrinkles in my skirt. Paul steps forward and says, "She's way ahead of you. Invited me to the show last week and I'm taking her out for dinner tonight."

"Ah, that is good news," says Zarina, but her smile is weak. Her energy spent, she closes her eyes.

"Zarina, I can see you need to get some rest. We'll leave you and I'll visit again soon."

"Fine Maudy," she murmurs. "And thank you, thank you for saving my life," she adds without opening her eyes.

"You're welcome," I whisper, before Paul and I walk silently from the room.

"Did you expect her to have remembered anything?" I ask, in the privacy of the elevator.

"I thought it unlikely but you never know with head injuries. She also suffered the complication of the stabbing and the loss of blood. Right now, we can be thankful she survived."

"She'll continue to receive protection, right?"

"Oh yes," he assures me.

"I've heard that in time, lost memories can return."

"But time is not something you want to give a murderer, unless it's time behind bars."

"Right. So the investigation continues."

We leave the hospital and walk toward the parking garage. Discovering we've parked on different levels, we say our good-byes and arrange to meet later at my apartment. It wasn't until I drive out of the parking lot that I remember my plans to visit Theo. Although I am a woman and can multitask with the best of them, I think there is something inherently dangerous in trying to dial a cell phone, talk and drive simultaneously. I pull into a strip mall and call Theo.

"I understand perfectly," she says when I explain the situation and apologise for cancelling our meeting on such short notice. "It is so good to hear that Zarina is improving. She's a strong girl, that one."

"She is," I agree. "Would you be amenable to a dinner on Friday evening?"

"Maud dear, I'm sure you have better things to do on a Friday night than take an old lady out to dinner."

"No I don't. Dining with you is exactly what I want to do."

"Well then, thank you. I would be honoured. Is six o'clock too early?"

I assure her that six is ideal. Returning my phone to my purse, I drive back to the office where both my uncle and my dog are overjoyed at my return.

"Was everything all right?" I ask Uncle Sid. "You seem unusually happy to see me."

"Everything was fabulous. I was just anxious to show you something. You sit down and watch this." I sit. "Okay, Holmes, let's show your Mom what we can do." He taps his thigh and Sherlock walks over to sit in front of him. "Shake a paw," he says, extending his hand. Sherlock's paw rises on command. "Good dog!" My uncle rewards him with a biscuit. "Okay, now lie down." He seems to need a little encouragement but when his teacher pulls another biscuit from his pocket, he drops to the floor. "And now, roll over." No response. "Come on, boy, roll over." Second time lucky—over he goes.

"Wow! You taught him that while I was out? I'm impressed. How many biscuits have you gone through?"

"Not that many," he insists. "He's a very smart fellow, aren't you boy?" He gives his student a pat. "So how was your lunch meeting?"

"Very enlightening. I'll get us a coffee and tell you all about it."

"So, the man was dying of AIDS," muses my uncle after I detail the conversation with Leona. "I'm not surprised she first thought it was a suicide. But why suspect Zarina?"

"I didn't have time to ask her. Maybe, she reasoned that if Zarina knew Charles had AIDS she'd want to save him from a horrible death."

"But, if that were the case, I think she would have used something more expedient than arsenic."

"Either that or give him one big whacking dose. Which makes me wonder if the method of poisoning was calculated for maximum suffering."

"I'm sure we can safely assume that Leona was the only one privy to his condition. Therefore, his murderer is someone with a serious grudge. To our knowledge, which one of the suspects had the most reason to hate him?"

"Alissa," we say in unison.

Chapter 18

Although I know my uncle is apprehensive about my return to the apartment, he insists I leave the office early to prepare for my big date. Perhaps he noticed that by three o'clock my carefully applied mascara made me look like a raccoon.

Home by three-thirty, I let Sherlock make a pit stop in the backyard before grabbing his leash and taking him back to the front door where I pick up my mail from the box.

As I climb the stairs, I will myself not to see Kora's lifeless body on the mat but it's no more effective than trying not to think of a pink elephant. I struggle with dark thoughts as I unpack my small suitcase and put Sherlock's two bowls in the kitchen, filling one with water and the other with food. His doggy bed, I put next to my own, although he's unlikely to make much use of it. I'd promised Uncle Sid I would put my gun under my pillow but I hoped he understood that as a figure of speech. It fits quite nicely into the drawer of my bedside table.

Permitting myself the luxury of an overlong shower helps to bring my mind into the moment and with my focus on the present I enjoy the scent of a hair product designed to soften my curls. A little make-up, a new summer dress the colour of fresh peaches, and my transformation is complete.

Looking the picture of health, I check my watch and find there's an hour to fill before Paul arrives. My empty easel calls for the portrait I'd started and letting go of the past also means I can't let some bastard stop me from doing what I love to do. Leaving her painting under the bed doomed Kora to remain forever as an inked drawing on canvas.

I place it on the easel, slip my artist's smock over my dress, and squeeze a little burnt umber onto my palette. I'm so engrossed in blocking in the darks, I drop my brush with the sound of a knock on the door and the almost simultaneous bark from my canine protector. After such careful preparation, I greet Paul in a paint-splattered apron.

"Hi Maud." He makes one step into the apartment before noticing a hound dog's glare.

"Friend, friend," I blurt out and Sherlock gives a tail wagging welcome.

Paul gives me a quizzical look but returns his greeting with affection. "Hey, Buddy, how ya doin'? Is he on loan or a new member of the family?"

I usher Paul into the living room, while reciting the story of my trip to the Humane Society and the meeting that resulted in my acquiring a bloodhound. Sitting in the chair opposite me, he asks if Sherlock has received some guard dog training, commenting that although they're wonderful trackers, they don't usually attack.

"Yes, actually. His previous owner trained him to protect. So far I've only seen him sit and look menacing. I don't know if he would actually attack someone."

"Well, let's hope we never have to find out." Paul's eyes scan my outfit. "Are you ready to go?"

"Sorry, yes. I'm quite presentable under this smock." I remove my protective covering.

"More than presentable." He smiles. "Is your boy here going to be okay?"

"I expect so. My uncle and I left him alone when we went to the firing range and we won't be too late, right?" I fight back the urge to comfort Sherlock, not wanting to transfer my anxiety.

"How about we go someplace in the neighbourhood? We could come back right after we eat and take him for a walk in High Park."

It's a pleasant stroll along Bloor Street with, for the most part a companionable silence, which is rare in the early part of a friendship.

"Your idea to stay local is a good one," I tell Paul after we're seated in a quaint little restaurant only ten minutes from my apartment.

"It's a nice part of the city. Have you lived here for long?"

I explain how I'd come to live with my aunt and uncle when my parents moved out west and that I chose to remain after graduation. "When it came time to get my own place I decided to stay in the neighbourhood. I like it here."

Throughout the meal we exchange life stories. I learn that Paul had considered a career in architecture but lacked the financial resources to go beyond a BA. He'd settled into the police force as a second choice and found it suited him. His marriage had been cut short by his wife's inability to deal with the long hours his work demanded.

"She found someone who worked nine to five and always had weekends off."

"Really? What does he do?" I ask.

"He's her dentist."

"That had to hurt."

Like me, he had grown up reading crime stories and mystery novels. His favourites were more of the hard-boiled variety. Our discussion of mysteries brings us to the case at hand and our waiter brings dessert, a piece of pecan pie for him and a chocolate mousse for me.

"Any leads on the attack and robbery at the studio?"

"Nothing very concrete to report there, I'm afraid." Paul slices a piece of pie with the edge of his fork and lifts it deftly to his mouth.

"We questioned those on your list of suspects. As we know, Ms. Tellman had dinner with Miss Hughes that evening. She and the others insist they spent the night in their respective beds but none have offered a witness to corroborate their stories."

I leave him to savour his first mouthful before asking, "And the missing paintings?"

He swallows. "Nada. But you know art theft is a tough one. Unless the paintings somehow come up for public auction or into the hands of a reputable dealer, they're almost impossible to trace. Many unscrupulous collectors have little concern for provenance and anyway by now they've likely been smuggled out of the country."

The mousse is lacking in the rich chocolate flavour I anticipated but it'll do. As it lingers on my taste buds, I imagine how one would smuggle a painting—taking it off the stretcher bars, rolling it up and storing it in a cardboard tube. It would then be possible to mail it out of the country. I have another thought. "What if the theft was not a real theft at all?"

"That's a possibility," he agrees.

"So if someone wanted us to believe his motive . . ."

"Or hers," he interjects.

"Yes, or hers, was stealing valuable works of art which he or she actually had no intention of selling, what would he or she do with them?"

"Well, he or she—the English language really needs a gender neutral pronoun—anyway, the thief could not run the risk of keeping them."

"But at the same time, an inexperienced thief is not likely to know how to safely dispose of them."

"Yeah, that could be a problem since he or she could never know when they might surface to become incriminating evidence. They would have to be hidden somewhere—a bus locker maybe or they may have been destroyed."

I swallow my last mouthful of dessert. "It's hard to imagine anyone destroying something so valuable."

"I think it would depend on the degree of desperation," says Paul. Reaching for his cup of coffee he asks, "What was Charles Venable like?"

Leaning back in my chair, I easily recall a vivid image of Charles. I see him in his favourite blue silk shirt—a colour that accentuated his eyes, magnifying them into ultramarine, and a pair of black pants, their creases razor sharp. I remember the many times he would look at me as if I was the only person in the world.

"Maud?"

"Sorry Paul, yes about Charles. He was a complicated man. Brilliant in his profession, quite the opposite in his personal life. A profound egotist, he could be quite a charmer when inclined. He had this way of looking at you."

"Yes?" Paul asks prompting me to continue. I'd stopped talking, seeing again the image inside my head. "Maud, I'm reading that look on your face and I have to ask, were you in love with him?"

"Maybe a little." I admit. "I think all his students were. He was often short tempered and impatient, but when it came to art, he willingly shared his knowledge."

"A good teacher, then?"

"Definitely. Many artists are secretive about their craft. Even those who teach, jealously guard their tricks and techniques, but Charles wasn't like that. If you earnestly wanted to learn, he would spend the time to ensure that you understood."

Paul finishes his coffee before asking, "And his personal life?"

"Ah, he wasn't quite so truthful in that area. Whatever he might tell you could be a reduction, an exaggeration or a complete fabrication."

"From your statement regarding the wife, I gather he was a bit of a philanderer."

"As it happens, I had an interesting chat with Leona today that I want to tell you about. It's a long story, so I'll save it for our walk in the park."

"Oh," he grins at me, "my interest is piqued. Let us make haste to collect your lonely canine."

Strolling along a tree-lined path with Sherlock in tow, I share the details of my conversation with Leona.

"So, he had AIDS. No wonder she thought it was suicide."

"That's just what my uncle said. I guess the new tests will reveal that, you know, after the exhumation."

"Yes, and the exhumation is scheduled for to-morrow. We ran into a delay when Mrs. Venable tried to block it, citing religious reasons."

"She did! That's rather incriminating, besides which . . ." I'm suddenly pulled along by a deter-mined dog. Craning my head around, I finish the sentence, " I don't think Charles was particularly religious."

Catching up with me and taking the leash, Paul held Sherlock next to him. "You need to teach him to walk behind you or beside you. If he gets in the lead he'll think he's the leader."

I rub my arm. He's probably right but there's something in the authoritative way in which he offered his advice and I see a tiny red flag. I'm trying to decide if I'm being overly sensitive when he asks, "Could he have infected his wife with AIDS?"

"I doubt it, since they hadn't been intimate for over a year."

Paul stops walking and stares at me. "A year! Crikey, she's one patient woman."

"Zarina suggested Alissa may have found companionship elsewhere, but when I talked to her, she made no hint of it."

"Speaking of Zarina," Paul begins as we walk amidst the gardens, beautiful in the early twilight, "she's quite a, um, an interesting personality. How old is she, anyway?"

"Thirty-something going on sixty-something."

"Well she's a bit odd."

"A bit?" I interject.

"Okay, more than a bit, but she was intuitive about one thing."

"Yes?"

He smiles and takes my hand. "She recognised our compatibility, didn't she?" He bends his head toward me and kisses my lips. His touch is tender and though I will myself to relax, my body refuses to obey. Once again my past rises up like a noxious gas to dampen a potential relationship.

"What's the matter?" His tone, thank God, is comforting rather than confrontational.

"Nothing, it's just that . . . well I hardly know you." I inwardly pray that he'll accept an excuse I seem to have picked from a 1950s movie.

"I think I told you most of my life story over dinner, but that's not really what you're talking about is it?"

"It's been a lovely evening and yes we are going to the art show. I'm really looking forward to it."

"That's good, me too, but. . ."

"Did you know High Park was given to the city of Toronto by its owner, John Howard?" I quickly interject.

"No, but . . ."

"He had a number of conditions though. One, that he and his wife could continue to live in Colborne Lodge, that no alcohol would ever be served in the park and that the City hold it for the free use and enjoyment of the citizens."

"I know High Park is the last 'dry' area in the city but I must admit I never knew why. Have you been to Shakespeare in the Park?"

As dusk falls and the lamps turn on in the park, we approach a bench under a spreading oak near the Bloor St. gates. and Paul invites me to sit with him.

"Maud, it's true, you don't know me very well." When I open my mouth to speak he gently places his fingers on my lips. "I don't expect you to confide in me until I've earned your trust but I've been in the police force for twelve years and I know that we sometimes think we've left the past behind only to have it resurface when certain events collide."

Tiny drops darken the orange of my cotton dress. I think it's rain until I realise I'm looking at my own tears. When Sherlock rests his head on my lap I stroke the short soft hairs of his bony head and inwardly thank him for covering those tell-tale drops.

"Whatever you're haunted by I hope you can forgive yourself so the past will lose the power it has over you."

I shrug away the tears while keeping my head down and my focus on the lovely dog by my side. "It was a long time ago."

"Forgiveness heals, Maud. Can you forgive yourself? Maybe you can even forgive the sorry bastard who hurt you, or at the very least, feel angry with him and not yourself."

"I kept telling myself that all men are not the same but that didn't help. I think I couldn't trust myself to recognise the good guys from the bad."

"That might explain your ability and interest in detective work."

He stands up and offers me his hand. I take it and together we walk along the path leading out of the park and toward my apartment. When we reach the cement walk leading to my building, Paul says, "I promised to have you home early and would say my good-byes at your front door, but I'd like to come in and make sure your apartment is secure. Okay?"

"Yes it's okay." I unlock the door. "My main concern is the fire-escape." I toss my keys on the table, point Paul in the direction of my bedroom and the window leading to the fire-escape. "I'm getting a glass of ice water, can I get you something?"

"Sure. A glass of ice water sounds good," Paul calls from my bedroom.

Sherlock follows me into the kitchen and I put some fresh water in his bowl. Watching him lap in mouthfuls I recognise the reassurance his presence gives me and know that as nice as Paul seems, he doesn't have my total trust.

"Everything looks fine. I suppose if I were to suggest you stay with your uncle tonight, it would be a suggestion unheeded?"

"Don't worry. I'll be all right, besides I have my ferocious hound to protect me."

"I thought we had doubts about his ferocity?" he says.

"Well, if he lets me down, I also have a loaded snubnosed .38 special."

His raised eyebrows prompt me to reassure him. "I have a licence and I'm a good shot."

"Okay, I won't worry, but keep your gun, your phone and your hound close by and I'll call you first thing in the morning. Oh and you better come downstairs with me and lock that bottom door."

After reassuring Sherlock of my imminent return, I close the door to my apartment and follow Paul to the foyer. He stops before opening the door. "A hug?" I walk into his embrace, comforted by his warmth and by the absence of my old feelings of anxiety. One sweet kiss goodnight and he's gone.

Back in my apartment, I pause before my painting of Kora. Finishing this portrait is going to be an emotional experience but for now it's just a set of shapes. My earlier application of the darks had begun the magic of transforming a two-dimensional surface into a three-dimensional image. I consider painting in the lights when I notice my brushes caked with paint.

After dunking them in mineral spirits, washing them with soap and water, I press the fine sable hairs back into their original shape. Perhaps tucking into the painting is a bit too ambitious. I get ready for bed and call Finella.

"I hope it's not too late to call you."

"No Maud, I never go to sleep until after eleven and I'm glad you called. I wanted to tell you I was deeply grieved to hear about Kora. How are you doing? Are you still at your uncle's or have you gone back to your apartment? Any news on Zarina? How's the investigation going?"

I wait, trying to keep track of each question.

"Maud are you there?"

"Yes, Finella. I just didn't know if you were finished."

"Sorry, see what happens when you don't call? I'll start again. First question, how are you?"

"I'm fine. It was a terrible shock but well, I'm okay now, and I'm back in my apartment." I continue to answer all her questions and bring her up to date on the case.

"It looks like the paintings could lead you to the murderer. Have the police searched the premises of your suspects?"

"Paul didn't say."

"Paul? Who's Paul?"

In the early days of a relationship one runs the risk of boring one's friends with 'he's wonderful' stories. I tried to avoid doing this but probably yak on about him a bit more than I intended.

"He sounds very nice. I would imagine this means your brief affection for Mr. T. Baer has dissipated?"

"I still think Teddy is a truly nice man but . . ."

"Not in that way," Finella finishes my thought.

"Are you coming to the opening of Charles's retrospective, on Saturday?"

"Yes, most definitely. It's at Tellman's in Yorkville, right?"

"Right. It'll be good to see you. Oh and I'm bringing Paul, so you'll get to meet him."

I said good-bye before she could express concern about my staying alone. Besides, I wasn't alone. There was a sleeping dog by my feet. He'd had such a long walk, he'd relieved everything that needed relieving and I was relieved not to have to take him out.

I knew Paul had done a thorough job of lock checking but I go through the apartment myself just to be sure. Leaving the light on in the hall will provide a little extra peace of mind. I put my portable phone and my cell phone on the table next to my gun and lay my head on the pillow. Sherlock lay on the end of my bed, after giving his own bed minimal consideration. The next thing to enter my awareness is the ringing of the phone. I awake with a feeling of panic. Who could be calling in the middle of the night?

"Good morning Maud, it's great to hear your voice."

"Paul? Did you say morning?"

"Yeah, it's five after seven. Did I wake you?"

"It's a good thing you did. I forgot to set my alarm."

"I wanted to hear your healthy voice and to tell you about some recent progress in the case. Mrs. Venable has been arrested."

"Alissa? When did this happen?"

"Late yesterday," he says. "A search warrant was obtained, and the stolen paintings were found in her basement, hidden behind some boxes."

"Wow! You know my uncle and I considered her the most likely suspect for the murder of Charles but I find it hard to believe she would attack and try to kill Zarina."

"If Zarina was getting close to exposing her then it was an act of sheer desperation."

"Yeah, I guess so." I try to visualise the scene at the studio. I had witnessed Alissa's temper but something didn't feel right. "If she killed Charles, and then tried to shut up Zarina, she also poisoned Kora and threatened me."

"That would seem to follow. For now though, she has been charged with theft and the attempted murder of Zarina. It's unlikely she will get bail so you can breathe a little easier." Before ringing off, we confirm the time he will pick me up for Saturday's art show.

When Sherlock and I arrive at the office, I tell my uncle about the recovery of the missing paintings in Alissa's basement and of her arrest.

"We thought she was the one most likely to have murdered Charles."

"I know. But the rest of it doesn't fit." The phone rings before I can explain. It's Paul.

"I realise that just a couple of hours ago I told you to breathe easier, but there's been some new developments." He sounds apologetic. "Mrs. Venable has just been released on bail. Apparently, someone stepped forward to provide her with an alibi for the attack on Wednesday night."

"So, she wasn't sleeping alone."

"No, it seems she was with Miss Evelyn Baer. Do you know her?" he asks.

"I've met her. She's Teddy's daughter. She told me they were good friends. I had no idea the relationship was, well, that close."

"If they are lovers, it explains Mrs. Venable's amazing patience where her husband's, um, affections were concerned."

"It explains a lot of things. Thanks for letting me know."

"Right. I'll talk to you soon. And Maud, keep that pistol handy."

"What was that all about?" Uncle Sid asks when I return the phone to its cradle.

When I relate the conversation he says, "So it looks like the Venables had what they call, a marriage of convenience."

"That's what it seems to have evolved into, if not what it started out to be."

My uncle leaves the office assuring me that he can be reached via his cell phone if I need him.

I try to tuck into my office chores but find it difficult to avoid sliding into memories of Charles and Alissa. I'd attended their small marriage ceremony in the backyard of their house in the Beaches. I recalled the obvious pride of Charles's aunt Theo. Although her attitude to Alissa would later turn sour, at the time of their wedding she seemed more than content to see her nephew finally settling down. And they were in love or at least they were giving a darn good imitation of it. Had Alissa sought comfort in the arms of another woman because her husband betrayed her with other men? And why did Charles marry? Some experts insist the human race is essentially bisexual and given the circumstances can form intimate attachments with either gender. I thought of Oscar Wilde. I'd read that he had started his fateful affair after contracting venereal disease and being told to avoid his wife's bed. These and other speculations intrude upon my work. Finally, at four o'clock I resolve to work harder tomorrow and head for home.

Before going up to my apartment, I take Sherlock for a long walk in the park. I attempt to empty my mind and let my subconscious mull over the details of the case. There's an important bit of information just below the surface and maybe if I don't try too hard it will emerge. One image keeps returning—my painting of Hamlet. Is there a clue in the picture I've overlooked?

I return home feeling mentally weary and physically hungry. While Sherlock does a sniff search of the premises, I make dinner. By the time I finish eating, the last thing I want to do is pack up my art supplies and go to class. It's six o'clock and I need a fifteen-minute power nap. But I sleep twice that long and then make a mad dash to the studio.

I'm fifteen minutes late and Grace is posing on the stage with the students intently at work. Holding my art case against my chest I tiptoe to the back of the room. Posed like a sprinter on the starting line I know Grace will not hold that position for long and so decide to wait before approaching my drawing horse. From my vantage point I'm surprised to see Alissa working at the easel next to mine. When she turns to look at me I automatically smile and nod but she returns my greeting with an icy stare and an abrupt turn of her head.

"Thank you Grace. You can take another pose. Maud, we're doing some five minute warm-up poses right now," Rupert says curtly.

I grab a drawing board and step toward my easel. "Sorry I'm late."

"Our next poses will be ten minutes and after the break we'll set up the long pose," he continues, ignoring my apology.

I put my head down and get to work, while at the same time wishing I'd stayed home. When we finally take our break, I'm anxious to talk to Grace, if only to experience an amiable encounter. I put down my pencil and stand up, hoping she will come over but once she donned her robe, Rupert engages her in a lengthy discussion.

Alissa leans close to my ear and whispers, "Remember, Maud, curiosity killed the cat." Her words smack me across the face and without thinking about it I leave my easel to chase after her.

"And what exactly did you mean by that comment?" I contain my anger and keep my voice low.

"You have always been an overly curious person, Maud. This time your meddling helped get me arrested and I have never been so humiliated in my life," she hisses.

"So you were humiliated. Well, someone killed my cat and threatened me. Was it you?" I practically spit at her.

"Someone killed your cat! of course it wasn't me. Christ Maud! Look, I'm sorry and I'm sorry if I sounded threatening—really, I had no idea. Your poor cat, what the hell is going on?"

"I don't know Alissa but I intend to find out."

I watch her hands shake as she pours a cup of coffee and like an offering of peace, hands it to me. I take it as a sign of acceptance but when she leaves the kitchen I replace it with caffeine-free water.

A few minutes later Rupert says, "We will now continue with the long pose, during which, Grace will take two, five minute breaks. If you work attentively, you should finish this drawing tonight and next week we will have a pose in costume. I would like some costume suggestions at the conclusion of this lesson, so get your imaginations going."

Returning to my drawing horse, Alissa smiles sympathetically when I sit down next to her. Grace takes her pose and as I work on my drawing, I consider some ideas for a costume. Whatever she wore, I knew Grace would be a pleasure to draw. After the second short break, Rupert begins a tour of the class. He pauses at each student's work and from what I can hear, makes at least one positive comment to everyone. When he reaches Alissa he says, "This is your first night drawing this pose, so you haven't had the advantage of the others, but you're doing a fine job."

She thanks him, and gestures toward my drawing.

"Maud's is excellent. Don't you think so?"

If she had earlier complained to him about my interference, I thought she was now letting him know it was misplaced. He's reluctant at first but finally agrees that I've done some fine work. Raising his voice he asks the class, "So, have you thought of any costumes for Grace?"

One student suggests a toga and laurel leaf. In the same vein, someone else mentions Venus and a third thinks Alice from *Alice in Wonderland*. One strange soul recommends Robin Hood but Alissa has the most unique idea. "How about Madeleine Smith?" No one knows who she's talking about, but I do.

Chapter 19

Arriving home before ten, I know it's early enough to call Finella and tell her about these latest developments.

"Alissa's costume suggestion for Grace was that she dress like Madeleine Smith? How did everyone react to that? "she asks.

"I know. Madeleine Smith is hardly a household name."

"But Alissa obviously knows who she was, right?"

"When I was at her place for lunch and mentioned the name, she had no idea and wondered if the woman had been a friend of Charles."

"Well, she may not have recognised the name then," said Finella, "but I found her on the Internet, so I'm thinking, Alissa did some research too. It looks to me like Charles's widow is telling you that she suspects Grace. What do you think?"

"I never considered Grace a suspect. She didn't get a painting. And what about her motive?"

"Everything she told you could have been a lie," she says.

"I think Alissa is just trying to take the heat off herself."

"Maybe. But even if we have no knowledge of a motive, we do know that Grace had opportunity. Sounds like she was a frequent visitor to the studio."

We discuss possible motives. Could she have wanted revenge for something? Could it have been jealousy or was money somehow involved? We ponder each of these ideas but lack enough information to substantiate any of them.

At the office, the next morning, I relate Alissa's comments and the discussion I'd had with Finella to my uncle.

"Somehow, I doubt she would have made the comment about curiosity killing cats if she had actually poisoned Kora. Bit too much of a giveaway isn't it?"

"True, but maybe she's trying to psych me out in a perverse attempt to have me come to that exact conclusion."

"While at the same time incriminating Grace by indicating that she played the role of reluctant lover? I don't know honey, it's a stretch. By the way," he adds, "I looked into the accounts of that agent fellow, Teddy, and they seem to be in order, on the surface anyway. He must handle some high-powered artists."

"Oh, that's great," I say before being interrupted by the phone. It's Theo.

"Sorry to bother you, Maud dear, but I was wondering if we could drop by the hospital and visit Zarina before going for dinner?"

"Sure, if you'd like, we can do that."

"Fine then, I'll call her and let her know. What time will you pick me up?"

I put her on hold while I ask Uncle Sid if he'll take Sherlock to his place, promising to come by after dinner to collect him. When my uncle agrees, I tell Theo to expect me at five-thirty.

I'm feeling guilty about leaving my pup yet again so on my lunch hour, I take him to the pet store and buy a couple of new toys and a bag of biscuits. At five o'clock, I leave him happily chewing on a big rawhide bone.

After picking up Theo, we drive to the hospital. I can't find parking near the front door so I drop her off and drive to the parking garage. I meet up with her again in the gift shop just inside the hospital entrance.

"I want to get Zarina a small gift," she says. "What do you think she would like?"

"Gosh, Theo, I don't know."

We spend a few minutes browsing when I spot some brightly coloured scarves. "How about one of these?" I ask, holding it up for her to see.

"I think that would be perfect. She loves colour, doesn't she?" She chooses the gaudiest one, and has it gift-wrapped. When we arrive at Zarina's room, she's sitting up in bed reading a book about women in the arts.

"My visitors!" She beams, closing her book.

Theo walks over to her bed and accepts her outstretched hand. "How are you, Zarina?"

"I'm much better now. Thank you, Miss Venable." Turning to me, her smile illuminating her eyes she asks, "And Maudy, how is that attractive young constable?"

"As far as I know he's fine."

"Oh, we are going to be mysterious, are we?" She wants to know more and why not? The poor woman doesn't have much in the way of entertainment. I tell her about our dinner on Wednesday night and hint at romance. She's delighted.

"Have you met Matty's new beau, Miss Venable?"

"Not yet, Zarina, but I expect to see him tomorrow at the gallery."

Zarina smacks her book onto the bedside table. "These Gestapo doctors are not going to let me go. I just hate the thought of missing Charles's opening."

She says it as if Charles would actually be there. "And Maudy, I'm very concerned about the safety of the paintings."

"I'm sure Leona has some kind of security system."

"Yes, but you know how things are in the city. Alarms go off so frequently that nobody pays much attention, and it takes the police forever to respond."

"I'm sure everything will be fine," I tell her, but I wasn't. "As far as the opening goes, I'll take pictures and notes and tell you all about it."

"Ah, Maudlin, you would do that for me? I'm touched."

"That is nice of you Maud," says Theo. "And I brought you a little something too." She presents Zarina with her gift.

Tearing at the wrapping, Zarina quickly unfurls the scarf and her eyes fill with tears.

"Miss Venable, it is wondrous! Thank you, thank you so much." With great expertise she spreads the scarf on her lap and makes intricate folds before wrapping it tightly around her head. "You've no doubt noticed that my hair is hideous. I tried that dry shampoo, but to little effect. Now, this is the perfect thing." She opens the top of the hospital table next to her bed and checks herself in the mirror.

"Infinitely better, is it not? I look positively elegant."

"You do indeed, my dear," says Theo. "I'm so glad you like it."

We chat about the boredom of confinement and different ways to keep the mind active. Theo suggests crossword puzzles and I remind Zarina that Henri Matisse was so often confined to his bed that he attached his brush to a long pole and painted on paper taped to the ceiling. We're discussing these possibilities when a young man enters her room with her dinner. Before he can make his getaway, Zarina stops him. She lifts the lids covering each plate and checks each dish.

"Everything looks in order. I trust the tea is hot this time?" He insists it is then flees from the room. Zarina looks toward us both but addresses Theo, "You know Miss Venable, the service here is sorely lacking. For the past two evenings they have brought me the wrong order."

"How unfortunate," Theo commiserates. "Have they given you any indication of when you might be going home?"

"Apparently Monday is a possibility, providing my Aunt Frances will come to look after me."

"That is excellent news."

"Zarina, I'm sure you would have said something, but I have to ask," she turns to me, eyebrows raised, "have you remembered anything from the night of the attack?"

"Oh Maudy, it's a source of immense pain. I have tried and tried. The only result is a headache. I can't even recall why I went to the studio."

"Could it have been something Leona said over dinner?" I suggest.

"Perhaps."

"If it's all right with you, I'll ask Leona to come here and maybe if she related your conversation from that evening, it will prompt your memory."

A nod of her head is her answer. I also offer to talk to Leona when I see her on Saturday.

Theo gently touches my arm. "You know Maud, Zarina's tea will be getting cold, along with the rest of her dinner. We really should be on our way."

Once in the elevator, Theo comments that although she thinks Zarina has a good heart, she wouldn't like the job of looking after her. Recalling her peevish instruction to the nurse on the fine points of bed making, I have to agree. When we arrive on the main floor, I leave Theo at the front door to retrieve the car. I pick her up, and she asks if I'd like to dine again at Bellini's. I assure her that I'm looking forward to it.

Mr. Bellini is equally happy to see us. We enjoy our meal and our conversation. It's satisfying talking to Theo. She's acquired a wisdom that helps put everything in perspective. We discuss the evil and the good in the world, the grief of losing a loved one, including the loss of a pet and how to cope with it. I wait until we're back at her home and sitting comfortably in her sun-room before broaching the subject of Charles's exhumation. I begin by talking about his trip to Italy and his visit to his doctor friend.

"Theo, the exhumation is going to reveal something I would rather you hear from me, than from a pathologist or the police." Her expression offers me comfort. "They will no doubt discover the poison but they will also find out that Charles had AIDS. I am sorry to have to tell you that."

It's a long time before she responds. Finally she says, "None of this is your fault, my dear. I see now that I did not really know my nephew and part of that has to be my fault, but he was secretive and perhaps no one really knew him. In a grotesque fashion, he was spared months of agony. I have dealt with much and I will learn to deal with this too."

"I believe you will. I told you before that I would do my best to find Charles's murderer and I want you to know that I am not giving up."

"Thank you, Maud but you must take care of yourself. Your safety is more important than anything you might discover."

"I'll be all right." I finish my tea and take the cup to the sink.

"Zarina's comment about the safety of Charles's paintings has me a little spooked. I think I'll drive by the gallery on my way home just to satisfy myself that all is well."

"Maud, it's getting dark."

"I'll be fine," I say, tightly clutching the purse that holds my pistol. "I'll see you tomorrow at the opening."

The sun has set by the time I arrive at the gallery and if there's a moon, it's hidden by smog and clouds. Parking my car in front of the building, the interior lights provide a good view of my 'Hamlet.' I'm about to release the brake and pull away from the curb when I see someone disappear into the shadows of the alley. They may have been taking an innocent short cut between the buildings, but I need to be sure. Exiting my vehicle, I'd partially closed the door when I see my voice recorder on the dash. On impulse, I stick it into my pocket. My quick sprint to the alley's entrance slows down to a cautious crawl when I enter the darkened lane and follow at what I hope is a safe distance.

Stretching my neck muscles to their fullest, I peek around the side of the building, and see someone closing the back door of the gallery. Oh God! Maybe Zarina was right. Before approaching the door, I pull my gun from the bottom of my purse, and will my hand to stop shaking. Behind the gallery is a dimly lit parking lot. In front of me are three metal steps ascending to the backdoor. Placing my weight as lightly as possible on each step, I climb to the landing, take two deep breaths, and exhale silently. My finger tips are pressed against the door when Hamlet's words pop into my head. "O Villany! Ho! Let the door be locked: Treachery! Seek it out."

But the door isn't locked and I know I must find this villain. I step over the threshold and for a few anguished seconds, shake so much I almost drop the gun.

As my eyes become accustomed to the faint light, I see that I am in a workroom. There are boxes piled against one wall and framing materials neatly stacked in open shelves on another. To my left is a mat cutting machine and next to it, a large chop saw. I'm sure the door on the far wall will lead to the main room of the gallery and the paintings. Creeping toward it, I'm crossing the Rubicon. The decision made, I ready my gun.

The interior lights are off but because of the street lamps I can see into the front room. From the safety of the shadows, the unmistakable odour of gasoline reaches my nostrils. Weaving back and forth in the gallery's main room, splashing the volatile liquid is the shrouded figure I'd seen turning into the alley. I can think of only one reason for someone pouring gas around a room and the knowledge immobilises me. Moving only my eyes,

I see the light switch on the wall to my left and hanging beside it, a painting of two men. I recognise them both and know that one of them is about to start a devastating fire.

My hand slips into my pocket, and turns on my recorder. If it transpires that I'm unable to speak for myself, it might do some explaining for me. Knowing my enemy I'm able to hold the pistol steady. With my left hand I flick on the lights. "Don't even think of reaching for a match, Rupert."

Startled, he drops the gas can, and turns toward me, his eyelids flapping against the bright light. Keeping my gun pointed at his chest, I take out my cell phone and dial 911. Relieved that the police are on their way, I ask Rupert one question, "Why?"

"I loved him," he whispers. His sorrowful expression changes to one of anger.

"I loved him," he snarls, "and then I hated him." He looks toward the painting depicting Socrates and Meletus.

"He used me, Maud. He said we would be equal partners but he made me his slave. And then his ridiculous affair with Leona. He took her to Italy, you know, when he had promised to take me. And if that wasn't enough he went after Grace. He gave her all his time and he gave me nothing. Jesus Christ, she was just a child! He was evil Maud, he was evil and he had to die."

"So like Meletus, you had to remove the world of a corrupting influence, but with arsenic not hemlock."

He tilts his head back and after a hollow laugh says, "One has to use what's available."

Wanting to get as much information on tape as possible, I continue as if there isn't a gun between us.

"How available is arsenic?"

"We work in what used to be a ceramics factory, Miss Gibbons. If you knew anything about the manufacture of ceramics, you would know they use arsenic."

His snotty tone is really grating on me. I finger the trigger of my .38.

"But why hurt Zarina?"

"She shouldn't have come to the studio." He spits out the words like a vengeful child. The puzzle finds its final piece.

"You were stealing Charles's painting of City Hall, weren't you? Then you tried to make it look like a break-in."

Staring at the depiction of Socrates and Meletus, he whines, "He left me nothing. Everything I did for him and he left me nothing but that mockery, a work I intend to burn."

He must have had a lighter palmed secretly in one hand for with an elaborate flourish he is suddenly dangling it between his thumb and forefinger above the puddle of gasoline.

"Rupert, don't light that! There are bullets in this gun and I know how to use them."

"You won't kill me Maud. You couldn't kill anyone."

Before he can utter another word, I lower my aim and fire. The lighter falls harmlessly to the floor as Rupert collapses clutching his knee. A crumpled mass, his body twists away from the lighter, allowing me to scoop it off the hardwood floor. Rupert swivels around like a wounded break-dancer and makes a frantic lunge for my foot. His aim is less than accurate and I easily step away. Having failed to disarm me his focus returns to his knee. He screams,

"You shot me, you bitch!"

"I have five bullets left in this gun. I only need to use one more."

His head bowed and his hands making a vain attempt to staunch the blood, Rupert raises his eyes toward mine.

"Please Maud, don't kill me."

In the distance, I hear the wail of sirens.

"You stay still until the police get here and I won't have to." I keep my gun aimed at his chest.

Curling his body into the foetal position he moans, "It was perfect. It was perfect and you spoiled it all."

"No Rupert. It wasn't perfect. You murdered a dying man."

"What!"

"Charles had AIDS." My captive looks at me in disbelief but I press on.

"Perhaps he ended his relationship with you to save your life. I think Charles really loved you Rupert. What do you think?"

He raises one arm and with his fist pounds the floor.

"No! No! No! You're lying, Maud. You're lying!" Eyes squeezed shut, he violently rolls his head from side to side. Finally, anger gives into exhaustion and the face he shows begs me to admit deceit, but I just stand there, slowly shaking my head until Rupert convulses with racking sobs. The heavy knock at the door alerts me to the arrival of the police and I quietly slip my gun back into my bag.

Letting them in to the main room of the gallery, the man they are here to take away has already left his senses. Murdering Charles had pushed his sanity to the edge. Learning the truth has pushed it over. Handcuffed and placed on a stretcher, his emotional motor is burned out and he stares catatonically at the ceiling.

Through the window, I watch while they carry him out to a waiting ambulance, his mouth once again moving frantically, saying words I can no longer hear. A police officer approaches me and places his arm around my shoulder.

"Maud. Are you all right?"

I look blankly into his eyes before recognising Paul. "It was Rupert. Rupert killed Charles. He attacked Zarina and he poisoned Kora."

"Yes Maud." His voice is so gentle.

"Come on let's get you out of here."

"I shot him."

"I know. We won't worry about that now." Like an usher, Paul begins to guide me toward the front door of the gallery.

I resist. Looking at the spilled gasoline and the blood from Rupert's knee, I say, "What about the gallery? There's a show tomorrow, I need to clean up this mess."

"It's okay, Maud. Miss Tellman has been called and should be here shortly. Everything will be taken care of." He's directing me toward the door again.

"But the show? Charles's art show—tomorrow."

A smile crosses his face. "Yes Maud, you said that already and now, thanks to you, the show can go on."

"Yes, yes it can." I smile then too. "Okay, I'm ready."

Keeping a protective arm on my shoulder, Paul walks me out to my car. I fumble in my purse, diving my fingers into each corner, ready to empty the contents on the sidewalk when I finally find the keys and hand them to Paul. He unlocks the passenger's door and guides me into the seat. I feel like a soldier, controlled during battle, but when the battle ends, shock takes hold. My senses are heightened, but numbness blankets my emotions. As Paul slips into the driver's seat and starts the engine, I'm keenly mindful of the deep whir of the motor and as he manoeuvres the car out onto the city streets, I have a kind of out-of-body sensation.

"Your uncle's place is on Russell, isn't it? Maud?"

I'm immersed in the scenery, barely aware of the man driving my car. Finally, I respond to a soft touch on my shoulder.

"My uncle's? Aren't you taking me home?"

"No, I don't think you should be alone."

"I forgot. He's got Sherlock and was expecting me right after dinner. He'll be worried."

"Yes, I'm sure he will be. Now what's his address?"

My mind goes blank and I stare helplessly at Paul.

"Wait," I tell him. "I need a second." In that moment I close my eyes and visualise the house.

"He's at 355 Russell. Do you know how to get there?"

"I'll find it," he says, turning the car on to Bloor Street.

"I'm sorry, Paul. I feel kind of weird, disconnected I guess."

"That's understandable." His voice is soothing. "Firing your gun into somebody's kneecap, even though he more than deserved it, is quite a bit different from shooting at the range. And by the way, why the kneecap? Pretty small target, isn't it? What if you'd missed?"

I turn and face him.

"Well, I didn't want to kill him," I say more emphatically than I intend.

"Yeah, I understand that." He takes his eyes off the road a second to look at me.

"It's just that the shoulder is a bigger target, if you know what I mean."

"Yes, but the shoulder is too close to the heart and if I had missed, I might have killed him."

Paul counters with, "But if you had missed the kneecap, he might have killed you."

I cross my arms over my chest and stare out the windshield. "Well, I'm actually a very good shot. I don't expect to miss."

He clicks his tongue in exasperation.

"Then you could have hit him in the shoulder," he says pulling the car into my uncle's driveway. I burst into tears.

"Oh Jesus Maud, I'm sorry." Paul turns off the engine and leans over to hug me.

"That was stupid, I didn't mean to argue with you. I guess I'm just worried, which is also stupid because you're fine. You're fine and you did great, really, really great!"

"Am I going to get into a lot of trouble for carrying and using my gun?"

I wipe away my tears on the back of my sleeve. I wasn't even sure why I was crying, but I couldn't seem to stop. It wasn't that I felt guilty for shooting Rupert, though maybe I should have. Still, I didn't see that I'd had an alternative. Of course, if I were an expert in the martial arts I could have kicked the lighter out of his hand.

"This is Canada," Paul begins but I'm only half listening. In my mind's eye, I'm leaping through space, my foot extended in perfect aim for Rupert's lighter. I blink the thought away and hear Paul saying, "We're very strict about firearms. However, given the extenuating circumstances, your life being threatened, hopefully there won't be any charges."

"That's good news." I find I can smile at him again.

"Shall we go in and talk to your uncle?"

"Yes, this should prove interesting."

Chapter 20

"Hello," I call out when Paul and I enter my uncle's house. Sherlock's the first to bound toward us, followed quickly by Uncle Sid.

"Cripes, Maud! I was getting worried. Where have you been?" He turns with surprise to Paul, but regains his composure. "Evenin' constable."

Paul dips his head in salute. "Evenin' sir."

My uncle takes a step closer to me and examines my face. "Maud, honey, what's up? Have you been crying?"

I glance in the hall mirror. Bright red nose, face various tints of pink.

"Sure is hard to deceive a good detective."

Paul intercedes on my behalf. "I think Maud is fine now, but we have quite a story for you."

"Well, then come on in. Would anyone like a drink?"

"Maud, maybe you should have a brandy."

I look at Paul in horror. "Oh God, not brandy! Let's all have a beer."

Uncle Sid leaves us for the kitchen. "Coming right up."

I lead Paul into the living room and drop into a worn but comfortable old armchair. Paul sizes up the offerings in the room and chooses the recliner opposite me. It was the favourite chair of the master of the house but I don't have the energy or inclination to warn him. When my uncle joins us with the beer, he pauses in front of his chair, holds his tongue and after handing each of us a bottle, sits down on the sofa.

"Okay Maud, what happened?"

I tell him I had driven to the gallery for a quick peek at my painting and how events had evolved from there.

"When I saw the painting Charles had done of Socrates and Meletus, I knew that the figure pouring the gasoline in the darkened gallery had to be Rupert."

"Why?" my uncle asks. "What did the painting tell you?"

"Remember you said that it was likely Charles had stronger suspicions toward one of the suspects? Well, in Rupert's painting, Charles portrayed himself as Socrates, no big surprise, I know, and Rupert as Meletus, once again not surprising. Historically, Socrates is said to have willingly taken the cup of poison, but in his painting, Charles, depicted Meletus forcing the poison upon him."

"Would have been nice to have seen that painting earlier," he says.

"I should also mention," I tell them both, "that I had my voice recorder running during my conversation with Rupert. It's here in my pocket, if you want to listen to it."

Each of them voice an emphatic 'yes' so I pull it out, rewind the tape and place it on the coffee table. Our voices were a bit muffled, thanks to the lining of my pocket, but still fairly easy to understand. I reach over and hit the stop button when we begin to hear the discussion Paul and I had after the ambulance arrived.

"Sorry, I forgot to turn it off."

Uncle Sid leans forward, elbows on his knees. "So, it was Rupert eh? Thought he'd committed the perfect crime, the little weasel. But you got him Maud. Good for you!" Seeing the expression on my face he adds, "I know what you're thinking, sweet niece of mine. Sure I could scold you for toting that gun, but hey, it saved your life. I could also rail at you for going into the gallery alone, but that's exactly what I would have done. Truth is, I'm really proud of you honey."

"Gee, thanks."

"And," he gives his knee a smack, "pocketing that recorder and getting Rupert's confession, well, that was a stroke of genius!"

I don't know what to say. My uncle's words calm me in a way no artificial substance could. I put down my drink, go to him and give him a big hug.

"I love you." I sit down next to him and plant a kiss on his cheek.

"Love you too, sweetheart." He squeezes my hand. "We may face some repercussions due to the illegal use of your firearm but we'll deal with that, when and if it happens."

Paul leans his head on the back of the recliner. "As I was telling Maud, the extenuating circumstances will have a mitigating influence. It was, after all, self-defence."

"Right you are, young man. Can I get anyone another drink?"

Paul lifts himself from the chair. "Thanks but I should get going. Maud, I'm sure you'll be safe in your apartment, but if you'd rather stay here, I'll call a cab."

"No Paul, I think I'm ready to go home now," I say and get to my feet. Paul gently drapes his arm around my shoulder as we walk to the front door. I grab Sherlock's leash from the hall table, attach it to his collar, handing the other end to Paul. After a grateful hug for my uncle I ask, "You coming to the opening tomorrow? It's your chance to see all the paintings."

"Wouldn't miss it."

"Paul and I thought we would go for around four thirty and then out for dinner afterward. You'll join us won't you? I thought I would invite Finella and Theo too."

"Sounds like a plan. You take care and I'll see you tomorrow."

He remains standing in the doorway as we walk to the car and as we pull out of the driveway he returns my wave.

"That's a very special uncle you have there, Maud." We watch until he steps back inside and closes the door.

"I know, Paul. I know."

"I could learn a lot from him," he says, more to himself than to me.

"Maud, I'd like to apologise again for what I said earlier. I should have been congratulating you on a job well done, instead of criticising."

"I do understand your reaction but I also accept your apology." He takes his right hand off the wheel to give my knee a light squeeze.

"Thank you."

When we arrive at my building, Paul offers to take Sherlock out to the backyard. I go in ahead and with each step up to my apartment, feel my energy drain. By the time I unlock the door my exhaustion is total. When Paul comes in with the dog, they find me stretched out on the sofa.

"Do you think you can get yourself into bed or should I get you a blanket?" he asks.

"I'll be okay." I'm half asleep and tugging at the afghan over the back of the sofa.

"I'll just call a cab then."

"No, take my car. You can bring it back tomorrow."

He bends down near my feet and gently removes my sandals. Picking up the keys from the table he says, "Okay, if you don't need your car in the morning I'll be back before four. Call me though if you need anything and sleep well."

I don't recall if he said anything else, but I remember his kiss goodnight. I would have slept till noon, if Finella had let me. She called, according to my watch, at ten after nine.

"What time are you going to the gallery?" Her voice was alert and chipper. I stifle a yawn.

"Paul's picking me up at four."

"Sorry Maud. Did I wake you? I thought you were an early riser."

"I usually am but I had a late night last night."

"Ooo, did you have a hot date?" she asks.

"I guess you could say that." I tell her about finding Rupert ready to burn down the gallery and all that followed.

"Rupert, sniffling little Rupert, who'd have thought!" She's silent for a moment, then continues, "Wait a minute, Maud, what were you thinking? You could have been killed!"

"I suppose so," I mutter, pondering her reaction. It's what I had expected from my uncle.

"Don't get me wrong," she says. "You did a good job. I mean you caught the bastard. But it might have been wiser to have called the police from outside the gallery, you know, when you saw Rupert going to the back door."

I could tell her I didn't know it was Rupert when I was standing outside the gallery but I don't feel like justifying my actions so I say, "I hear ya."

"Of course, I guess at that point you didn't know it was Rupert."

"Right." I can see she's going to work this out on her own.

"And also, if you hadn't gone in, you wouldn't have that taped confession, or saved the gallery."

"Right."

She laughs. "Okay. I'll quit harping and just congratulate you on succeeding at what you set out to do. Charles was right to have asked for your help."

"Well, thank you Finella. Speaking of Charles, if you want to meet us at the gallery early, say between four-thirty and five, Paul, my uncle and I, are going out for dinner after the show. We'd like you to join us."

She agrees to meet us there. I no sooner hang up the phone and Theo calls. I relate my oft-repeated story and wait. Her reaction is to thank me for the arrest of Charles's killer.

"I know it won't bring Charles back," she says, "but I feel with his killer behind bars, there's a sense of closure, not to mention how much easier we'll rest, especially you, my dear. You were very brave and I'm sure Charles, in whatever form the afterlife takes, is pleased."

Before saying good-bye, I invite Theo to join our dinner party and she cheerfully accepts. I add that I'd thought of going to Bellini's, unless she would like a change of venue.

"I think it would be quite fitting to have dinner there. It was, after all, Charles's favourite restaurant."

As a relatively new dog owner and someone more than a little distracted that morning, I shouldn't have been too surprised to find a large wet spot on my bath mat. I'm annoyed, but know I need to take some of the blame when I note that it's well after ten. I rinse the mat out in the tub and hang it on the railing of the fire escape. When I walk into my bedroom Sherlock's hindquarters are protruding from under the bed. I let him think he's well hidden until I get dressed, run a brush through my hair and slip into my sandals.

"Come on, Buddy," I say, patting his very visible butt. "Mommy owes you a long walk in the park." He shimmies himself from his self-imposed exile and we're soon walking among the trees. I hope this walk will be therapeutic for me too. I need the mental clarity that might help put recent events into perspective.

Strolling beside a bed of boisterous pink impatiens, I remind myself that the world holds good as well as evil and make a mental note to remove the gun from my purse as soon as I get back home. I would lock it away with the hope that I'd never have to use it again. Maybe I should study a martial art, not that a carefully placed blow couldn't be as lethal as a bullet but weapons make killing so easy. I'd always prided myself in the belief that I could never hurt anyone. But I'd hurt Rupert and if necessary, would have aimed to kill. As Zarina had reminded me, we are all capable of murder. Perhaps the only difference is our capacity for regret.

Sherlock pulls on the leash, looking back at me as if to say 'Are we going for a walk or what?' "Okay let's do this thing." I put my shoulders back and pull myself into the present. We wander the pathways for another half hour, finally breaking into a run as we head for home.

Once back in my apartment, the shower I take is especially cleansing. I towel dry my hair, leaving it to fall in natural curls, while I apply a light blush to my cheeks and a new mascara to my lashes—one guaranteed not to smudge. Selecting an outfit poses a problem, since I forgot to take my linen suit to the dry cleaners. I push some clothes around the closet, give up and make a sandwich for lunch.

According to the weather report on the radio, it's to be another hot and humid afternoon. Sipping my ice tea, I envision a house on the shores of the Atlantic where ocean breezes cool the air. This jogs a memory of a cotton sun-dress the saleswoman had called Ocean Blue. I bought it last year at the end of the season and pulling it from my closet, I'm pleased to see it's just as pretty as I remembered.

Having chosen my outfit, I begin tidying the apartment. I'd given it minimal attention since receiving my painting of Hamlet. I wash my lunch dishes, retrieve the bath mat from the railing—still a bit damp but good enough to drape over the edge of the tub. I lock my gun back in the jewellery box, remembering to put a small camera in my purse for the pictures I promised Zarina. Finally, I dress, retouch my makeup and by the time Paul arrives, both my surroundings and I are looking pretty good.

With a deep bow, Paul says, "You are a vision in blue, Miss Gibbons."

I curtsy. "Why thank you kindly, Constable Marlow."

Taking my hand he asks, "You do look terrific, but how are you feeling?"

I keep hold of his hand and lead him into the living room, where we sit together on the sofa.

"This morning, I took Sherlock for a long walk and used the time to sort through a few things. You know Rupert taunted me by saying that I couldn't kill anyone, but he was wrong."

"But Maud, you didn't kill him."

"I know but I was prepared to and it's likely he'll never fully recover from the damage to his knee."

"He brought that on himself—acts of evil have consequences. I'm sure you'd like to know that late last night there was a search done of the studio basement. They found a container of arsenic among the old supplies from the previous tenant, the ceramics factory."

"Any prints?"

"Nothing on the arsenic container, it had been wiped clean, which is evidence in itself. But it seems Rupert left his prints on the box in which it had been stored."

"Well, that's good news."

Still holding my hand, he pushes his weight forward and stands up. "What do you say, shall we go?"

"Sure, I'm ready and I can't wait to see these paintings."

We arrive at the gallery to find the parking lot full and cars lining the side streets. The only available space turns out to be three blocks away at an overpriced lot.

"Looks like a great turnout," Paul remarks as we walk back to the gallery. Mounting the steps to the front door, I hear my name being called. Turning around, I see Finella coming up the walk.

"You made it. Excellent. Where'd you park?"

"The other side of the moon, I think," she says. "Quite a crowd, eh?"

"You're sounding very Canadian." She squeezes in next to us. "Aren't you supposed to say, 'Quite a crowd, what?'"

"I guess I've been here too long."

I introduce Paul and Finella. More people arrive and Paul pushes ahead of us and through the door, creating a space for us to enter. I'd never seen so many people at an art exhibit. Looking at the crowds, Paul says, "Wow, I had no idea art shows attracted so much attention."

With her small stature Finella is almost lost among the shoulders. "They usually don't, unless," she continues cynically, "the artist is dead."

"Well, then," he begins, "wait until the news hits the press. When the public reads about the circumstances of his death, the show may go on indefinitely."

Stopping at the desk, I look from Paul to Finella and back to Paul. "I'm going to be in the papers, aren't I?"

Paul nods. "I expect so."

"And you'll likely be hounded by reporters," adds Finella.

It's not a welcome image but I shrug it off. "Well, no point brooding about that now. Let's enjoy the show. Paul if you can get a hand near that desk, grab a program. We can start our tour with painting number one."

Paul reaches ahead to snatch a pamphlet. Checking it, I note that Leona has gathered more than fifty pieces. Judging by the dates, she started with his early works, many likely borrowed from Theo. She hung them in a room off the main hall. Leading the way, I'm pleased to see only a small group of viewers and even more pleased to see that Theo is one of them. She returns my greeting with a hug.

"Maud, dear, it's so good to see you. This must be your charming constable. A pleasure to meet you." She extends her hand to Paul. Taking it, he replies, "The pleasure is mine, Miss Venable."

I step beside her. Theo, do you remember Finella Finnegan?"

"A former student of Charles, I think."

"Indeed I was. Are some of these paintings from your personal collection?"

Theo animatedly describes the works she's lent the gallery and continues her commentary as we go around the room. Before leaving, I pull out my camera and get a few pictures for Zarina. Heading into the second of the three rooms, we find many of Charles's portraits and his landscapes of Italy. Unfortunately, we're now competing with a large crowd.

"I'm afraid I can't tell you much about these," says Theo. There may be something in the program."

I read out the short blurb about each work and we slowly parade around the room as I continue my photographic record for Zarina. Within half an hour, we enter the large main room of the gallery, holding Charles's most recent works. The painting of Old City Hall is there, as well as some rare narrative illustrations in pen and ink. On the left-hand wall, next to the light switch I'd turned on a scant twenty hours earlier, is the painting of Charles and Rupert.

When he sees it Paul says, "I can see why you concluded that the intruder was Rupert."

"Yes, look!" Finella pointed at the picture. "Socrates isn't holding the cup of hemlock. Meletus, AKA, Rupert is pouring it down his throat."

Theo's hand jumps to cover her mouth. "Oh my!"

"This must be difficult for you Miss Venable." Paul slips a hand under her elbow.

"Shall we move on to the next picture? The woman in this one looks like Zarina."

I move along with them.

"This is 'Guinevere and Sir Gawain.' Finella is familiar with this story." Pulling herself away from Rupert's painting, Finella explains, "A jealous knight has given an apple to Guinevere and she is expected to give it to Sir Gawain. She doesn't know that the apple is laced with poison. However, in Charles's work, and I guess that's a blonde Zarina as Guinevere, she's offering a glass of wine rather than an apple. Although his back is facing us, I assume the knight is meant to be Charles."

"It seems to suggest," I say, "that although Zarina gave him wine, she was unaware of the poison."

Paul reads out the label on the next painting.

"This one is called 'Hercules and Deianira.' "

"Then it's Alissa's," I tell him. "According to the myth, Deianira thought she was losing the love of Hercules, so she presented him with what she thought was a robe soaked in a love potion, but it was poison."

"And in the picture she is holding the robe over her arm and handing him a goblet of wine."

"You're right, Paul," Theo adjusts her glasses. "Do you think Charles was suggesting that the drink would somehow make him dependent?"

"Possibly, certainly making him sick would mean he would need Alissa's help. Shall we have a look at the next one?" I spin around and bump into someone towering over the next painting. When he turns I apologise.

"Oh Teddy, I'm sorry."

"Don't mention it Maud. It's always a pleasure bumping into you. Leona told me you had quite a time last night."

"Yes, I did. You know, I haven't even seen Leona yet."

"Hard to find anybody in this crowd. It's really something, isn't it?"

I express my agreement before introducing Teddy to Paul. When we turn our attention back to the painting, Theo says, "Good likeness of you, Mr. Baer, I assume as Nero." In this work, both toga-clad figures were holding glasses of wine, but the figure of Nero had his hand raised, as if to prevent Britannicus from taking a sip.

"Did you and Charles often share a glass of wine?" I ask.

"I admit it was a common occurrence, up until a month or so before he died. He stopped offering, unless I brought the wine. The one time I went ahead and poured myself a glass from the bottle he always kept in the fridge, he seemed so offended I never did it again. Obviously, I had no idea that bastard Rupert was putting poison in it."

Moving to the last of the set, we see the painting Charles had done for Leona. Here was the image of Perseus and Medea, beautifully drawn and as glorious in its use of colour as the others.

"Medea," I begin, "did not want to lose her power so she put poison in a cup she intended her husband to give Perseus." In this work, Charles had painted Leona as Medea, himself as Perseus, and the man offering the cup resembled Rupert.

"All of his paintings would certainly suggest that Charles believed the poison to be in his wine," says Paul.

"You're right," Finella agrees, "so why did he keep drinking it?"

"Perhaps he deemed it a better way to die." These words came from Leona, who stood directly behind us.

"Oh yes, I forgot he had . . ." Finella doesn't finish the sentence.

Quickly changing the subject, Theo smiles up at Teddy. "Your painting would suggest that Charles never really considered you a suspect."

He put his arm gently around her shoulder. "But he couldn't be entirely positive, could he? I may have drunk that glass of wine to throw him off—a small amount of arsenic is seldom fatal."

"Looking at all the paintings," Paul adds, "Charles focused his suspicions as we now know on Rupert, but also on his own wife."

"And me," says Leona, sadness in her voice. "My painting suggests that I poisoned the wine and Rupert merely conveyed it."

"Quite so," murmurs Theo. "Where's Maud's painting of Hamlet?"

"Over there, close to the window." Leona directs our gaze. "Hard to see, through all these people." She leads the way, stopping in front of my picture.

"I deliberately set this one apart from the others. Won't mean much to the general public, yet anyway, but it will be understood by the rest of us."

Theo is mesmerised by the painting. "You know, I think this is one of his finest. It conveys so much emotion."

"Certainly a great way to say thank you isn't it."

Recognising my uncle's voice, I turn to greet him.

"I was wondering when you'd get here. Let me introduce you."

The introductions made, I suggest to the others that they enjoy some refreshments while I take my uncle back to the other paintings. He's most interested in those given to the suspects. Looking each one over carefully, he comments that had I seen them initially, I would surely have focused my attention on Rupert and Alissa.

"I know. And if I had, Zarina might not have been injured and Kora would still be alive."

"But Maud, you also know that Rupert would never have let you see his painting."

The gallery begins to empty out as the dinner hour approaches. Leona asks, if we're finished looking at the work, to follow her to her office as there's someone who wants to see me. I hesitate with a questioning look toward my uncle.

"Well, I don't know either," he confesses. "Let's follow the woman and find out."

When we enter, I see a similar gathering to the one we'd had at the lawyers' office. Mr. Andrew Smith and Ms. Katherine Wilson are standing next to Leona's desk with Alissa and Teddy. We're missing Zarina, unfortunately and Rupert, thank God, but Paul, Theo and Finella are also in attendance.

"It's nice to see you again, Miss Gibbons," says Mr. Smith. "Hearing of your successful capture of Rupert Jaynes, my colleague and I have something for you. Before he died, Mr. Charles Venable told me he had given you an assignment. He did not say what it was, only that I would be sure to recognise it when it happened. At that time, I was to convey his thanks and present you with this painting."

Ms. Wilson set the painting on the desk, holding it upright for all to see. We seem to simultaneously inhale. It depicts a young woman sitting in front of drapery the colour of lapis lazuli. Her hair is piled loosely on her head and around her neck hangs a strand of pearls. The ceramic box she holds in her elegant hands is partially open.

"This painting depicts Pandora," Ms. Wilson told us. "And it's called 'The Gift.' "

I manage one word. "Gosh!"

"Gosh, indeed," added Finella. This was followed by laughter and applause.

"Charles also wanted you to have this letter," says Ms. Wilson, handing it to me.

"Maud, could we hang the painting on the wall so we can have a closer look?" asks Finella. I nod and Leona picks it up, expertly placing the wire over a nail on the wall. While everyone moves in to admire the work, I step back and open the letter. I read it through twice. When I look up, I find the group facing me.

Her voice just above a whisper, Alissa says, "Is it something you can read aloud?"

I struggle to get my emotions under control, give up and begin to read through my tears:

Dear Maud,
Pandora is said to have been the first woman. Some say she was created by Jupiter to punish men, others, to bless them. She came to earth with a box equipped by the Gods and was told never to open it. Her insatiable curiosity prevented her from following these instructions. The box was opened, the truth revealed but hope remained. You were my hope for revealing the truth. Thank you.

'Adieu, adieu! Hamlet, remember me.'
Charles Venable